CALISTA GREEN

By A. J. Butcher

CALISTA GREEN

a Spy High novel

A. J. Butcher

www.atombooks.co.uk

A paperback original from *Atom* Books

First published in Great Britain by Atom 2005

Copyright © 2005 by Atom Books

Based on concepts devised by Ben Sharpe
Story by A. J. Butcher

The right of A. J. Butcher to be identified as author of this Work
has been asserted by him in accordance with the Copyright,
Designs and Patents Act 1988.

A CIP catalogue record for this book is available from
the British Library.

ISBN 1 90423 337 6

Typeset in Cochin by M Rules
Printed and bound in Great Britain
by Bookmarque Ltd, Croydon, Surrey

Atom
An imprint of
Time Warner Book Group UK
Brettenham House
Lancaster Place
London WC2E 7EN

www.twbg.co.uk

For Molly
knitter extraordinaire

PROLOGUE

For a man who would be dead before morning, Professor Werner Wagner was in great shape. He knew because his body sensors told him so. The e-broidery stitched into his clothes, the monitors of his heart rate, his blood pressure, his body temperature, the electrical activity of his brain, all were sending the same reassuring signals. Professor Werner Wagner was a man in the full bloom of health, like a machine functioning in peak condition.

It was a pity for him that the sensors had not been programmed with the ability to see the future.

He'd returned home late that night. His speech to the International Association of Nanosurgeons had been, and he was modest enough to admit it, a triumph. He wouldn't have had to buy a drink however long he'd stayed in the bar afterwards. But he'd torn himself away from the admiration of his peers as promptly as he could without causing offence. Professor Werner Wagner preferred to keep his successes, like his secrets, to himself.

'Lights on,' he said, stepping from his personal elevator into his penthouse apartment. And there was light. 'Muted.' And it was softened, smudged. 'Mozart.' And the soothing strains of a string orchestra filled the rooms. 'Muted.' Romance relegated to the background.

His three favourite girls waved to him from the wall. Triplets with identical faces, features that his body sensors, after analysis of his physical responses to the images of five thousand females, had identified as those of optimum appeal to him. Here they'd been recreated in blonde, brunette and a fiery redhead, like flavours of ice-cream.

His three favourite girls, none of them with names, waving to him, calling to him silently, keen to come out and play. But they were doomed to remain two-dimensional tonight. Professor Werner Wagner was beginning to feel tired after his exertions at the conference. He only wanted to relax.

He made his way directly to the womb-room.

In the past, of course, people would have called this softly curving sanctuary a bedroom, in the days when furniture was fixed and could generally only accommodate a single function. Now, though, in the era of smart furniture and multi-purpose, computer-controlled living spaces, such rigid demarcations were obsolete. Indeed, this had been a theme on which Professor Werner Wagner had been waxing lyrical earlier that evening: people welcomed the enhancements and flexibility nanotechnology and other scientific advances could bring to their immediate environment, so why were so many still reluctant to apply the same principles to themselves, to human beings? E-volution not evolution was the way forward for Mankind, he'd declared. The phrase amused him. He chuckled. He didn't realise it, but that was the last time he would ever express amusement in this life.

The womb-room. Its single colour changed as it interpreted Professor Werner Wagner's mood from its connection to his body sensors, became the blue of lying on one's back on a summer afternoon and staring at the sky, the deep and distant blue of peaceful oblivion. The room's sole other occupant, a leather and plastic object too long to be a chair yet too vertical to be a bed, leaned towards the man with the eagerness of a pet delighted by the return of its owner.

'Ah, Mother,' said Professor Werner Wagner, 'did you miss me? I've missed you, too.' He settled into the embrace of the bed-chair, which shifted its shape to maximise his comfort. 'Just a little diversion before sleep, I think.' He addressed the room at large. 'Woodland,' he selected.

And the trees grew tall through the floor of the womb-room and thrust their topmost branches through its ceiling. Rounded walls fell away into hazy forest perspectives. The light filtering through leaf-laden branches was golden and green, the air fresh and tinctured with the odour of loam. Deer grazed in the glade where Professor Werner Wagner lay on his bed-chair and they were unafraid. Neither did they seem puzzled by the tranquil music that wafted past them on the breeze. It helped that the deer, like the rest of the wildlife in the scene, like the forest itself, were not real. They just seemed that way.

'Here, boy. Here, little fellow.' Professor Werner

Wagner reached out his hand to stroke the young deer nearest to him, as he had done countless times before.

But not tonight. The virtual animal suddenly jerked up its head, its eyes wide with alarm, and it fled. Its companions fled. The squirrels, the birds, the entire woodland population, they too fled into the invisible recesses of the forest. Professor Werner Wagner was left alone.

'That's not supposed to happen,' he said.

And the wind was picking up now, too, and the sky was darkening. It looked like a storm was on its way.

None of which, needless to say, was part of the program.

'Computer,' said Professor Werner Wagner, annoyed, 'check woodland program for viruses. Oral feedback required.'

The leaves were dying on the boughs. Autumn had come early and the leaves were falling as a cold wind shook them. And their colour was not red or yellow or brown. Their colour was funereal black.

'Computer,' demanded Professor Werner Wagner, 'oral feedback at once. Is there a virus in the system?'

The computer was saying nothing. The music was no longer pastoral and harmonious but janglingly discordant, the soundtrack to *Bambi* swapped for *Halloween*. Violin bows rose and plunged like daggers. The trees twisted and bent, their trunks gnarled as if by a sudden injection of poison. The rich soil withered and cracked, as if something long buried craved release.

'Computer, speak to me! Restore woodland program. Exit present scenario and reboot.'

And there were howls from the dark and distant

forest, and screeches in the night that had descended. They were not human.

For a second, Professor Werner Wagner froze.

His body sensors registered the fact. Heart rate, up. Blood pressure, up. Perspiration count, up. Stress indicators, engaged.

'Computer, exit woodland. Initiate lonely cove scenario immediately. Immediately!'

No sign of a cove, lonely or otherwise. In the midnight forest, dark shapes moved. Branches clutched like witches' claws.

Heart rate, up. Blood pressure, up.

'Computer, exit all virtual programs. Return room to neutral. Do it. Do it!'

The forest didn't want to go. Unlike Professor Werner Wagner.

'What's happening here . . .?'

Brain activity, fear centres stimulated. Stress levels, within tolerable limits but rising.

He swung his legs from the bed-chair, stood. The air was ice around him. He didn't understand it. What was going on? *There were things in the dark, shapeless, shambling things.* What kind of glitch had corrupted his system? *They were coming towards him. They were closing in.*

Heart rate, up. Blood pressure, up.

It didn't matter. He'd sort it out. The door was only over here. The door to the rest of his apartment, his safe, secure, controlled apartment. There was no danger. He could see its outline, a yellow frame between two trees. He only had to open the door and step through and everything would be back to normal, everything would be . . .

The door wouldn't open.

Booming laughter from blackened skies. Shrill shrieks of glee from creeping, crawling, unnatural things. A low moan in the throat of Professor Werner Wagner.

Heart rate, up. Blood pressure, up. Stress levels, becoming dangerous.

And they were nearer now, the creatures, the things. They *wanted* him.

'Somebody . . . computer . . . somebody help me . . .'

No way out. The door was locked. There was no way out.

Something was twining around his ankles. Something plump and slimy. Not real. It wasn't real. Nothing could hurt him, not *hurt* him.

Brain activity, fear centres stimulated beyond advisable limits. Warning.

He didn't look down anyway.

'Somebody! Computer! Help me!' He was yelling. He was screaming.

Larynx, strained. Warning.

Heart rate, up. Warning. Blood pressure, up. Warning.

And behind him. Something was behind him. Something hideous and huge, he knew it. He could feel its hot, reeking breath on the back of his neck. He should turn and face it. He had no choice. There was no way out.

Stress levels, critical. Heart rate, critical. Blood pressure, critical.

Cardiac arrest, imminent.

Professor Werner Wagner snapped his head around.

His scream still echoed through the restored glade as the innocent deer foraged, rippled through the golden afternoon like the legacy of an ancient curse. The animals didn't hear it because they weren't real. They didn't notice the still, prostrate body of Professor Werner Wagner either. And they certainly weren't in a position to consult his body sensors.

Though if they could, they'd have soon discovered he was dead.

'So this is Cally.'

'Correct, Field Handler Kwan. Cally Cross. Calista Cross. While on active duty, Calista *Green*.'

'A lot of names for one girl, sir. Sounds kind of complicated.'

'Agent Cross' present situation might well be called that, Field Handler Kwan. It's why you're here.'

Here was the private quarters of Jonathan Deveraux, founder and, as far as the general public was concerned, headmaster of the elite educational establishment named after him, the Deveraux College, sited in leafy seclusion some distance north of Boston, Massachusetts. The idea of the principal of such an institution discussing one of its graduates with one of its members of staff would strike most people as far from unusual. Unless, of course, they were granted access to the interview itself, admitted to the top floor of the imposing gothic building that housed the school, allowed to enter Deveraux's rooms. Then they might have to think again.

Even in 2066, headteachers' studies usually came with bookcases fat with books, oak desks, hard-backed leather chairs. Not here. Paper and leather and wood did not feature significantly in a room that hummed with electric power, that gleamed with metal and shone with screens

8

A.J. Butcher

and flickered with computers and circuits and sensors of every description. Equally, at least at first glance, the majority of headteachers tended to be alive, in order to more effectively discharge their duties. Jonathan Deveraux had not been truly alive, not flesh and blood alive, for over ten years. His computerised brain patterns and digitalised image ran the Deveraux College.

Perhaps that was why he employed staff who would not have made it past the CV stage at other select centres of excellence. Field Handler Kwan, for example. Chinese, not a problem, but kind of young, in his early twenties, only a handful of years older than some of the girls he'd be working with, and teenage crushes were always a risk. Good-looking, too, with something of the Bruce Lees about him. But that hair, dyed blond and unnaturally spiky, that didn't create a good impression. Neither did the dragon tattoos that breathed fire along the backs of his hands, the scaled tip of a tail tickling at the nape of his neck – and who knew where *else* they might be hiding? No, Field Handler Kwan would not have made an appropriate addition to the faculty at any normal school.

But then, the Deveraux College was not a normal school. Above ground it mostly appeared so, but at Deveraux, as anywhere else, appearances could be deceptive. Below ground there was no pretence. Below ground there were holo-gyms and cyber-cradles and sleepshot and SkyBikes. Below ground there was another kind of school for a different kind of training. Below ground was Spy High.

'I trust you are ready for the challenge, Field Handler Kwan,' said Jonathan Deveraux, his austere and unblinking face peering down at the man from the ring of screens suspended from the ceiling.

'Yes, sir.' The reply was quick and confident. 'I didn't qualify as a field handler to shirk my first assignment.'

'Good. Then tell me what you know about Agent Cross.'

Kwan had done his homework. He circled the dread-locked African-American girl as respectfully as if it was really Cally in his presence rather than a hologram. 'Parents assumed dead. Cally never knew them, at any rate. Grew up on the street. Not an easy early life. First noted by Deveraux when she was ten years old and living at the refuge operated by Selector Agent Mac Luther. Mac spotted her potential, took her under his wing, became the closest thing to a father Cally had ever known. Didn't quite manage to stop her turning to crime, though, always a danger for a kid with her back-ground.' The field handler paused briefly as if distracted by memories of his own.

Jonathan Deveraux, being software, was never dis-tracted. 'Go on,' he instructed.

'Saved from a life of possible self-destruction by the intervention of former Senior Tutor Elmore Grant. Recruited for Spy High four years ago when she was fourteen. Joined Bond Team. Proved to be a fine all-round agent but exceptionally skilled with computers. A natural, instinctive. The best hacker Deveraux has ever produced. After graduation, assigned to Region Green, China, Japan, and my own old stamping ground, Hong Kong. Has maintained a highly successful record there under Field Handler Mei Ataki ever since.' Kwan paused again. 'At least, until recently . . .'

'Indeed.' If Jonathan Deveraux's voice had been permitted inflections, it might have sounded disapproving, but it had not. Human inflections suggested human weakness. 'Until the loss of Agent Stanton.'

'Ben Stanton, Benjamin White, former leader of Bond Team and Cally's boyfriend.' Field Handler Kwan knew that, too. 'Apparently killed last month in Wallachia fighting President Tepesch. Atomised while trying to disengage the starstone. Not surprisingly, Cally – Agent Cross – hasn't taken it well.'

'Indeed not.' Compassion didn't register in Deveraux's voice tone either. 'Agent Cross has indulged herself in an emotional response to events.'

'Well, that may be true, sir,' said Kwan, 'but she can hardly be blamed for it.' He regarded Cally's hologram as if considering a physical demonstration of sympathy. 'You lose someone you . . . feel strongly about, you don't recover from that easily. Sometimes you don't recover at all.'

'A Deveraux agent knows the risks implicit in the work before he or she sets foot in Spy High,' remarked the founder.

'Agreed, sir,' said Kwan, 'but we're only hu—' He redirected himself in time. 'She's still young.'

'And she still has a chance, Kwan.'

'A chance to what, sir?'

'To remain a Deveraux agent. But she must rouse herself from her stupor. She must regain her energy and her focus. That is why I have assigned you to be Agent Cross' new field handler. You will provide her with a fresh start, persuade her to think about the present rather than the past. Following the unfortunate incident in Shanghai we decided to place her again on compassionate leave, but she cannot mourn Agent Stanton indefinitely. She must return to the field at some point, and the mission we have for her now ought to be a straightforward one.'

'Yes, sir,' said Kwan.

'Unlike the Shanghai incident, there must be no mistakes. Calista Green has reached a pivotal moment in her secret agent career. If she fails a second time,' warned Jonathan Deveraux, 'there will be only one option available to us.' His perfectly sculpted features seemed cold and impassive. 'She will be mind-wiped.'

It may not have been the *worst* thing, but seeing Ben's parents sure hadn't been *good*. Cally had only visited the Stanton estate in Newport, Rhode Island, once before, on the occasion of Ben's sixteenth birthday party. Then great marquees had sprouted in the grounds like festive white mushrooms, and the soundtrack had been of dance and celebration. This time the place had seemed shrouded in gloom, the vast lawns empty, lonely, the mansion itself perched above Rhode Island Sound like a suicide about to jump. She hadn't enjoyed her previous visit, had felt out of place among the rich and powerful who'd flocked here to mark the birthday of one of their own. She'd felt similarly uncomfortable on her return, even though the East Coast elite were notable by their absence. There was little dancing for the missing, presumed dead.

Mr and Mrs Stanton had received her in a room apparently designed for unpleasant news and awkward silences. Portraits of the Stantons of the past looked lifelessly down on them: maybe, somewhere, there was a space already cleared for Ben.

And Ben was why she was here, she'd constantly had to remind herself. She'd rather have been elsewhere, trying, learning to cope in her own way, but it had been her duty as Ben's girlfriend to come, her responsibility. Ben had always been big on responsibility.

'They still aren't telling us very much,' Mr Stanton had said. 'However often we contact them it's the same. Ben's solocopter lost in terrible weather while flying to join his InterAid colleagues in a remote province of the Tsarist Federation. No sign of wreckage yet found, which I still take to be hopeful' – a half grunt from his wife had suggested that she felt otherwise – 'but no contact from Ben, either, which . . .'

'I know,' Cally had said.

'But we're not satisfied with the Tsarist Government's response.' Mr Stanton had grown temporarily defiant. 'We don't trust them to do everything necessary to find Ben alive, everything possible. We're sending a search team of our own, a *Stanton* team. Access papers are being drawn up even now and we don't care how much it costs. Money is no object. We'll bribe every official in the country if we have to. We'll find Ben.'

No you won't, Cally had thought sadly, not if you paid the whole world to scour the soil of the Tsarist Federation. Because Ben wasn't there, dead or alive. There had been no flight in dangerous conditions, no solocopter crash. That was a lie, a cover story organised by Deveraux to keep the truth secret, that Benjamin White had been killed in the line of duty as a graduate of Spy High. Correction: *possibly* killed. In the absence of a body there was still hope, albeit a clutching-at-straws kind of hope. That was why Ben's public fate had been left open, on the anorexically slim chance that one day it might still be possible for him to emerge from the wilderness with a miraculous tale of survival against the odds. Cally dreamed of that day, but she knew too that dreams were not reality.

'There's nothing I can say.' She'd not been able to look Ben's parents in the eye. 'Ben and I were very close.' Mrs Stanton's half-grunt seemed to have become habitual. 'What we had was special. I'd like to think I made him happy in the time we were together. I know he made me happy. I just thought . . . That's why I came. I wanted you to know that. And if there's anything I can do . . .'

'You can leave.' Mrs Stanton had entered the conversation. 'That's what you can do. Leave and not come back.'

'I beg your pardon?'

'You heard. You're not deaf.'

'Nancy, please . . .' Mr Stanton had endeavoured to restrain his wife, but there'd been no stopping her.

'This is your fault, Cally or whatever you call yourself, all of it.' She'd jumped to her feet, had advanced on Cally with accusation and disgust in her eyes. 'Our son would be here today if it wasn't for you. Here. Happy. Alive.'

Cally had flinched. She'd retreated, the woman's verbal assault as punishing as anything she'd ever had to face in the field. 'That's not true. It's not.'

'It *is*.' Mrs Stanton had been irresistible. 'You took our son from us. You *stole* him. What was he doing in the Tsarist Federation in the first place? Backward, impoverished, nobody of any sense goes there. And working for *InterAid*, of all things, squandering his talents and his family name doling hand-outs to peasants and degenerates. When he could have been at Harvard. When he *should* have been preparing for his rightful place on the board of the Stanton Foundation.'

'Ben made his own choices, Mrs —'

'No. *You* did this to him, young lady. Our son was perfect until you crawled out from whatever ghetto it was. You took him and you changed him, and now you've killed him. You're to blame, Calista Cross. You've killed our son.'

'Steady on, Nancy . . .'

'Mrs Stanton, I'm sorry . . .'

'Sorry from you is like a slap in the face. Why couldn't you have stayed away? Why did you have to set your sights on our son? He was happy with Lori. What right had you to ruin his life? And ours. You've ruined our lives, too.' The sobs had started then, bitter and racking. 'What am I going to do without my *son*?'

'Mrs Stanton, I . . .'

'Cally.' Ben's father had silenced her. 'I think you should go now, don't you?'

So no, maybe not the worst thing, but hardly a sparkling social event either.

And all the way back to Deveraux Cally had been lost in thought. About Ben, mostly. It was odd, but she was only beginning to realise how much he meant to her now that he was no longer around for her to tell him. Ironic, really, if that wasn't too intellectual a word to use to describe the pain that clutched her heart like a fist. But she wanted to tell someone. She *had* to tell someone. Who was there?

It was at times like these that she missed her own parents most. She didn't remember them, of course, didn't know their names or what they looked like, or even if they were alive or dead (maybe her parents and Ben could start up a club). It had occurred to her in the past that she might have crossed the path of her mother or her father many times and never been aware of it, on the street, in a hoverbus, might even have exchanged a 'pardon' or 'excuse me' with either of her parents and never realised. One thing she was certain of, though, they'd never been like Mr and Mrs Stanton. Her parents were warm and loving and understanding. Had to be. And if they were here now, she could go to them and tell them about Ben and the hurt inside her and why nothing seemed to matter any more. Her parents would have words to say to heal her. And then maybe she'd ask them why they abandoned her in city streets at three years old.

Who else was there? There was Mei, of course, her field handler. Cally trusted Mei. But she was in Hong Kong, and heart-to-hearts by holophone were never the same. But there were others she trusted who were due to be at Spy High tomorrow, resting up between missions, two friends from her Bond Team days.

Lori and Bex couldn't arrive soon enough.

The three girls stood at the top of the steps to the club. They made a striking group. The dreadlocked girl and her friend with the bewitching blue eyes and the long blonde hair, they were clothed in a style appropriate for the premiere of the latest blockbuster, in figure-hugging dresses of red and black. Their companion was equally arresting, if for slightly different reasons, those including a hairstyle reminiscent of an ice-cream cone, in pink, a rash of piercings across most of her visible flesh, in gold, and a dress that if she were to take it off would most likely quickly find use as a means of refuse collection, in black.

'Are you sure this is a good idea?' said Lori Angel.

'It's a great idea.' The blonde girl's worries were dismissed with the wave of a hand boasting blood-red fingernails of unfeasible length. 'It's just what Cally needs. It's just what you need, isn't that right, Cal? Quality time with your best mates. A girls' night out. Come on.' Bex Deveraux led the way down the steps.

'Yeah, but Bex,' Cally pursued. Her next words were lost in a blast of music crashing through the club's opening door like a brawler hurled through a window.

'What's that, Cal?' Bex asked.

'I said I was hoping for somewhere *quiet*.'

'Are you kidding?' Bex gave the laugh of someone with experience. 'This is *comatose* for the Inferno Club. Wait till things *really* start cooking.'

'Remind me of the one, if you can't stand the heat get out of the kitchen,' Lori whispered in Cally's ear. *Would* have whispered, had they been anywhere else but the Inferno Club. Here, whispers sounded uncannily like yells.

'Is it too late to change our minds?' Cally whispered back.

'What's that, Cal?'

'I said this is great, Bex.'

Bex winked an eye she'd evidently borrowed from a panda. 'I told you you'd love it. It's one of my favourites. You can trust ol' Bex.'

'Trust, yeah,' grumbled Lori, 'but I'd just as soon hear her, as well.'

To be fair, audibility improved after Bex had led them to a table about as distant from the dance floor as it was possible to get without tunnelling through the wall, a wall painted in lurid flames of orange and red, and embellished with a series of screaming heads.

'What's left of last night's clientele, maybe?' pondered Lori.

'Hell's Angels,' corrected Bex brightly. 'Inferno. Hell. It's like the club's theme. A lot of bikers come here.'

'I can see that – just about.' Lori squinted through thick swathes of smoke at the long-haired and leather-jacketed mobs of men at the bar. 'Well here's one Angel who still prefers Heaven. I'll go get us some drinks. What's the club special, Bex? Axle grease?'

And they talked, and Cally was glad to have Bex and Lori with her. She could be candid with her fellow Spy High graduates in a way that would have been possible with no one else, nobody who didn't know the truth about the Deveraux College or what had really happened to Ben.

'I'm so sorry, Cal,' said Lori, 'but I still can't believe he's gone. Not Ben. Any of the rest of us, maybe, but Ben . . . He was the best of us all. And listen, I know he and I were together back in our Bond Team days, but Ben found something with you that we never had, Cally. I mean it. You were *right* together. Hold on to that.'

'I'm going to. With both hands,' Cally said. 'Thanks, Lo.'

'And remember,' Bex added, 'no one was there when

Ben . . . at the end. No one saw it. The techs are still carrying out experiments on the starstone, aren't they? Dad
hasn't given up on him. There's no hologram of Ben
Stanton yet in the Hall of Heroes.'

'No,' mused Cally. 'I almost wish there were.'

'What?' From both her friends.

'The ceremony. Ben commemorated among the Fallen.
It'd be difficult, but at least it'd maybe bring a sense of
closure, help me move on, get on with my life. Right now
I'm no good to anyone.'

'What are you talking about?' Bex protested. 'You're
good to *us*.'

'Bex is right,' supported Lori. 'Where's this coming
from, Cal?'

'Haven't you heard about Shanghai?' Cally smiled
wanly. 'It's okay. I've done the Facial Expression
Analysis Modules too. So you *have* heard about
Shanghai. Those terrorists got away because of my
incompetence. They might kill again someday because *I*
didn't have my mind on the mission.'

'That wasn't your fault, Cal,' said Lori. 'They returned
you to the field too soon. It wasn't right. You needed
more time.'

'Dad knows it,' Bex reassured her. 'Why else do you
think he went and extended your compassionate leave?'

'Not for long,' Cally said. 'I get a new assignment in a
couple of days. I just hope I'm up to it.'

'You will be,' Lori assured her. She squeezed Cally's
hand. 'You will be, Cal.'

'Say, a little bit of girl-on-girl bonding.' A male voice,
flavoured with arrogance and an aftertaste of threat.
'What about letting us in on the action?'

Three of them. One each, Cally presumed. Leering faces and torn jeans. Too much drink and too little brain.

'Oh, great,' Lori sighed, then, politely: 'I'm sorry, but as you can see, we're having a private conversation here.'

'You don't come to the Inferno to talk,' the boy made clear. 'You come here to dance. For starters. So who wants to dance?'

'*We* don't,' said Bex, 'but it looks like you've got two little partners all ready and waiting for you, Big Guy. We hope you'll all be very happy. What, you're still here? You want me to spell it out for you? G-E-T-L-O-S . . .'

The three boys slouched away gloweringly.

'That was diplomatic, Bex,' observed Lori.

'Diplomacy's lost on the guys who come here, Lo,' said Bex. 'So is any word with more than one syllable. Forget 'em. But Cal, this stuff about closure. I mean, I understand what you mean, but all the while we don't know for *sure*, like *irrefutably*, that Ben's gone for good, then there's still a chance, however ridiculous or far-fetched. Look at me. For years I thought my dad was dead. Then I find out he's a computer program and he's founded a school for secret agents. Out of left field or what? It's just you never know. Life. Death. They're full of surprises.'

'Talking of which,' groaned Lori.

The boys were back. And they'd multiplied. Six of them. Stubborn jaws. Narrow eyes. Not looking for a dance now. Looking for trouble.

'Not you guys *again*,' Bex complained. 'What, you suffer from some repetitive action syndrome or something?'

'You're gonna dance with us,' declared the ringleader.

'Why don't you just go wash your hair or something?' suggested Lori. 'Let me tell you, it needs it.'

'You're gonna dance with us *now*.'

'What if we don't *want* to dance with you now?' wondered Cally. She felt her muscles tensing, an excitement growing. It felt surprisingly good. 'Or, to tell you the truth, *ever*?'

'You're gonna dance with us now,' the thug amended, 'or *else*.'

'Oh. Or *else*.' Bex nodded at her companions as if impressed. 'We haven't had an *or else* for a while, have we, girls? I think that decides it, don't you? Cal?'

'I think it does.' Cally stood. Bex and Lori followed her lead. They stepped out from behind their table to confront the six grinning youths. '*Or else* it is.'

They didn't even work up a sweat. Cally was throwing the ringleader before he was aware his feet were no longer on the ground. To her right and left the fleeting embraces of Lori and Bex's judo moves were the only moments of female contact the thugs were likely to get that night. And while their heads never quite reached the clouds, their entire bodies quickly came down to earth with a pretty emphatic bang, or more like a thud.

The reinforcements fared no better. One of them actually tried to aim a blow at Cally. He missed. She didn't. Bex was ruffling her assailant's hair as he sank to his knees. Lori eliminated the final obstacle with the disdainful grace of a ballet dancer.

By now, the club's bouncers were aware there was trouble, were zeroing in on the Deveraux girls. 'Catch us if you can!' dared Bex. They couldn't. Avoiding the lunges and grabs of the average security man was to students trained at Spy High like dodging a plantation of oak trees. They were past them in seconds, racing to the door, up the steps and into the street, laughing, patting each other on the back, gulping mouthfuls of cool night air.

Feeling good. Cally could scarcely believe it. She'd almost forgotten that such a thing was possible.

'Well, I don't reckon I'll be able to show my face in *there* again,' announced Bex.

'Who would *want* to?' huffed Lori. 'So what now? What do we do now? Cal? You want to head back?'

'To Deveraux? I don't think so.' A slow smile crept across her face. 'The night is yet young.'

'That's the spirit, Cal,' approved Bex. 'And I know this other club, the Velvet Dungeon . . .'

'No way, Bex!' Cally and Lori in unison. All three of them in unison, really.

And she was going to be fine. When she was with her friends, at least, Cally was going to be fine.

On her own, though, that was still another matter.

But she didn't have to be on her own, after all. She could be with Ben if she wanted to be.

He was waiting for her at the table in the restaurant, amid the popping of champagne corks and the blur of rushing waiters. He was wearing a tux and his blue eyes were bright with animation. He spoke to her: 'I was beginning to think you weren't coming, Cal, but I didn't mind waiting. I'd wait for you for ever. Sit down.'

She did. She was elegant in a slinky blue number. A menu was in her hands. 'I don't know what to have,' she said.

'Order whatever you like,' Ben grinned. 'We don't have to pay for it. And it doesn't matter if it's not on the menu, either. It's *that* kind of restaurant.'

'I don't feel like eating anything at all,' Cally said.

'I guess you want us to be alone together,' Ben surmised. 'Me too.'

And they were, on a beach silvered by the stars. They were holding hands and Ben's was warm and strong in hers like it had been when he was alive. Only it didn't belong to Ben any more. Cally pulled away from him.

'What's the matter, Cal?'

'I can't do this. I can't.'

'What do you mean?' Ben seemed hurt. 'This is what you wanted, isn't it? You and me, together again on a night programmed for love. Well, I'm here. The moonlit beach is here. What say we take advantage of both?'

'No.' Cally shook her head. It took an effort to do so. 'You're not here. *Ben*'s not here. You're not Ben.'

'I am if you want me to be, Cal, and as a bonus, I'm Ben with all the good bits intact and all the bad bits taken out. I'm your *ideal* Ben.'

'No. You're a virtual reality representation of Ben. You're an illusion and I don't want you.'

'But you created me, Cally. This is your program.'

'I was stupid. This is wrong.'

'Come on.' Temptingly, his hands on her shoulders. 'Let me make it *right*. I can, you know. Anything's possible here.'

'Anything but the truth,' said Cally. 'I'm sorry. In the end the truth's what we have to live with. The truth's what we have to face up to. Computer. Transfer.'

And there was no beach, no Ben. There was only Cally's cyber-cradle exhaling gently open in the virtual reality chamber at Deveraux.

She sighed sadly. 'Even if we have to face up to it alone.'

ONE

'Jimmy Kwan?'

'Just Jimmy, please. And can I call you Cally?'

'My new field handler?' She let him take her hand as if it was dead. 'But what about Mei?'

'Field Handler Ataki has been transferred to other duties,' said Jonathan Deveraux. 'I trust you will quickly form an efficient and productive working relationship with her successor, Agent Cross.'

'We'll get along fine, won't we, Cally?' prompted Jimmy Kwan.

'Sure,' said Cally. 'Sure we will.' But she spoke from duty rather than conviction.

'Then let us begin the briefing,' said Deveraux.

So what were they up to? Cally speculated as she seated herself at the table in Briefing Room One. Was springing this refugee from a martial arts movie on her in place of Mei Ataki a means of testing her out, piling on pressure, pushing her to see how far she'd really recovered from Ben? Didn't Deveraux have faith in her any more? (Though bearing Shanghai in mind, maybe he was wise not to.) The founder's grave and greying visage on the screen gave nothing away as usual. But what was Jimmy Kwan's game? He was trying to catch her eye and slip her a smile across the table like a guy who fancied his chances. Well, he could forget *that*. And didn't field handlers have to be over thirty or something, hadn't she read that in the Deveraux regulations somewhere? She was relieved when a hologram of a middle-aged Caucasian man with an academic air about him interposed itself between her and Kwan.

'This is Professor Werner Wagner,' Deveraux introduced. 'Perhaps the world's foremost nanosurgeon, a pioneer in techniques applying nanotechnology to human bone and tissue. You are familiar with nanotechnology, I trust, Agent Cross?'

'Yes, sir,' said Cally. 'It's the precision manipulation of the atoms that make up matter.' He wasn't going to catch her out on *that* one.

'Good,' acknowledged Deveraux. 'Professor Werner Wagner was in the process of developing a range of grafts, implants and other artificial enhancements that might not only have radically transformed medical science but altered for all time the way human beings think of themselves and their bodies.'

'*Was*, sir?' said Cally.

'Three days ago, Wagner was found dead in his apartment. The official cause of death is a simple heart attack, and no evidence of foul play has been discovered at the scene.'

However, Cally anticipated. There had to be a however.

'However,' said Jonathan Deveraux (and Cally would have smiled if she hadn't wanted to preserve a poker face for Jimmy Kwan), 'we feel that there is more to this fatality than meets the eye. We were alerted by the IGC's anomaly files to certain tangential information that suggests Professor Werner Wagner may have been murdered.'

The old IGC coming through again, Cally thought. She sometimes wondered what Spy High would do *without* the news and the knowledge supplied by the Intelligence Gathering Centre.

'It appears,' Deveraux continued, 'that Wagner is not the only expert in nanotechnology and related fields to have died suddenly over the past year. None of the deaths alone is suspicious, all accidental or by natural causes, but as the anomaly files correctly bring to our attention, a pattern of deceases has clearly been established.'

It was one of Spy High's truisms: there is no such thing as coincidence, only a plan that has yet to be understood.

'Six deaths. Chronologically Dr Vijay Sharma, Professor Ronald Stoneham, Troy Cutter, Professor Larissa Kratilova, Dr Carlita Sanchez, and Professor Werner Wagner. Further investigation into the group has yielded some interesting findings.'

The late Professor Wagner suddenly lost thirty years and gained seven friends. The holo-photo showed them raising unanimous glasses as if in response to some unknown toast.

'They knew each other?' Cally deduced.

'Exactly,' said Deveraux. 'The entire group was at Princeton together. More than that, they seem to have been close.'

'Six deaths. *Eight* students,' Cally counted. 'Which are the lucky two still alive?'

'None of them,' returned Deveraux. 'Everyone in this photo is dead, but your thinking is leading you in the right direction, Agent Cross.' Six smiling young people, including Werner Wagner, dissolved as if smitten with sudden decay. The pair who remained, a male and a female, had their arms that were not occupied with the glasses tightly clasped around each other's shoulders. Those two looked like they'd been *very* close, Cally thought. 'Darius Thornchild and Joanna Wade, soon to become Joanna Thornchild. The only members of the group to marry and have offspring. The only members of the group not to have died within the past year. Darius and Joanna were killed in a wheelless crash over five years ago, but it is with the Thornchilds that you will be principally concerned, Agent Cross.'

'Sir?' Cally didn't understand.

'I think at this point Field Handler Kwan can take charge of the rest of the briefing, tell you precisely what your assignment will be. There are other matters that require my attention.' JD sure had a way of making you feel special sometimes, didn't he? Cally thought. 'Discharge your duties well, Agent Cross.'

Deveraux vanished from the screen. The Thornchilds disappeared from the holo-frame. Two real people were forced to look at each other across the briefing table.

'So, Mr Kwan,' Cally said frostily. 'The Thornchilds.'

'Jimmy. It's Jimmy,' revised the field handler. 'And I'm sorry you obviously weren't expecting me to be taking over from Mei Ataki, Cally. I imagined that Mr Deveraux would have informed you in advance.'

'Must have been other matters that required his attention.'

'I have spoken to Mei about you. She thinks of you very highly.'

'Mutual,' said Cally.

'And I've read your file.' Jimmy scrutinised Cally's face as if he was a burglar and it was a safe he needed to crack. 'I realise you've had a particularly difficult time lately with what happened to Agent Stanton and I just wanted to say that if there's anything you'd like to talk about, anything at all, I'm here for you.'

'That's cool,' said Cally. A total stranger, there for her. She felt better already. 'What say we talk about the Thornchilds?'

Jimmy seemed disappointed, but he obliged. 'One of the reasons Mr Deveraux is keen to act on the anomaly files' report is the company that the Thornchilds formed. Thornchild Silicon Systems – Bringing the Future to Birth. It's run by their son Adam now and it's a big player in the global computer systems market. Plenty of sensitive contracts, *government* contracts. Even *we've* placed orders with them for some of our new equipment. Mr Deveraux wants to ensure that nothing happens to undermine the company.'

'Such as?' Which sounded more confrontational than maybe Cally had intended.

Jimmy either didn't notice, or pretended not to. 'If somebody *is* murdering nanoscientists, a group of terrorist futurephobes, perhaps, and if for whatever reason they're targeting Professor Wagner and the rest of them from the holophoto, then the closest candidate to next in line is Adam Thornchild. Your mission, Cally, will be to protect him while Deveraux investigations into the six deaths proceed.'

'You're kidding.'

'Thornchild has its head office in Region Green, Hong Kong itself, so it's perfect for us. You could walk there from the Shop if you wanted to, Cally.'

'Yeah. Perfect.'

'You'll present yourself as a security consultant specialising in countering industrial espionage. Your papers and backlife are already being prepared. We'll say that certain key Thornchild customers are concerned about the information they supply with their orders getting into the wrong hands, confidentiality being compromised, that kind of thing. We'll say they've hired you to carry out a review of all aspects of company security.'

'But in fact I'm just there to keep watch over one guy,' Cally interrupted unhappily.

'Adam Thornchild, yes, and there's something—'

'A guy who we have no concrete evidence is actually under any threat, is that right?'

'You know what Mr Deveraux says, Cally. It's better to save a life than to avenge a death.'

'Oh, that's good. That's very good.' Cally felt a surge of indignation inside her, a sense that somebody somewhere was not treating her with the respect she deserved. 'You don't need a graduate agent for this. This is low-level stuff. Routine Deveraux security could handle it. What do you want me for?'

'It's the mission you've been assigned, Cally,' said Jimmy Kwan carefully. But not carefully enough.

Cally was on her feet and railing. 'This isn't a mission. Fighting the Diluvians or Nemesis, leading an assault on the Guardian Star, those are missions. Those are what I'm trained for. *This*, this is pat-a-cake. This is worthless. It's all about Shanghai, isn't it? And about Ben. Mr Deveraux doesn't think I can cope any more, does he?'

'Of course he does,' asserted Jimmy. 'We both do.'

'You *both* do. I'm privileged.'

'So this might not be the most dangerous mission you've ever undertaken. So what? Use it to ease yourself back into active duty. Use it to help *you*. I know you're still hurting over Ben, Cally . . .'

'Do you? You know that?'

'But it was a brave step to come out of the VR program when you—'

'What?' Cally stiffened. 'You've been monitoring my VR sessions? You've been *spying* on me?'

'Not spying, no,' Jimmy defended himself. 'Not exactly. I shouldn't have said that. I'm not sure you're supposed to know, but a new directive from Mr Deveraux means that all students' and graduate agents' virtual reality sessions are now recorded and downloaded to their files as a matter of course in order to assist their tutors and field handlers with psychological profiling.'

'I don't believe it.' And Cally *looked* like she didn't. 'What happened to privacy, the rights of the individual? What's going on in this place?'

'Please, Cally, this isn't the start I wanted for us. Let's get back to the briefing. Sit down, please,' pleaded Jimmy Kwan.

And she might have done had her belt communicator not at that moment bleeped. Jimmy had no idea who was calling her, but from the sudden urgency of Cally's expression, it was important.

'I've got to go,' she said tersely.

'Now? But you can't. We haven't finished the briefing yet.'

'Download the mission file to my computer,' Cally said. 'I'll see you in Hong Kong.'

'But Cally, there's something you should know about Adam —'

But the something would evidently have to wait. Calista Green would not. The door to Briefing Room One slid stubbornly shut behind her.

Jimmy Kwan slumped back in his chair and ground his fists in his eyes, moaned aloud. *That* had gone well. He and Cally had struck up a *real* rapport. They were going to make a great team, like Bond and Blofeld or Holmes and Moriarty. But then, whoever said this job was going to be easy? And he *had* read his charge's file. He *did* know what she'd been through. And he knew what she still had to offer.

He wasn't giving up on Cally Cross by a long chalk.

While Spy High was the cornerstone of Deveraux's empire, it was hardly the only facility the computerised man owned. Others were dotted around the world, each of them engaged in some or other aspect of the organisation's espionage and related activities. One such, a modestly sized scientific research installation, was located among the orange groves of the Sunshine State, but Cally did not fly down to Florida for the weather.

It was here that the starstone was kept.

'Thanks for calling,' she said to the Head Tech, a bespectacled man called Thurby, as he led her to the central control room.

'You asked to be kept informed whenever we had something worth reporting, Agent Cross,' Thurby replied. 'I think you'll find what we've established interesting.'

They entered a textbook control room, computers, screens, and men and women in white coats, the latter collectively boosting the profits of the nation's opticians by a considerable amount.

'I thought you were going to show me the starstone,' Cally said.

'The starstone has been sealed in a titanium vault one hundred metres below us,' the Head Tech informed her, 'for reasons of safety while we continue our experiments. I'm afraid the screen will have to suffice, Agent Cross. Angela, please.'

A tech hit a button and there it was, looming above them on screens that extended from waist height to the ceiling. The so-called starstone. The mysterious alien device that had been discovered on the Moon, stolen by the Wallachians, taken to Vlad Tepesch's capital city and partially activated. Partially had been enough to obliterate Ben. This was the last thing Ben had seen, Cally knew, the jagged, multi-pointed grey-green star, fourteen feet high, fourteen feet wide, carved from something like marble, the control panels in its centre flickering a fatal countdown as the end came. It wasn't right. The last thing someone should see should be the face of a loved one. If only she'd been with him. Cally felt her fists clench.

But the starstone seemed safe enough now, like a wild beast sleeping.

'We've been experimenting with partial activations of

the starstone,' Thurby was explaining, 'controlled discharges of its power, in order to try to gauge not only the effect of the energy it can generate but its nature also.'

'I can tell you what it does,' said Cally grimly. 'It *eats* people.'

Thurby offered an embarrassed laugh. 'Not the most scientific form of words, Agent Cross,' he observed, 'but not entirely inappropriate. Let me show you something. Angela, playback, please. Experiment Thirteen.'

On the screen, the present melted into the past. The viewers' perspective widened. The starstone in its lonely vault had company, a much smaller instrument bristling with antennae and flashing with excited lights. Or perhaps the lights were anxious. The highest point of the alien artefact was glowing green, humming like a dynamo, emerald mist emitting from the body and drifting upwards. The starstone was about to detonate.

'We placed a probe in with our alien friend,' Thurby said, 'a probe designed to measure and analyse energy. We also equipped the probe with a state-of-the-art communications system so that it could continue to send us data even through the explosion.'

'I think you wasted Mr Deveraux's money then, if you don't mind me saying so, Thurby,' commented Cally. 'Difficult to communicate when you've been atomised.'

There was a flash of savage power that even on the screen was blinding. A bolt of consuming green energy stabbed from the starstone. For several seconds nothing in the vault could be seen. Then, like an ocean commanded by the tides, the energy receded, flowed back towards its source, was absorbed again by the marble frame of the device. The starstone stood as undamaged and uncaring as ever. The vault's titanium surrounds had been dissolved by more than a foot. Of the probe there was no sign. It might never have existed.

'Hope you've got the budget for a replacement, Thurby.' Cally smiled thinly.

The Head Tech smiled too, but there was a knowingness about him that made Cally wonder. 'I'm not yet convinced we'll need one, Agent Cross,' he said. 'Listen to this.' He pressed a switch himself this time, perhaps feeling that Angela would benefit from a rest. A pinging sound like a heart monitoring machine in a hospital could be heard in the control room.

'Sorry, modern music isn't my thing.'

'This is the probe's locator signal,' Thurby said, 'so that if we were to lose visual contact with it in the field, we'd still be able to find it. You're hearing the signal *before* the events of Experiment Thirteen.' He pressed another switch. It produced an identical pinging sound, but now it was softer, remote as the stars, as if all the Head Tech had done was to turn down the volume. 'And this is the signal now.'

'Now?' Cally frowned. 'What do you mean, now? How can it be? The probe was destroyed. We just saw it—'

'We saw it *disappear*,' Thurby revised. 'That's not *necessarily* the same thing. It includes an assumption that the purpose of the starstone's energy emissions is destructive.'

'But . . .' Cally groped. 'So, what? You're saying they're not?'

'I'm drawing no absolute conclusions at this point,

Agent Cross, but let me say, we have traced the probe's locator signal to its present position.'

'And where's that?' Cally wanted to know.

Head Tech Thurby turned to the screen. 'Inside the starstone.'

He'd said more as well, and Cally had gone over every word a thousand times during her flight to Hong Kong. There was a strange feeling inside her. It had to do with Ben, the starstone and the probe. It had to do with a tension, an expectation, a wild and as yet formless hope, an impossible hope. 'Perhaps,' Thurby had told her, 'whatever is immersed in the starstone's energy field is not actually disintegrated. Perhaps it is simply *displaced*.' Displaced. A good word. It didn't have the finality of death about it. Cally nursed it gently in her mind like a mother with a sickly child.

The private Deveraux jet was over India before she remembered that she had yet to read her mission file. Jimmy Kwan had downloaded it on to her PC as she'd rather rudely requested, and she hadn't even glanced at it. She'd better start now. Her relationship with her new field handler had already commenced a little coolly: if she wasn't careful it would end up arctic.

But there were distractions keeping Cally from Adam Thornchild. Not just Ben and the starstone, but some of the more general material Jimmy Kwan had included in his package. Especially Professor Werner Wagner making the paralytic walk.

Footage of one of the late nanosurgeon's demonstrations of the miracles of modern technology. There he was, surrounded by acolytes and wide-eyed sensation-seekers, taking centre stage in a theatre more likely to host a play than a medical procedure. There was the paralysed man, lying on the operating table before him, his useless legs extended and naked and pale. There was the syringe-gun in Professor Wagner's hand.

'Religion? Faith? Belief?' he was sneering. 'Overrated. If you don't want to be sick or ill or crippled in the twenty-first century, don't waste your time praying to God, spend it *paying* your nanosurgeon.' General laughter. Even the paralysed man managed something of a grin. 'And miracles? Meaningless. In an age of science there are no miracles, only the marvels we create ourselves. Observe!'

He pressed the barrel of the syringe-gun firmly against the fleshless thigh of the paralytic's right leg, squeezed the trigger. 'You'll feel nothing at first,' Wagner said, 'but then you'll be used to that, won't you?' He repeated the process with his patient's other leg. 'But wait and you'll see. The nanografts will take a few moments to knit themselves to the bones of your legs, the fibula and femur, the patella, the tarsals and metatarsals of the feet. The nanofluid will require the same to mingle with your blood and seep into your sadly wasted muscles. But have no fear. Nanotechnology, nano*surgery*, will make you walk.'

Wagner addressed his eager audience more expansively. 'No one need ever suffer again. With nanotechnology we can make the blind man see and the deaf man hear. We can drive out disease like demons, and as for lepers, we can cure lepers ten a penny before breakfast. We can control the body. We can control the mind. And healing is just the start of it. What we can accomplish now, what is within our grasp—'

'Something's happening,' uttered the paralysed man in awe. 'I can feel them. I can feel my legs!'

'We have it within our power to create the perfect human being, to design and construct a new race, a new humanity . . .'

'I can feel them. I can feel them and they're so *strong* . . .'

'. . . who will be to us what we are to the neanderthals who once grunted and slouched their way across the world. All this we can do, all this we can achieve, if we find the courage within ourselves to view Mankind not as a pinnacle, not as an end product, but as work in progress. And let me conclude by assuring you, my friends, that the time will swiftly be upon us when to think like this will be as natural and as easy as it is for me now to say to this man before us, *take up thy bed and walk*.'

'I can do it. I can *feel* them.' And the man – paralysed no longer – swung his legs from the table and placed his feet on the floor. He stood. 'I can walk! I can *walk*!' The audience erupted in jubilation.

Not Cally, though. She sat back in her chair as the video ended and her brow was furrowed. Maybe her mission wasn't such a waste of time, after all. What she'd just watched would surely have provided *some* with a motive for murder, extreme futurephobes, as Jimmy Kwan had suggested, or certain fundamentalist religious groups. The incredible potential of nanotechnology might terrify as well as inspire, and nanoscientists could be seen as devils just as mistakenly as gods.

Out of the window the skyscrapers of Hong Kong were thrusting for the heavens. Cally thought she'd give the Shop a miss for the moment. Not to avoid Jimmy Kwan, however.

She felt it might be an idea to get to Adam Thornchild as quickly as possible.

From the helicopter the city seemed like a man-made mountain range. Its peaks of metal and concrete and glass dazzled in the afternoon sunlight, clamouring and competing one with another to reach the cleanest air. Hundreds of metres below the sheer and sparkling precipices, in the swarm of dark and cavernous streets, life teemed in all its exuberance and unpredictability, the citizens of Hong Kong invisible insects from Cally's lofty vantage point. The chopper swooped over Hong Kong Island itself, crossed Victoria Peak and Causeway Bay, the star ferries bobbing like green and white stones in the harbour waters, and headed for the business district of Kowloon, the mainland. Soaring above its peers rose the Thornchild Building. Its uppermost floors were constructed entirely from glasteel so that the people Cally could see working within and their desks and their computers seemed to be hovering in mid-air, as if levitation skills were a prerequisite for employment here. Cally hoped none of them suffered from vertigo.

The pilot lowered the chopper to the rooftop heliport. It was probably as well he'd landed here before, with no visible surface to guide him. Cally thanked him and disembarked – cautiously.

She'd left a message to let Jimmy know what she was doing, and in between plane and helicopter had slipped into something less comfortable for the purpose, a sober grey outfit that had been tailored for her as suitable for a freelance security consultant specialising in countering industrial espionage.

She was greeted by a party of three men in expensive suits, but only one of them seemed likely to concern her. He was tall, thin, and from his aspect probably difficult to beat at either business or cards: his face gave nothing away, appeared entirely without emotion. His companions were obviously underlings, their eyes fixed on his lips for instructions like a pair of matching Uriah Heeps. It was the first man who came forward, extended a palm in welcome.

'We've been expecting you, Ms Cross,' he said.

Cally shook his hand and did the maths. He looked a little *old*, but . . . 'Mr Adam Thornchild, I presume?'

'I'm afraid not. My name is Lucas Thornchild. Please, if you'd care to follow me . . .'

Cally was escorted to a transparent elevator that whisked them from the roof to the confines of the Thornchild Building. They emerged on to a level where at least the interior walls and floors looked as well as felt solid. Elegant oak and mahogany panelling had replaced the glasteel. 'An impressive place you've got here, sir,' she thought it polite to say.

'Mr Thornchild's office is this way, Ms Cross.'

And now Cally seriously began to wish she'd completed her briefing. Then she'd doubtless already know what relationship Lucas was to Adam, instead of wondering whether she ought to ask him. Just as she decided that to do so would appear unprofessional, it was too late in any case. They'd come to a door at the end of a corridor. Emblazoned upon it: 'Adam Thornchild –

President.' Lucas Thornchild knocked, opened the door. 'Ms Cross,' he invited.

Cally entered, the tall man behind her. Their erstwhile companions did not join them. The holy of holies, Cally thought. The company president's office.

And now she *totally* seriously wished she'd completed her briefing, because Jimmy Kwan had tried to tell her.

She'd got her expression all worked out, confident and businesslike but with a hint of put-'em-at-their-ease humour in her eyes. She'd got her line prepared too – 'Calista Cross, Mr Thornchild, freelance security consultant. It's an honour to meet you' – and her handshake, bold yet sensitive.

Then she saw him. She saw what he was doing. She saw what was with him. And then Cally could do nothing but stare.

Jimmy Kwan had wanted to warn her.

Adam Thornchild could not have been more than twelve years old.

TWO

He was dressed in a suit that seemed too big for him, like a school uniform his mother might have bought for his first day in the belief that eventually he'd grow into it. He was pale and thin, almost delicate, as if rehearsing to be an invalid in later life. His hair was blond, but not vigorously or emphatically so (not like Ben, Cally thought), rather as if it lacked the energy to be anything else. It was in keeping with Adam Thornchild's general physical appearance. He was a picture that had yet to be coloured in. He was a doll that needed a ventriloquist to make it speak.

The president of Thornchild Silicon Systems was seated behind an expansive oak desk playing what looked to Cally suspiciously like a computer game on his mini-PC. Stretched out on either side of the desk, mouths open and panting, were two huge dogs. If they'd been canines of the flesh, blood and fur variety, their breed might have been Alsatian. As it was, their gleaming metal bodies and electronic eyes, coupled with the fact that they were more than twice the size of the living dogs on which they'd been modelled, rendered such a consideration irrelevant. Maybe Thornchild Silicon Systems operated a Pets Manufacturing Division on the quiet.

Adam looked up with faint interest on Cally's entry. 'Hello,' he said. 'Who are you?'

'This is Ms Cross, Adam,' supplied Lucas Thornchild. 'She's come to talk to us about our security. I told you about her.' Though the man's face remained virtually impassive, Cally detected a note of exasperation in his voice.

'Told me? Did you, Uncle Lucas? I forget.' Adam shrugged and was all but swallowed by his collar. 'Sorry, Ms Crass.'

'Cross,' corrected Cally. 'Calista Cross, Mr Thornchild, freelance security consultant. It's an honour to meet you.' She was back on track after her initial surprise. Now to step forward for the handshake.

The steel dogs stirred at once. They sat up, growled threateningly, baring fangs like butchers' knives.

'Rover. Rex,' frowned Adam. 'Be quiet. Lie down.' The mechanical creatures obeyed on both counts. 'I'm sorry, Ms Cross. My dogs are very protective. They don't like it when strangers come near me.'

'That's fine. No problem,' said Cally. 'Only I hope I won't qualify as a stranger for too long, Mr Thornchild.'

'Oh, Adam, please,' the boy responded. 'My Uncle Lucas is the only *Mister* Thornchild around here. And I'll call you Calista, I think, if that's all right with you.'

'Of course.' Cally smiled like a babysitter with an unexpectedly agreeable charge. She indicated the mini-PC he was holding. 'What are you doing, Adam? Playing games?'

The boy seemed almost offended. 'No, I never play games, Calista. This isn't an entertainment program. See for yourself.' He showed her the screen and Cally saw what looked like the end of the Universe pixellated in miniature, all exploding planets and worlds rent asunder. But it wasn't a vision of the cosmos in chaos. The configuration of the globes gave their secret away. Protons. Neutrons. Electrons. Cally recognised them all. This was devastation at a sub-atomic level. 'I'm working on ways of refining and upgrading our smart atom technology,' Adam explained with something of pride in his voice.

'*Smart* atoms?'

'Oh, yes. It's easy to *split* the atom – they were making bombs that way back in the middle of the last century, after all. But to break an atom down and then put it back together again in an *improved* form, programmed the way you want it, programmed to be intelligent, a *smart* atom, that's a little trickier. Sometimes it keeps me up all night just thinking about it. I don't get a lot of sleep, Calista. The ideas in my brain won't let me.' He grinned apologetically. 'So smart atoms, yes. What do you think?'

'Incredible,' Cally admitted, though she was astonished as much by Adam Thornchild as by his work. 'I guess you must be top of your science class at school, right?'

'Adam doesn't attend school,' said Lucas Thornchild. 'It isn't necessary. Adam is a genius in all subject areas.'

'And it'd look bad for the school if a student knew more than the teachers, don't you think, Calista?' The boy put down his mini-PC and hopped off his chair. Cally noticed that a cushion had been placed on it to allow Adam to reach the desk. He called to his dogs –

'Rover! Rex!' – and they came to him, wagging tails like lengths of steel cable. They were very nearly as tall as him. 'Rover and Rex are made of smart atoms. They can do everything a biological dog can do and a little bit more besides.' Adam patted the constructs' shiny metal backs. They seemed to like the attention, didn't want it to end. Their steel skin became liquid and curled around their owners' wrists to keep his hands in contact. Elongated tongues snaked from their mouths and licked moisturelessly at his adjacent cheeks. 'Actually, they can do a *lot* more than living dogs. They've been programmed for loyalty and love. They'll never let me down or leave me. They'll never die. No vets' fees. No food bill. They don't even need to be exercised. The pets of the future, I think, courtesy of smart atoms, a Thornchild Silicon Systems product.'

'You never know,' said Cally, but somehow she doubted that animals in cold metal, however faithful or long-lasting, would ever replace creatures you could cuddle that were furry and warm.

'That's enough, boys, lie down,' Adam instructed Rover and Rex. He extended his hand now to Cally. 'I like you, Calista. I think you're nice.'

'Well, thank you.' She took his hand. It was cold, like it had been stored in a refrigerator. 'I'm glad.'

'Would you like to come to a party tomorrow night?'

'Party?' Cally knew that Deveraux agents were pretty much expected to do whatever was necessary for the successful completion of a mission, to go to any lengths, make every sacrifice. But still, dating a twelve-year-old seemed a bit extreme.

'It's my birthday. I'm thirteen tomorrow. Uncle Lucas

tells me I ought to mark the occasion with a party so apparently I'm having one. I'd like you to come.'

'Adam,' interrupted Lucas Thornchild, 'I'm sure Ms Cross will have work to do tomorrow, *won't* you, Ms Cross?'

'I think so, Mr Thornchild,' said Cally, taking the hint.

'Can I remind you that Ms Cross is here as a security consultant and we haven't yet even begun to discuss —'

'No, Uncle Lucas.' Adam's lower lip jutted out petulantly. 'You *can't* remind me of that.' Low growls of disapproval in the throats of the dogs. 'I'm busy with smart atoms today. We can discuss Thornchild's security with Ms Cross another time.' And suddenly he was all charm again, turning to Cally. 'What about tomorrow at my house, before the party? You could come for lunch. What do you think?'

Little alternative. 'Well,' said Cally, 'that's very kind of you, Adam . . .'

'Then it's settled.' Adam leaned forward confidentially. 'And don't worry about Uncle Lucas, Calista. He thinks that because he's my only living relative and my legal guardian to boot he can tell me what to do. But he can't, not really.'

'Adam, please,' protested Lucas Thornchild.

'I let him deal with the day-to-day running of the company – he likes to feel he's important, don't you, Uncle Lucas? – but I make all the big decisions and I come up with all the big ideas. Isn't that right, Uncle?'

'If you say so, Adam, I'm sure it must be,' winced Lucas Thornchild.

'So Calista's coming to the island tomorrow,' Adam stated. 'Have arrangements made.' Lucas nodded.

'Good.' Adam refocused on Cally. 'Uncle Lucas will remain my guardian until I come of age, of course, Calista, which I know is technically sixteen, but somehow I feel that tomorrow is my most significant birthday. Thirteen. A teenager. Time for me to come into my own.' He smiled and shook Cally's hand a second time. 'I'm glad you'll be there to share it with me.'

If someone was tailing Cally after she left the Thornchild Building, an enemy agent, say, at first he'd have found it difficult to keep the object of his pursuit in sight. The streets of Kowloon were thick with people, so many that it seemed surprising there was enough air to go round. He could have lost Cally a hundred times. If he'd persisted, though, if he was good at his job, he'd have managed to follow her into Nathan Road, a shopping street that had seen better days and more numerous shoppers, and from there into a dingy, dishevelled arcade, which sadly for it had seen neither. A simple matter to keep her in sight now, to watch her as she paused briefly before the shabby façade of a tailor's shop and then went in without a backward glance.

If the stalker was keen or impatient, he might have ventured inside too. It was a public place, after all, albeit one that the public seemed to have forgotten. There were suits to be bought here, hung up on racks like the victims of some cruel medieval torture, and looking nearly as old. Perhaps it would be a better deal to have a garment made to measure. Our pursuer would have clearly seen – at least, as clearly as the exhausted lightbulb would allow – a Chinese gentleman of advanced years, monumental spectacles and a tape measure round his neck directing Cally to a changing room at the back, perhaps for a fitting. He'd have seen her enter the changing room alone.

And then our stalker, our spy, would surely have abandoned all pretence of purchase in any case. He'd have borne down on the changing room knowing that Cally was behind its frail wooden door, that he had her now, that she was at his mercy. And maybe, if such a pursuer had existed, he'd have flung the door wide open. It would have matched his mouth. He'd have discovered the changing room absolutely empty.

But of course, there was no stalker. Nobody followed Cally to Chung's tailor's in the arcade off Nathan Road. The Shop, as everyone called it who knew what it really was, what it hid beyond and beneath the rows of suits that would never be bought. Cally had exchanged a few words with Ling Po, and entered the changing room. On three sides, glass walls. It didn't matter which she pressed her hand against – each of them would register her palm print, identify her as Calista Green, Spy High graduate, and slide open to grant her access to the Deveraux organisation's Hong Kong base. Labs, holo-gyms, SkyBike bays, they were all at her disposal, all ready and waiting for her.

As was Jimmy Kwan.

He steered her into the meeting room. He was wearing a black shirt and trousers that clung to his admittedly impressive musculature like a love-struck girl. His sleeves didn't extend to his forearms, allowing Cally to view the sinuous dragon tattoos that provided artwork for his skin. She found herself feeling slightly uncomfortable – no doubt the tattoos reminded her of Talon and the tragic confrontation they'd had with the Serpents during their training. For whatever reason, she tried to keep her eyes on Jimmy's face rather than the rest of him.

'So did you meet Adam Thornchild, Cally? How did it go?'

'I won't say you should have told me he was a kid because you tried to,' Cally conceded, 'though I don't think *anything* you could have said would have prepared me for what he's actually like.'

Jimmy nodded. 'I don't doubt it. Child prodigies are always a little disconcerting, mature in some ways, immature in others.'

'Disconcerting,' Cally mused. 'That's field handler for *weird*, right?'

'I think you might be doing him an injustice,' Jimmy cautioned. 'Adam Thornchild is to computer science what Mozart was to music. He thinks in a different way. It's not so much that it's *outside* the box, it's more as if the box never existed in the first place. A total original. A genius. A radically new approach to fields like nano-technology, atomic engineering . . .'

'Smart atoms,' added Cally.

'Exactly. Adam patented the first generation of those when he was four years old, while the rest of us were still probably sucking our thumbs and having A is for Apple drummed into us.'

'You were sucking your thumb at four, Jimmy?' Cally sounded intrigued.

'That was an example, not a confession, Cally,' Jimmy grinned.

'Sure it was. And anyway, maybe we should all have started with A is for Atom. Or Adam.'

'Or even Are you going to tell me what happened?'

Cally did. She reported every detail of her interview with Adam Thornchild, culminating in her invitation to the prodigy's thirteenth birthday party tomorrow. And while she was speaking, she found herself feeling that maybe this Jimmy Kwan wasn't so bad after all. He was much nearer her own age than Mei Ataki had been – she had friends who *dated* guys in their early twenties. She could joke with him: Mei had been a generous and understanding field handler, but she hadn't exactly majored in humour. Maybe Cally hadn't really given him a chance back at Deveraux. Maybe she should put that right.

'Well, you did a good job,' Jimmy acknowledged once she'd finished, 'and without the benefit of my full briefing either.'

'Yeah, I wanted to apologise about that,' Cally said. 'About my behaviour before in general, actually. I wasn't being fair to you, Jimmy. It's not an excuse but I suppose I just wasn't expecting—'

Jimmy Kwan shook his head. 'Forget it. It's not important. That was then, this is now. Each new dawn is a new beginning.'

'Who said that? Confucius?'

'No, it was in a fortune cookie I got once. I've been waiting for a chance to use it in a conversation for years.'

Cally laughed. 'So we can, like, start again?'

'We'd better.' Jimmy laughed too. 'An agent and her field handler are a team, and this mission has got to work, Cally, or . . .'

'Or what?' Cally smiled. Until she saw the moment of panic in Jimmy's eyes, the realisation that he'd said more than he should have done. 'Or *what*?' And a smile seemed suddenly inappropriate.

'Nothing. It doesn't matter.' Jimmy could have cursed himself. He was still new to this job. He had to learn to vet his words before coming out with them. First the monitoring of the VR sessions, now this. From Cally's accusing glare, starting again was looking unlikely. Each new dawn – same old foul-up.

'No, it's not nothing. What were you going to say, Jimmy? This mission's got to work or what?'

Or Mr Deveraux's going to have you mind-wiped, Cally, Jimmy knew. But he couldn't tell *her* that. He *wouldn't* tell her that.

'You're worried about your job, aren't you?' His silence led Cally to leap not only to her feet but to conclusions of her own. 'That's it. You're afraid that if I blow it, it's going to reflect badly on you as a first-time field handler. Well thank you very much for your confidence. Why don't you tell Mr D, Jimmy? Maybe there's still a chance for you to get reassigned to an agent with greater potential who doesn't come with a dead boyfriend for baggage.'

'No. Cally. It's nothing like that. Sit down, will you, please? Let's talk about . . . no, don't even *think* about storming out. Cally!' He was fighting a losing battle. 'Where do you think you're going?'

She was at the door already. 'Sorry, boss, but I've got a party to get ready for.'

'But that's not until tomorrow.'

'A girl needs to look her best for a boy's thirteenth,'

Cally remarked acidly, ' 'specially when her mission's got to work *or*. Guess I should have trusted my first impressions after all, hey, Jimmy?'

'No. Cally, you're wrong about me. And you can't keep—' But she did. The meeting room door slammed shut behind her. 'I don't believe it,' groaned Jimmy. 'She's done it to me *again*!'

The islands off the coast of Hong Kong seemed to have been thrown from the mainland like dice. The South China Sea shimmered around them, but Cally didn't have time to admire the view. That was one of the downsides of working for Deveraux: you got to travel the world but you never got to enjoy it. There was always the mission to think of; you always had to concentrate less on sightseeing and more on simply staying alive.

At the moment, to be fair, as a Thornchild helicopter transported her to the island owned by the family, she didn't feel she was in any danger of sudden death, but there was still plenty on her mind. Jimmy Kwan for example. They were getting off on the wrong foot so often she feared their relationship would be permanently lamed. That would be bad. Because Jimmy had been right about one thing: agent and field handler *should* function as a team. Cally supposed she'd no choice but to try to be professional about it: she might have to work with Jimmy Kwan, but she didn't have to *like* him. Add another problem to the list. She was just about holding on by her fingertips as it was.

The helicopter was beginning its descent. Thornchild Island lay below. Its crescent shape cradled a sandy bay, protecting it from the deeper waters that buffeted the craggy cliff sides of the island's outer rim. From the beach on all sides the land rose steeply, passage facilitated by moving walkways cut into the rock and leading to the only building on the island, a domed construction evidently designed to blend in with the natural environment. A pity such a large section of the natural environment had had to be cleared for the helipad, Cally thought.

It was déjà vu. She was met again by Lucas Thornchild, who once more took on the responsibility of escorting her to Adam. He even appeared to be wearing the same suit. Cally, however, had changed into a lighter, less formal dress, bearing in mind the festivities planned for later. She carried a laptop with her too, though – freelance security consultants never went anywhere without one.

There was no evidence in the house that its owner was celebrating his birthday today. Lucas led her through accommodation more akin to offices than lounges or living rooms. There were servants and there were Thornchild employees and there were men with heads like the rocks outside who were obviously the security, but there was no warmth and no welcome and not a sign of an individual personality. It was a house, sure, but it was nobody's *home*.

'The private quarters are this way, Ms Cross,' Lucas informed her.

'Does Adam live here on his *own*?' Cally wondered. 'I mean, other than the people who work for him, of course.'

'Not quite,' said Thornchild. 'I reside here too. My rooms are close to Adam's. I like to keep an eye on him. But here we are.'

He knocked on a door. Cally half expected to see the words 'Adam Thornchild – President' written on it. They weren't, but Adam himself was on the other side. He was wearing a T-shirt and jeans this time, though they still looked like hand-me-downs from an older brother, and Rover and Rex remained in attendance. He seemed pleased to see Cally, at least remembered she'd been invited. Lucas Thornchild he dismissed peremptorily. 'He wants to talk business with you, Calista,' Adam confided, 'but then Uncle Lucas *always* wants to talk business. Let him wait.'

Cally looked around. Adam's so-called private quarters were as soullessly neat and spotless as if they belonged to someone who'd recently died rather than a newly teenaged boy. No socks strewn across the floor. No holo-posters of starlets or sportsmen on the walls. No music blaring loudly. Just the hum of a VR room and more computer equipment than most stores. Cally began to feel sorry for Adam Thornchild, boy genius. 'Happy birthday,' she said.

'Thanks. Hey, I think I've made some advances with the smart atoms program I was working on,' he enthused. 'Do you want to see?'

'Sure,' said Cally, 'but shouldn't you be getting ready for the party or something?'

'Nah.' Adam wrinkled his nose in distaste. 'The party was Uncle Lucas' idea, not mine. I didn't want one. I might not even go.'

'Might not go? Adam . . .'

'What's the big deal?' the boy shrugged. 'I don't like parties. You have to have people at parties and I don't really *do* people. People make me nervous. With one or two notable exceptions, Calista, such as yourself. Nah, Uncle Lucas expects over a hundred guests tonight. I think I might just stay here with Rover and Rex.' On cue, the oversized dogs brought their metal snouts within fondling distance. 'I know where I am with Rover and Rex.'

'Can I say something, Adam?' Cally ventured. 'Kind of a personal something?'

'Sure,' Adam consented. 'You can say whatever you want, Calista.'

'I think you should give people a chance. I know your *abilities* make you a special case, you're not maybe like other thirteen-year-old boys, but I think if you allow that to isolate you, to set you apart from everybody else, I think that'll be a mistake, and one that eventually you'll regret.'

'Do you?' said Adam interestedly.

'It's difficult forming relationships. Believe me, I know—'

'Do you have a boyfriend, Calista?' Adam interjected.

'I *did* have.' She wasn't going to go *there*. 'But I'm not just talking about boyfriend-girlfriend stuff. *Any* relationship. *Every* relationship. Friends. Family. They can be hard. They can hurt you. But they can bring you good things, too, happiness, love, *good* emotions. And in the end, it's relationships that make life worth living. Without them, it can be a pretty lonely world. Don't give up on people just yet, Adam.'

'No?' Adam Thornchild smiled thinly. 'You don't know much about me, do you, Calista?'

'I know your parents died when you were seven. I know how you must have felt.'

'Do you?' Adam seemed dubious. 'How?'

'Because I lost my parents too.' Cally wasn't sure she should say this, whether the truth contradicted anything in the backlife that Deveraux had created for Calista Cross, freelance security consultant, but she wasn't sure she cared, either. Right now she needed to reach pale, lonely Adam Thornchild on a human level. The secret agent stuff would have to wait. 'I don't know whether they're alive or dead. It *feels* like they're dead. I was found wandering the streets when I was about three. When I was old enough to be told that, I felt alone, rejected. I did some bad things. I resented people. But I learned better, Adam, I learned that whatever terrible things, tragic things, might happen to you, you can get through them, but you need people to help you do that. Don't shut yourself away with your mechanical dogs and your computers. Go to your party. Meet someone. Make friends. You'll be glad you did.'

'Maybe I will.' Adam narrowed his eyes contemplatively. 'You've certainly given me plenty to think about, Calista. And just in time, too. Here's Uncle Lucas back again.'

Almost as if he'd been lurking outside the door.

'I apologise if I'm intruding,' Thornchild said, 'but I really *must* have a few words with Ms Cross myself before lunch.'

'If you insist, Uncle Lucas,' sighed Adam, 'but I know what they're going to be. Uncle Lucas doesn't think Thornchild needs your services, Calista. He thinks our present levels of security can cope with any problems that might arise. Convince him he's wrong, won't you? I don't know, but I think I'm beginning to make a friend.'

Lucas Thornchild conducted Cally from Adam's rooms like a servant preparing to show her to the door. They'd hardly left the boy's hearing range, however, when the tall man's normally bland features finally decided on an expression, and it was one that would not be found on the face of any servant who wished to remain in his or her employment. Blazing eyes. Twisted sneer. Cally might or might not be making a friend of Adam. That she'd made an enemy of his uncle was certain.

'Now that we're alone I think we can drop the pretence, don't you, *Ms Cross*?' Her name couched in contempt.

'I don't know what you mean, Mr Thornchild.' Had Lucas somehow seen through her?

'I think you do. I know what you're up to, young lady. Fluttering your eyelashes and tossing those dreadful dreadlocks, ingratiating yourself with my nephew, insinuating yourself into the trust of an impressionable boy. I have no doubt you clapped your mercenary hands with joy when you were hired for this assignment. A chance to exploit the heir to the Thornchild billions?'

'Actually, no, Mr Thornchild.' Panic over. Lucas knew nothing. 'I'm here to help you out, not rip you off. I'm a professional freelance—'

'Yes, yes,' snapped Lucas. 'You've been checked out. I know who you are. And I want *you* to know *this*. I will not allow *anyone* to come between myself and my nephew, especially not a grubby little fortune-hunter like you. I tolerate Adam's outbursts and insolence because he is young and knows no better, but he's not as clever as he thinks he is. *I* run the company, Ms Cross, and *I* know what is best for my nephew. I also have many friends in positions of importance in the business community. Keep away from Adam, or you may soon find freelance security consultancy work rather difficult to come by. Do we understand each other, *Ms Cross*?'

'Oh, I think so,' said Cally, not flinching from Thornchild's threats. 'I understand you perfectly.'

Maybe he'd expected her to leave before the party. If so, Lucas Thornchild was going to be disappointed. Cally was still on the island when the guests began to arrive by helicopter and by boat in the late afternoon sun.

She made her way down to the beachside terrace. Music and food were due to be provided from here. Numerous poles with light-globes atop them had been sunk into the sand, ready to replace the natural light as evening descended. There were to be games and entertainment with a midnight climax of a fireworks display above the bay. To be honest, Cally wasn't interested in any of that. She was on the look-out for . . . 'Adam. Adam!'

'Calista.' He'd made an effort to smarten himself up, though the brighter colours he now wore made his pale complexion resemble that of a ghost even more closely. Rover and Rex must have been left in the house. 'I took your advice. Here I am.'

'That's good,' Cally smiled. 'I'm glad. Now all you have to do is relax and have a great time.'

A cluster of girls in party frocks stepped on to the terrace from the moving walkway, saw Adam, and huddled together giggling.

'I don't know who any of these people are,' Adam said.

Cally winked encouragingly. 'So now's your chance to find out.'

Little chance, as it happened. It seemed that Uncle Lucas wanted not only Calista Cross to keep her distance from the birthday boy, but the other guests as well. Why else would he have organised a high-backed chair like a throne for Adam to sit on, raised on a podium and guarded by a pair of most *un*-party-like security men? 'I know what's best for my nephew,' he'd claimed. As if. Cally watched the subdued youngsters file past their host offering him presents and congratulations, but looking as if they were paying their last respects to a dead king or somebody lying in state. It wasn't *Cally* who was using Adam Thornchild for their own ends.

The atmosphere lifted a little with the clowns. Traditional clowns, all bowler hats and cartoon boots, white faces and red noses, bulging eyes and sprouting hair. Loud check suits with flowers in the lapels that squirted water. White-gloved hands with buzzers concealed that shocked you when the clown's hand closed on yours. Lunatic smiles sawn on the faces in the colour of blood. There was no act as such, no performance. The clowns simply milled among the revellers and played whatever tricks took their fancy on whoever they chose.

Cally kept out of their way. She'd never been partial to clowns. There was something manic about them, something crazed and unpredictable that she found disturbing rather than amusing. The kids didn't seem to share her hang-up, however. Hoots and squeals of laughter from the beach and terrace. Even Adam on his perch seemed to be chuckling, though no clown had yet dared to approach the prodigy. Probably under kindly, protective Uncle Lucas' orders.

Maybe she herself should go to the boy, coax him down, get him involved. Some of the kids were dancing. Maybe she should . . .

And one of them was screaming.

A shrill, hysterical sound that most people wouldn't have been able to differentiate from all the other shrieks and yells of the party. But most people hadn't undergone aural sensitivity training at Spy High. It was a scream. And for an agent in the field, to hear it was to pinpoint its location.

Cally's head snapped round to the beach. A girl, sprawled in the sand, hair matted, tears of shock and pain coursing down her cheeks. Reason obvious: the badly burned hand that she was holding up to her friends. Cally could almost see the reddened flesh smouldering.

A clown was lumbering stiffly, bow-legged from the beach. Towards Adam.

'Excuse me. Excuse me.' Cally pushed past the queue for the food in the same direction. The clown was wearing a yellow and green check suit and a bow tie that was spinning round like the rotors of a helicopter out of control.

One of the screaming girl's friends, a boy, was racing after the clown, shouting the kind of words you didn't like to hear at thirteenth birthday parties. Those nearest to him were frowning, sensing now that something was wrong.

'Excuse me. *Excuse* me.'

The clown's left arm dangled at his side. His right

hand was raised. The white glove on it was blackening and smoking. The clown seemed to find this humorous. He was laughing.

Even when the boy caught up with him, swung him round, aimed a punch at his very red nose. Even when his right hand intercepted the blow, seized the boy's fist and squeezed. Especially when the boy's screams matched the girl's, and he collapsed to the sand with his own hand stripped of skin and a smell like roasting meat in the air.

The screaming was, as always, contagious. It spread. So did panic. Those who'd been more than happy to take advantage of Adam Thornchild's hospitality were reluctant to demonstrate a similar willingness to rush to his aid. Only two guests seemed intent on reaching him. One was the clown. The other was Cally.

But maybe she wouldn't be needed. Uncle Lucas' security men.

'Where do you think you're going, mate?' The first of them, confronting the clown. The clown just laughing. 'Stop there. Stop there.' The clown not stopping there but plodding forward on ungainly feet. 'I'm warning you, mate. I don't wanna hurt you . . .'

The glove on the clown's right hand flickering with flame. The hand itself striking like a cobra, seizing, sizzling the security man's face. Muffled agony. Adam's official protection reduced by half.

No spoken warnings from the second guard. He had a gun in his shoulder holster and he knew how to use it. He emptied a full clip of bullets into the clown's oncoming form. They shredded the jacket of his suit and tore through the vile yellow shirt beneath and they even mortally wounded the frantic bow tie, which spun no more, but not a single shot wiped the smile from the clown's psychotic face. *And he did not stop*.

'An animate,' breathed Cally.

The security man just had time for a wail of despair before the hand did its work. The clown lifted it again. Now the glove had burned away entirely and the steel fingers and palm were revealed, crackling with murderous power, fully and fatally energised.

The clown laughed. He had plenty to laugh about. Who was left to oppose him now?

'Calista!' Frozen to his throne, Adam's eyes were wide with fear. Cally couldn't really blame them.

'It's all right, Adam. I'm here.' She squeezed his hand briefly, turned to face the clown's. 'I won't let anything happen to you.'

Cally tensed for action. If she was going to save Adam Thornchild, she'd have to do it alone.

THREE

There was this game she'd played with the other kids at the refuge when she was small. *It*. One of the kids was 'It', and in order to save themselves from a possible life-time of social exclusion, they had to chase after the other kids and turn one of *them* into 'It' in their place. They effected the transformation by touching their victim with their hand. The idea, if you wanted to stay safe, was to keep clear of the hand.

You never knew when these things were going to come in useful in mission situations.

Cally launched a kick at the clown, pile-driving her foot into his solid metal chest, staggering him backwards. She didn't want him anywhere near Adam, either. She landed, pivoted on her left hip. Her right foot smashed into the animate's chin with a reckless force she might have partially restrained had her assailant been human. The good thing about battling mechanical enemies was that you could afford to give it everything you'd got. Cally followed up with a scything blow from her left foot. The clown's lower jaw shattered from its synthetic hinges, dangled down across his chest, made his obscene smile very big indeed. And he was still laughing. Damage minimal.

Cally corrected herself. Battling mechanical enemies, you *had* to give it everything you'd got. A pity she hadn't brought a shock blaster or thought to wear her sleepshot wristbands. She hadn't realised it was going to be *that* kind of party.

The clown lunged for her. She felt the heat from his hand as she ducked below it, exploded upwards with both fists. The lower jaw gave up the ghost and clattered to the terrace. An electronic eye glared from the ruined left side of the animate's face.

She'd been right about clowns all along.

'Calista! Look out!'

Adam's warning was welcome but unnecessary. She saw the animate's swipe, twisted her lithe form to avoid it. But even though she'd torn her dress with her first kick, it was still restricting her legs a little, slowing her down. Should have worn trousers. Girls always had that *extra* obstacle to overcome.

This time she fended off the hand with her forearm, taking care to make contact with only the *clown*'s forearm. But his other hand, it was grabbing her by the hair, jerking her head back cruelly, painfully. She went with it, rammed into him hard, bent suddenly low, shifted her weight, lifted, threw him.

The clown crashed on to his back in a shower of sparks. The limbs twitched at unnatural angles. If they'd been made of flesh and blood, at least two would have been broken. And the animate looked *in*animate. Maybe she'd won.

'Calista! You've done it!' Adam seemed to think so.

Cally edged forward, closer. What would Ben have said? 'Shoot it again, just to make sure.' She leaned over the body. And he'd have said, 'A good secret agent always makes sure. Otherwise these guys just keep coming back.'

The clown's hand lashed out. Cally recoiled. Instinctively. Swiftly. Not quite swiftly enough. It scorched through the tatters of her lower dress, seared across her thigh, burning, blistering.

Cally cried out, dropped to her knees.

The clown was on his feet, reaching for her head.

One chance. She had to ignore the pain. If she didn't, there was going to be a lot more of it. One chance. Seemed animates could get overconfident too. The clown filled the world above her and from his hollow mouth came a crescendo of laughter.

Cally sprang, propelling herself upwards like a missile. Both hands clutched the clown's forearm, her momentum carrying it with her, thrusting it towards him.

The animate's mouth was in a very good position to gape its astonishment.

Murderous hand connected with mechanical face. There wasn't so much an explosion as a hissing, a fizzing, like hot metal plunged into cold water, like a hundred circuits shorting out simultaneously. The clown didn't scream, but at least he wasn't laughing any more. His limbs fused. A grotesque statue now, he fell.

Not even an animate made sound when it was dead.

And now Cally could afford to wallow in her pain. Her thigh looked like it had been served from a barbecue. But she supposed it wasn't too bad. The medtechs' accelerated healing treatments back at the Shop would have her good as new, though she'd probably have to attend a public hospital first along with the other casualties. Truth was, any injury you could inspect yourself was a *good* injury.

And suddenly, a lot of people wanted to congratulate her and pat her on the back. Words like *amazing* and *fantastic* and *unbelievable* and *very, very brave* gleamed in the air like medals. Nobody apologised for not helping her out.

Adam was by her side. 'That was something *else*, Calista.' His eyes shone almost euphorically. 'I thought for a second you might not . . . but you did it. Without you, I'd be . . .'

Lucas Thornchild and an assortment of armed security guards were belatedly pushing their way through the crowd. So much for liking to keep an eye on his valuable nephew. Cally wondered who would inherit Thornchild Silicon Systems in the untimely event of Adam's death.

'Adam. Adam. Are you all right?' Thornchild allowed himself an expression fifty-fifty shock and sympathy. 'I can't believe what happened.'

'I'm fine, Uncle Lucas,' frowned Adam. 'No thanks to you.'

'I'll recover too, Mr Thornchild,' Cally jibed, 'though I think your security arrangements are pretty much on the critical list.'

'*Exactly.*' Adam quaked with anger. 'Calista could have *died* protecting me. Where were *your* security men, Uncle Lucas? How did this *thing* even get on the island? Don't we have *vetting* procedures any more? No *rules* against homicidal animates?'

'I'm sorry, Adam.' Lucas Thornchild's face flushed the

colour of the burns. 'I'll have an investigation commenced immediately.'

'*You* won't, Uncle Lucas,' retorted Adam. '*Calista* will.
I'm appointing her temporary head of Thornchild's security until we learn who's behind this attack, and I expect
her to have your full cooperation.'

'Of course, Adam,' said Thornchild through gritted
teeth.

Adam smiled grimly at Cally. 'Looks like you arrived
just in time, Calista.'

Cally couldn't have agreed more.

The crisis point with Jimmy Kwan came out of nothing.

He was waiting for her in the gym. He seemed to be
en route to his big scene in *Enter the Dragon*, robed in a
dramatic black judogi. The uniform's loosely belted
jacket revealed that his profusion of dragon tattoos had
spread at least as far as his chest, feral eyes staring out
from his pectorals. He carried a second belt in his hand
but this was nothing to do with the martial arts. It was a
Deveraux issue mission belt.

Cally entered wearing a judogi of her own, regulation
white and not as flamboyant as her field handler's.
Maybe Jimmy felt he had to make more of an impression.

'How's the leg, Cally?' he enquired.

'Not fallen off yet. It works.' She thought about
adding a *thanks* but couldn't quite make it.

'Good. That's good. And any update on the animate?'

'Not yet. It's a little limiting having to be restricted to
the normal authorities' technology, but short of stealing
the thing and bringing it back to the Shop, I guess I'll

just have to make do. Whoever built it, though, they knew how to cover their tracks.'

'You'll find them, Cally,' said Jimmy. 'I have faith in you.'

'Yeah?' Cally was sceptical. 'Really truly, or just in public to keep me sweet?'

Jimmy declined to answer directly. What could he say? Words weren't going to win Cally round. Only actions could do that.

Cally wished he'd cover up his pecs. They were distracting. And that dragon's tail, it wiggled all the way down to his navel.

'Well, I called you to the gym because I've got something from the techs here that might help you in the field.'

'Being as I need a lot of help, you mean. After Shanghai. After Ben. Hey, I even almost got my butt kicked by a clown.' Where was Mei? Why couldn't Mei still be here?

'Cally, it's an agent's duty and responsibility to keep informed of all technological developments that might be of benefit both in preserving the agent's life and in facilitating the successful completion of their mission.'

'You've read the manual. Nice one, Jimmy.' But he was still right. She knew it. 'Okay, so what have we got?'

'I-Shields,' Jimmy said.

'Eye what?'

He shook the belt. 'I-Shields. A personal force-field generated from your mission belt. It's active to a five-centimetre distance from your body and powerful enough to deflect anything short of a shock blast without injury.'

'Sounds like it might come in useful if your date got a

bit frisky,' grinned Cally, but not for long. 'If you *had* a date, that is.'

'Not intended for romantic liaisons,' Jimmy dismissed. 'It's for hand-to-hand combat situations. Could help even the odds, give you an edge over a stronger or more skilful opponent.'

'What? As in, and there must be lots of opponents stronger and more skilful than *you*, Cally? That's not a *weapon*, Jimmy, it's a comfort blanket.'

Jimmy sighed. They were getting nowhere. 'This attitude of yours, Cally, I know you don't think you can trust me, but it's not helping matters.'

'Is it not?' Fingertips. She was holding on by her fingertips. She thought of Ben. She thought of Mei. She looked at Jimmy, patiently offering her the belt. What the heck was she doing here?

'Buckle it on over your judogi. I'll show you how the I-Shields work.'

Suddenly it was all too much. And suddenly the stress of the last few weeks washed over her and her fingertips slipped and in her mind she was falling.

'I don't think so,' she heard her voice saying. 'Don't bother. Thanks.' There were tears pricking the backs of her eyes, bitter, frustrated tears, and they'd been brewing a long time. 'Why don't we just pass for now, Jimmy, hey? I mean, you'll only go easy on me anyway, won't you? Wouldn't want your student to look bad.' She turned towards the door, didn't want him to see her. 'Think I'll just go get changed.'

With quicksilver speed Jimmy was in front of her again. 'Oh no, Cally. Not this time. Three strikes and you'd be most definitely out.'

'So? What do you care? You can't be held to blame, Jimmy, not for me. I was in a mess before you even took over. Mr D won't mind.'

'*I'll* mind,' said Jimmy Kwan, and meant it. 'And I *do* care.'

'Field handler manual page ninety-six.' Cally averted her gaze. 'Tell the suckers what they want to hear. Look, just let me past. I'll put in for more compassionate leave. I shouldn't have . . . I'm not . . . someone else can take over with Adam Thornchild . . .'

'I can't let you do that, Cally.' Jimmy was adamant. 'You leave now and that's it. Game over. You're too good an agent for that.'

'That's what those terrorists in Shanghai said – when they were making their getaway.'

Jimmy's eyes narrowed. 'Okay. And they were right.'

'What?'

'You messed up. You messed up big-time. I reckon they're on the holo-phone to all their terrorist buddies right now saying, next time you go on a job to kill all those inno- cent people you just gotta *hope* they send Calista Green after you. That way you've got *no* chance of getting caught.'

'Don't, Jimmy. Don't say that.'

' 'Cause not only is Calista Green the most abject, woeful, worst-prepared agent the Deveraux organisation has ever put into the field . . .'

'No, that's not . . . Jimmy . . .'

'. . . but she's also the most self-pitying and childish and defeatist one as well. No backbone. No courage. No stomach for a fight.'

'Let me past, Jimmy.' He wouldn't. 'I'm warning you . . .' The tears had dried.

'Whoever let you into Spy High in the first place, Cally?' Jimmy Kwan mocked. 'I reckon Deveraux must have had a glitch in his circuits that day. Just proves not even a computer's infallible. Hopeless, Cally, hopeless!'

'I'm not hopeless, and if you don't get out of my way, Jimmy, *now* . . .'

'What? What are you gonna do? Throw a tantrum?'

Her lips curled back over clenched teeth. Her fists balled.

'I reckon you should have stayed on the streets, Cally. That's where you belong. That's all you're good—'

'No!'

Cally's blow lifted her field handler off his feet and sent him thudding on to his back. He was dazed by the ferocity of the attack. Cally followed up with a textbook offensive stance to a fallen foe, her legs braced and her fists poised at his head.

'I'm *better* than the streets! I've *earned* my place here. You've got no right to speak to me like that. I've proved myself a *hundred* times.'

'I know you have,' groaned Jimmy.

'And I'll do it again. I'll show you how good I am and how good I can be.'

'I know you will.'

Cally relaxed a little. For a man lying flat on his back with a bloody nose and maybe damage to the lower lumbar region, Jimmy Kwan seemed rather content with life. He was even smiling. (Quite a nice smile, actually, even *with* the blood.) 'You *know* I will?'

'Sure,' grinned Jimmy. 'I know what you can do. But you wouldn't have believed it if *I'd* said it, would you? You had to say it for yourself. Whatever her field handler

says or does, an agent of Spy High has to believe in
herself.'

'So you didn't mean . . . those things? You were just
trying to goad me, so I'd stop feeling sorry for
myself . . .?'

'Seemed like a good plan at the time,' Jimmy said ruefully. 'Until you *hit* me, that is. Maybe I should have put
some I-Shields on first.' He paused. 'Do you forgive me?'

Cally considered. 'I don't think Mei Ataki would have
gone for those kinds of tactics, but then I guess Mei
Ataki isn't my field handler.' She held out her hand. 'And
you can't lie there all day. You've got to show me how the
I-Shields work.'

Jimmy took Cally's hand. Her grip was strong and
steady and confident. He let her help him to his feet.
'Lesson One,' he said. 'Emotion can be a powerful
weapon.'

'I know,' said Cally. And for the first time, she smiled
properly at Jimmy Kwan.

It was later that evening. Jimmy was standing Ling Po
to a Chinese meal at the Jumbo hoverestaurant above
the harbour. He'd invited Cally along as well but she'd
declined. 'I wouldn't want to be a gooseberry,' she'd
joked, 'or is it a lychee in these parts?' She thought one
step at a time building on this newly positive relationship
with her field handler was the best approach. 'You're
missing out on the best crispy duck in Hong Kong,'
Jimmy had tempted her. And part of her had wanted to
go, and not because of the allure of the crispy duck
either. 'Another time,' she'd promised.

She returned to her quarters in good spirits. Looked

like things were on the up. Light at the end of the tunnel, etc. After their little showdown in the gym she felt she could finally believe in Jimmy Kwan. She was even beginning to like him – what with that punk haircut, though, maybe she should introduce him to Bex's stylist. Her mission was going well, she'd earned Adam Thornchild's trust. She'd reminded herself that she could cope with the whole espionage business after all.

And she hadn't thought of Ben for at least five minutes.

'Computer on,' she called from her bedroom as she changed. Maybe she'd e-mail Lori and Bex, let them know they could stop worrying about her.

'You have e-mail,' the computer announced.

'Put it on speaker,' Cally said, expecting to hear the voice of one of her friends.

'Unable to comply,' returned the computer.

Which meant it was an old-fashioned text-only message. Which meant it couldn't have been sent by anyone she knew – everyone at Deveraux used vocal optioning. So how had the e-mail found its way on to her allegedly security-screened computer? Curious, Cally padded in her underwear to the desktop. The sender's identity was a simple question mark. Some sort of virus? Secret agent instincts. She didn't think so. 'Display text,' she said. And she was right. No virus. Something more disturbing.

Calista: if you want to learn the truth about your parents, come tonight. Come alone. And there was an address.

The tunnel had suddenly grown dark again.

'Someone's playing games,' Cally muttered. 'Someone who'll regret it. Computer, locate sender.'

'Unable to comply,' admitted the computer.

'Use your tracer program.'

'Unable to comply.' It was getting to be a habit.

Cally sat back and frowned. So the mysterious e-mailer was sufficiently skilled with computer systems to evade even a tracer program. Well, if she couldn't determine the note's origins by electronic means, there was only one course left to take.

The address was in the Seabound District. Cally memorised it instantly. It was some kind of set-up, obviously, tailor-made for Cally Cross. A new enemy or an old one, it didn't matter. In this line of work you picked up enemies like celebrity-hunters collected autographs. But whoever it was, they couldn't know anything about her parents, could they? After all this time? After countless hours wondering herself, dreaming, imagining?

Could they?

She had to know.

Seabound. The darkest, most dangerous district in Hong Kong. Triads. Muggers. Murderers. Nobody went there who had any choice, even by day. But that was just it, of course. Cally didn't *have* any choice.

From *The Secret Agent's Guide to the World* by
E.J. Grant
THE FAR EAST 5. HONG KONG

In any thriving and prosperous modern metropo-
lis there are losers as well as winners, the
destitute as well as the dignitaries, slums in
the shadows of the skyscrapers.

    In the last century and the early part of

this, the poor of Hong Kong tended to congregate in a ramshackle fleet of run-down and patched-up houseboats, moored on the far side of Victoria Peak, conveniently out of sight of the city's prosperity. Eventually this district was given a name, Seabound, and soon after that its nature began to change.

There were too many poor, too many boats, and the population kept rising. Sanitation became an increasing problem, with the waters thick with refuse and human sewage. It was said that on a bad day, if the wind was blowing off the sea, even the tourists at the Peak could smell the stench, and that would never do. In the end, the Chinese authorities had no choice but to clean up and renovate Seabound.

Thanks to advances in air cushion technology, they believed that this could be done without squandering precious resources. The boats were removed and destroyed, the sea was purged of its filth. A massive network of interconnecting air cushions linked to Hong Kong Island itself was constructed, each one capable of bearing houses, businesses, public utilities, every kind of building necessary to create and sustain a flourishing floating community. And as the numbers of people living in Seabound multiplied, new air cushions were to be added. Seabound's expansion would never need to cease.

Unfortunately, the government's plans did not quite reach fruition. Maintenance costs for the air cushions themselves, for the steel skirts

that protected them and for the giant pumps and
motors that kept them from capsizing proved to
be prohibitive, requiring major cutbacks in
other areas of the budget. Seabound did not
grow: it simply happened that more and more
people were forced to share the same space. In
the end, one type of floating ghetto was
exchanged for another.

Seabound now is a maze of islands, decaying
and decrepit, sagging, flimsy buildings, treacherous pontoon bridges, dirty, murky waterways.
It has been christened by one wit 'The Venice of
the Poor', but it is unlikely ever to replace
the Italian original, now refloated on air cushions too, in the affections of the public.

Indeed, Seabound is sadly notable for one
thing only. *Crime* . . .

Next time (not that Cally was particularly looking
forward to a next time), she'd bring her AquaBike. The
canals that crisscrossed Seabound like scars across a
dead man's face looked black and toxic, but at least if she
travelled by water she wouldn't have to pick her way
over the bodies of groaning drunks or watch her back for
sudden furtive movements from darkened doorways.
Several times she'd heard sinister chuckles from behind
her, as if the shadows were watching her. Several times
more she'd heard sobs, the crying of babies, voices
raised in argument, from somewhere among the crippled
wooden buildings a shrill laughter at the futility of it all.
Once she'd even been approached, a wizened Chinese
man like a rat drawn out by the prospect of food. 'Hello,

girl,' he'd said in broken English. 'You lost? You looking? I got what you looking for.' He'd tried to reach out for her but she'd simply knocked his arm aside. He'd scurried back into the night. Harmless, really. No need to employ her sleepshot or shock blaster. She was troubled by no one else.

A jaundiced yellow light seeped from the windows of the narrow streets and stained the air. It wasn't good, but it was the only assistance Cally had to match the memorised street-plan of Seabound with the reality. Where she was heading, though, even that pitiful illumination was swallowed up by the dark. She toyed with the idea of activating the belt-beam in her mission belt, but decided against. Stealth was probably preferable now she was close. It was why she'd worn a black infiltration suit, like she was going burgling. In a way, she supposed she was.

The address was of a so-called souvenir emporium, though who would delve this deeply into Seabound to buy a few trinkets Cally couldn't imagine. They'd be wasting their time, anyway. She crouched within sight of the forlorn shop. It clearly hadn't been in use for years. The boarded-up windows were a giveaway. And the absence of a door. Unless, of course, the latter had been removed just to tease her inside.

Well, if so, score one to the Bad Guy. It had worked.

Stupid, Cally, stupid, she scolded herself as she drew her shock blaster and darted nimbly and noiselessly to the gaping doorway. It was reckless enough to voluntarily enter what was patently a trap – *so* patently she wouldn't have been surprised to see the word TRAP printed above the doorway in big bold letters. But to do so without back-up, without having notified her field handler of her intentions, that was rash to the point of suicide. But she hadn't wanted to disturb Jimmy Kwan's crispy duck.

And besides, this was to do with nobody's parents but hers.

Cally edged inside, every sense taut with alertness. The slightest movement – none in the hollow, empty shopfront. The slightest sound – through the back, a tiny voice, electronic, and a green gleam of light from beneath a closed door. Storeroom, Cally guessed. The souvenirs for the emporium had to be kept somewhere.

She braced herself, confronted the door. Raised both blaster and sleepshot in readiness, arms extended ahead of her. Knock, knock, she mouthed silently.

Then she kicked the door open.

Unlike the shopfront, the storeroom was still lined with crates and packing cases and hulks of objects shrouded in sacking, all obscured by darkness. Nothing threatening. The green light came from a computer screen. The computer was all alone on a table in the middle of the room. It was obviously optimistic that it was due a visitor. 'Welcome,' it repeated. 'Welcome. Welcome.'

Cally took the greeting personally. She crossed to the computer. 'Welcome. Welcome.' On the screen it said to press any key to continue. She'd probably regret it, but to learn about her parents she'd risk anything. Cally pressed A.

'Goodbye, Calista,' said the computer.

And suddenly, from the corners of the storeroom, black shapes stirring, moving, coming alive . . .

FOUR

The fact that the trap was finally sprung didn't surprise Cally. (Ninjas, four of them, hooded, swathed in night like black bandages, the curved blades of their long swords, their katanas, flickering like bright tongues.) But their moves surprised her. She'd always thought she was quick, but the ninjas were lightning.

Sleepshot and shock blast she fired simultaneously. Targets left and right. Missed them both. The ninjas moved like liquid, like wind. The first katana flashed where her neck would have been had she not ducked. The second slashed down at her wrist, sliced the blaster from her grasp, her fingertips stinging but at least intact. The blur of burnished steel both high and low, the teamwork of death.

Cally threw herself between the blades, rolled on the hard storeroom floor. A third ninja in front of her, both hands gripping the hilt of his sword, the katana high above his head, beginning its guillotine descent. Cally rammed up hard, barrelled into the ninja, battered him backwards. A satisfying impact against solid flesh, *human* flesh. The ninjas were only mortal after all.

They could be beaten.

But they weren't going to make it easy for her. She was still surrounded.

She glanced towards the door but instantaneously a ninja moved to block that possible means of escape. Cally could only elude the thrusts of the katanas by retreating further back into the storeroom. It wasn't good. Not too much room to manoeuvre here, and her assailants' ability to avoid her sleepshot was uncanny, unbelievable, almost psychic. And the way they worked together, with seamless synchronicity. They hadn't uttered a syllable since the attack had begun, yet they seemed to be in perfect communication. It was like they could read each other's minds.

The backs of Cally's legs bumped against the table with the computer on it. This was one of those occasions when the I-Shields attachment on her mission belt might have come in useful. A pity she hadn't waited to have it fitted before she left for Seabound, but she'd thought that time was of the essence. It sure was now.

Here came the katana, scything down at her head. If it hit, it would split her skull in two.

Cally jerked to the right. Just in time. Just far enough. The sword continued on its arc, found another victim. It bit into the computer in an eruption of sparks. The ninja writhed as electricity jolted into him via his blade. Cally thought she'd do the caring thing and relieve him of his pain, along with his consciousness. Her blow pitched him to the floor. She snatched up the man's katana, the steel now simply warming her palms. The Good Guys were off the mark.

But there were still three of them to one of her.

She faced them boldly. 'Who are you?' she demanded. If she was going to die within the next few minutes, she wanted answers first. 'What do you know about my parents? Tell me.' Maybe this particular order of ninjas took a vow of silence when they signed on. 'Tell me!' They prepared to wield their katanas a final time.

Then suddenly the storeroom was dazzled with a brilliant white light. Somebody else was bursting in, Cally was aware of the outline of a human form. Whoever it was slammed into two of the ninjas, exploiting the element of surprise. Cally wasn't going to simply stand around, either. At virtually point-blank range, her final opponent couldn't avoid a burst of sleepshot.

The white glare was already fading. Light-grenade? Cally wondered. The newcomer was still standing. The ninjas were not. But Cally had already taken too many foolish chances tonight. She let the katana fall but trained her sleepshot on him, both wrists. 'I'd put your hands where I can see them if I were you,' she warned.

'If you like,' the newcomer said, raising his hands obligingly, 'but you're not going to be seeing anything too clearly for the next few minutes, are you? Which is why I forgive you, Cal. Otherwise I reckon I'd be pretty miffed if this is how you say hi to a former team-mate who's just saved your life.'

'Jake?' The light-burst hadn't affected her hearing. Cally laughed with delight. 'Jake, what are you *doing* here?'

'Getting a hug, maybe?' said Jake Daly.

'No maybe about it. Come here!' Cally flung her arms

around him, felt his presence warm and reassuringly strong. Jake Daly. The one-sixth of Bond Team filed under mean and moody. Cally's first real friend at Spy High, the first of her team-mates who'd genuinely believed in her. It was good to have him with her again now. 'Are the others around, too?'

'What?' Jake grinned. 'I'm not good enough for you on my own?'

'No, of course you are.' Cally slapped his shoulder playfully.

'So I should hope. But no, it's just me, Cal.'

'I'm *glad* it's you. It's *good* to see you, Jake.'

'Ditto, Cally, and maybe next time we can arrange somewhere a little more salubrious.' He peered round distastefully at the rotting storeroom.

'I know what you mean,' Cally concurred. 'What's an agent like you doing in a place like this?' She surveyed Jake as best she could in the dark and with her sight still recovering from what had certainly been a light-grenade. He was wearing a radar visor to protect himself from its effects, and an infiltration suit like hers besides. *Whatever* Jake was doing in Seabound, he was here on business, not pleasure.

'I guess we've both got questions,' he said, 'but we'd better get these jokers sorted out first.' Indicating the defeated ninjas. 'Your base is in Hong Kong, isn't it, Cally? Call the capture in. I reckon it's going to have to be interrogations before bedtime.'

'Yes, sir,' mocked Cally gently. Jake was assuming leadership the way Ben had used to do. She reached for her belt communicator.

'Wait, Cal.' Jake was suddenly frowning. He pulled

off his visor, knelt by one of the fallen ninjas, removed the man's black hood.

'What is it?'

'He's dead.'

'What?' Cally joined him. No need to check for a pulse. Spy High graduates knew dead when they saw it. This time it came with blind yet staring eyes and clotted dribbles of blood from the nostrils and ears. 'But how? You didn't . . .'

'I know how to knock someone out without killing them, Cally,' Jake remarked. 'I've been doing it for four years. Check the others.'

Cally did, even the man she'd eliminated with sleepshot, guaranteed to avoid fatalities in the field. So they were looking for another culprit. Because the ninja in question was as stone dead as his comrades. Cally and Jake, in a Seabound storeroom with four corpses, all of them with white eyes open, all of them having bled from nose and ears.

'Cyanide capsules, something like that?' Cally suggested. 'You know how these secret order type guys like to go in for suicide rather than surrender.'

'No evidence of any of them having swallowed any poisonous substance,' said Jake. 'Besides, the one you hit with your sleepshot wouldn't have had time for a capsule, Cal, and it looks like they all died the same way.'

'It does, doesn't it?' Cally shuddered.

'So I guess we can scratch the interrogations. Better tell the medtechs to get ready for four autopsies instead.'

Jimmy Kwan didn't have to ask for an explanation from Cally. 'I know I should have told you where I was going and why,' she said, having volunteered it first. 'As my field handler, you had a right to know. But Jimmy, that stuff about my parents, it pulled all my strings. It clouded my judgement. I *let* it cloud my judgement, acted like I was still in my first term at Spy High. I'm sorry.'

She appealed not only to Jimmy but to Jake for good measure. The three of them were in the briefing room beneath the Shop. It was the morning after the altercation before.

'You never have to apologise to me, Cal,' said Jake.

'Well,' contributed Jimmy more thoughtfully, 'you're still with us and that's the most important thing. The fact that this e-mail got through to your computer, though, Cally, that its sender clearly knows you're an agent and something of your past, this is all worrying. I'll initiate a review of Shop security immediately, and maybe we should consider withdrawing you from the Thornchild mission until we know more. From the sound of it the ninjas were playing for keeps.'

'I was holding my own,' Cally asserted. 'I could have taken them. Jake saved me time, that's all. Not that I'm not grateful, mind,' she added quickly.

'We aim to please.' Jake bowed with a flourish.

'What I mean is, Jimmy,' pursued Cally, 'I can cope. If someone wants to kill me, he can join the queue. I *don't* want to be taken off assignment, not now my cover's established.'

'Okay. Okay. You stay with Thornchild,' Jimmy conceded. He seemed pleased. 'But stay alert. As Mr Deveraux says, a good spy keeps his eyes open . . .'

'. . . even when they're closed,' concluded Cally and Jake together.

'Even when they're closed, exactly. And Cally, for what it's worth, if I'd been in your position, given a possible lead as to the fate of my parents, I'd have done the same thing.'

'Would you?' Cally met her field handler's gaze and realised she didn't want to look away. She almost wished that Jake wasn't there. Seemed there was more to Jimmy Kwan than tattoos and a bad haircut. Cally wondered how *much* more.

But Jimmy was turning to Jake. 'At least we know why one Deveraux operative was midnight-strolling in Seabound. What about the other? Jake?' He recognised Daly from Cally's files, which naturally contained complete reports of her Bond Team days. Jake didn't appear to have altered very much physically since then. His thick black hair still hadn't been combed, his eyes were still just as dark, intense, brooding, magnetic, and there remained a restlessness about him, a volatility, a potential for violence barely restrained. Jimmy had heard on the field handler grapevine, however, that Jake Daly had been growing increasingly impatient with the Deveraux organisation's rules and methods of late. Solo missions were suiting him, and it was known he liked to work on a long leash.

Jimmy hoped that Cally wouldn't find her old friend too changed.

'What was *I* doing in Seabound?' Jake was saying now. 'My job, of course. I'm on mission.'

'Care to share it with us?' prompted Jimmy. 'All spies together kind of thing?'

'I guess so.' Jake seemed a little reticent.

The smart desk's communicator saved him. It was the

medtechs. They'd established the ninjas' cause of death
and thought Field Handler Kwan and Agents Cross and
Daly might like a look at it.

'It?' said Cally.

'A neural implant,' explained the tech in the medlab.
He held it up between his thumb and forefinger, and if
he'd assured Cally the tiny speck of metal was a ball
bearing she'd have believed him. When he then placed it
under magnification and projected the image to a screen,
though, she realised it wasn't. It was more like a computer chip.

'Looks like it's been burned or something,' Cally
observed. The chip was reddened, scorched, useless.

'We think detonated,' said the medtech, 'and not by
the host himself. By an external agency. We found one in
the frontal lobes of all four of the deceased. I'm afraid
there wasn't much of their brains left.'

Cally cast a squeamish glance to where on a row of
examination tables a quartet of sheets considerately concealed the ninjas' remains. Something red was soaking
through at the head of one of them. Cally turned her
back to it. 'So somebody didn't want either their tech or
their men falling into our hands,' she said.

'What are the implants for?' Jimmy asked. 'Just to
kill?'

'I think I can help you there.' Jake stepped forward.
'Correct me if I'm wrong, Medtech, but these devices
look like neurotelepathy stimulators to me.'

'Well done, Agent Daly,' approved the tech. 'Indeed
they are.'

'Professor Daly, come on down,' Cally applauded, but
Jake did not smile.

'And highly sophisticated, too,' the tech continued meaningfully. 'More advanced than anything we have by a considerable margin. If only we'd secured just one of them intact . . .'

'Telepathy, though?' Jimmy seemed doubtful. 'Communication by the power of thought? I know this is 2066, but even so . . .'

'The implant adapts itself to the electrical activity of the brain,' the medtech explained, 'becomes part of the host brain in the same way that a transplanted organ becomes part of its new host body. Then, like e-mails between computer consoles sharing the same network, it can communicate with any other brain fitted with the same kind of implant. Direct communication brain-to-brain, no speech required. Neurotelepathy.'

'So that's how come they didn't speak,' Cally realised, 'and why they made such a good team. Until they came up against a better one.' She grinned at Jake who, given the grimness of his expression, at the moment at least seemed to be on a different wavelength.

'That's the theory,' added the medtech. 'I've never seen it in action myself. I know the nanosurgeon Professor Werner Wagner was developing work in this area before he died, but—'

'Wagner?' Cally looked enquiringly to Jimmy Kwan. 'Maybe he got further than he made public. Maybe someone wanted his ideas for themselves. Maybe there's more to this whole Wagner-Thornchild business than just a bunch of futurephobes offing scientists.' She narrowed her eyes speculatively. 'And maybe there's a connection between whoever was responsible for the clown attack on Adam and whoever tried to have me killed last night. And I wouldn't be surprised if the missing link didn't begin with the letters Lucas Thornchild.'

'Sorry, Cal,' interrupted Jake, 'but are you talking in code or what?'

'Cally can outline her mission for you in a moment, Jake,' said Jimmy, 'while I'm checking something out, but before she does, you still haven't told us what *you* were doing in Seabound.'

'That's right. I haven't.' He glanced at Jimmy as if he didn't appreciate being reminded. 'But it's why I recognise a neurotelepathy stimulator when I see one. I'm on the trail of a criminal ring manufacturing and trafficking illegal neural and nanotech implants. You know the kind of thing. Some of them are pretty straightforward muscle boosters, the kind of enhancement sportsmen get tested for these days, only my guys have them forcibly injected into the slave labour gangs they operate in the developing world. I'm talking untested high-performance implants that inevitably react against the host body and cause massive cardiac arrest, and if not death, total paralysis. Then there's the whole scene with neural stimulation. The computer chip of your choice. Syringe-gun to the temple. Squeeze the trigger. All-time high. You can directly manipulate the pleasure centres of the brain. Course, these implants are totally addictive. Do enough of them and you'll end up rotting your brain, and I mean literally, but what do the suppliers care? The profits are astronomical. Nanotech trafficking, it's the new drugs trade. I have it in mind to help close it down.'

'And you've traced this organisation to Hong Kong, Jake?' said Cally.

'Well it's a long way to come for a Chinese takeaway,' Jake grunted. 'Sure I traced them. And I'm close. I can *feel* it. One of my contacts gave me the address of that souvenir emporium in Seabound where I found you, Cal, which kind of suggests that we've both got ourselves involved with the same crims.'

'Could be,' agreed Cally. 'After all . . .'

'There's no such thing as coincidence, only a plan that has yet to be understood.' Jake reeled off the Deveraux mantra with a sigh of tedium.

'So are we saying we're going to pool our resources?' Cally sounded hopeful.

'I don't know, Cal.' Jake, on the other hand, sounded reluctant. 'I mean, it's not like we're in Bond Team any more. I might need to leave Hong Kong at any point to do my own thing . . .'

'But all the while you're here . . .'

'Cally's got a point, Jake,' intervened Jimmy. 'Having someone to watch your back is never a bad idea.'

Jake seemed to relent. 'Course. Sure. You're right, Cal. We can work together. It'll be good.'

'It'll be just like the old days.' Cally hugged her former partner. 'A team again!'

'A team in a dead end,' Jake said gloomily. 'The emporium was my *only* lead, and our late friends with the katanas aren't going to be of much use supplying us with another.'

'I wouldn't be too certain of that, Jake,' said Jimmy cryptically. 'Cally, fill Jake in on your mission while I . . . Sorenson, could you give me a hand with these bodies, please.'

Cally watched Jimmy and the medtech uncover the first of the ninjas, saw her field handler stoop to inspect the dead man's skin. That was enough for her. She was only too glad to tell Jake everything there was to tell about the Thornchild mission, and then some. Though their presence was sometimes a necessary evil given her line of work, corpses were not Cally's favourite people.

She was moving on to describe the interior decoration of the house on Thornchild Island when Jimmy announced the completion of his examination of the ninjas. 'I was looking for tattoos,' he informed the teenagers.

'Haven't you got enough of your own?' Cally quipped.

'Membership of a Triad is always denoted by a tattoo. A lotus blossom on the left shoulder. A scarlet pagoda on the right forearm. An eye in the small of the back.'

'I'm glad you didn't ask *me* to look for them,' Cally winced.

'It's not enough simply to belong to one of these criminal societies. You have to be *seen* to belong. Triad membership brings with it certain duties and responsibilities. You have to abide by a code of honour. If you break it, you're unclean, cast out.'

'Don't give me this Triad code of honour crap,' protested Jake. 'You're talking Chinese Mafia, Jimmy, not the Hong Kong golf club. These guys kill for a living. I don't want to know they send their old mum a birthday card. And anyway, what? Are you saying the ninjas belong to a Triad? Which one?'

'That's just it,' said Jimmy. 'They *don't* belong to any of the local Triads. There's not a single tattoo on their bodies. Which means, and let's assume they were employed by your implant traffickers, Jake, that this is an organisation setting up to rival the established Triads. Then these same established Triads might be only too happy for a third party to eliminate the newcomers for them. They might be willing to divulge any information they might have to that end.'

'They might,' Jake considered. 'Makes sense, I guess. So what do we do? Walk right into one of the local Triad dens and demand to see the Head of the Family?'

'Not quite. I make a few calls is what we do,' said Jimmy.

'You have contacts in the Triads, Jimmy?' Cally asked in surprise.

'I ought to have. I used to be one of them.'

Cally and Jake sat in Victoria Park on Hong Kong Island. Greenery was precious in the city, and the park was as popular as ever. People practised their t'ai chi in informal rows strung out across the open expanse of grass. In small groups clustered under the trees Chinese men gambled with dice, their heartfelt cries of victory or defeat drifting on the breeze. Others, mostly elderly, strolled the paths with songbirds in cages, as if showing them the sky was compensation for stopping them from reaching it. Jimmy had encouraged the teenagers to spend some time relaxing that afternoon. By evening, he might have some news for them.

'I can't believe Jimmy used to be a Triad member.' Cally seemed to be trying to picture him in that role. 'How can he have got involved in the first place?'

'Who knows?' Jake's shrug implied a silent *who cares*?

'Misspent childhood. Badly chosen role model. There's always something about our pasts we'd sooner forget, isn't there?'

'Maybe,' conceded Cally, 'but there's also plenty I want to remember. Bond Team, anybody?'

'Bond Team.' Jake smiled thinly and shook his head.

'What's the matter?' Cally frowned. 'We had good times together, didn't we?'

'Sure. Some. I guess when we weren't facing certain death at the hands of Frankenstein or the Diluvians or somebody. When Ben wasn't being a pain in the—' Jake suddenly seemed to realise what he was saying. 'Sorry, Cal, I didn't mean to . . .'

'It's okay. It's all right.' Cally smiled gently. 'You can talk about him as he was, Jake. Ben wasn't a saint. I know that as well as anybody. But he was all I ever wanted.'

Jake nodded. 'Ben and me, we didn't always get on as well as maybe we should have done for the team's sake,' he reflected. 'I'm not sure now whether that was because we were too different or too much the same. But I think, by the time we finished training, by the time we graduated, I'd *like* to think we understood each other a bit better, thought of each other as friends. I know I did.'

'Ben did too, Jake.' Cally squeezed his hand. 'There were never any resentments.'

'I always respected him, Cal,' Jake said. 'Nobody was a better agent than Ben Stanton. It's incredible that he's gone. I want you to know how sorry I am.'

'I do.'

'Jennifer dying was one thing. We were young then.

We loved her, but she made mistakes and you can't afford to make mistakes. But Ben . . .' Jake sighed. 'It's the end of an era, Cally. Nothing's the same for us now. The days of Bond Team are over. We're on our own.'

'Sounding bleak, Jake.' Cally's brow furrowed. 'You need Eddie around to cheer you up. Or Lori.'

'Lori and I are finished,' Jake stated flatly.

'Yeah, I did . . . I had heard that. I'm sorry. You were good together.'

'Not good enough.' Jake's dark eyes were cold. 'We grew apart, isn't that what people say?'

'I suppose so,' allowed Cally. 'Some people, I guess. So are you . . . seeing anyone else, Jake?'

'No. I'm not.' He seemed pretty certain about that. 'And I don't intend to be.'

'What? Never?' Cally laughed a little nervously. 'I didn't imagine the celibate life would ever suit Jake Daly.'

'I live for my work now,' Jake said. 'That's it. My missions are my life. The world's a more dangerous place than ever, Cally. There are new kinds of evil maniac out there, a new breed, ruthless, emotionless, totally without pity or compassion. Deveraux needs to wise up. We're gonna need more than sleepshot to take *them* out. We need to show the Bad Guys the same mercy they'd show us, i.e. none. I'm telling you, Cal. We need to learn to fight dirty. It's the only way.'

Cally looked far from convinced. She realised she'd drawn away a little from Jake and felt suddenly ashamed. 'I don't know.'

'Well look around you, Cal. See what's happening. Anyway, I've got no time for personal relationships now. Relationships are a distraction. I don't want them.'

'But Jake,' said Cally, 'then what are you fighting *for*?'

It was funny how your perceptions of people could change, Cally mused. A couple of days ago, if she'd been told she was going to be eating out in a Chinese restaurant with Jimmy Kwan and Jake Daly, she'd have envisaged herself chatting easily and good-humouredly with her former team-mate while scarcely exchanging a word with her current field handler. In reality, the opposite was nearer to the truth. After the exchange in Victoria Park, Cally no longer knew quite what to make of Jake, how to address him. She didn't feel *secure* with him any more. He was different, darker, somehow more dangerous, not the inexperienced boy from the Domes who'd first joined Bond Team. With Jimmy, on the other hand, she was quickly feeling more comfortable.

'So tell me about your days in the Triads,' she fished as he led them into the restaurant.

'Let's get seated first,' Jimmy said. 'Kwan,' he announced to an approaching waiter. 'Table for three. We're expected.'

The waiter raised his eyebrows as if impressed. 'Indeed you are, Mr Kwan,' he said. 'This way, please.'

The restaurant was busy, noisy with diners, but Cally still felt it to be a strange choice. It wasn't exactly in a *bad* part of town, but it was well off the beaten track, not a place you'd come across by chance, and it hadn't looked much from the outside. The other clientele were probably all regulars. Cally sensed their eyes on her as she passed. She didn't notice too many women, and no children.

'What are we doing here?' Jake was grumbling beside her. 'Couldn't he have told us his intelligence back at the Shop? Espionage isn't usually discussed over dinner.'

'Jimmy must have his reasons, Jake,' Cally defended her field handler, but she had wondered the same thing herself.

The waiter seated the small party at a table pretty much in the centre of the restaurant. 'I'll be with you in a moment,' he promised.

'How's the crispy duck here, Jimmy?' Cally grinned.

'Forget dead waterfowl,' Jake protested. 'Did you get anywhere with the Triads?'

'Oh, I think so,' Jimmy said.

'Well do you mind telling us about it?'

'I don't think I'll need to,' said Jimmy. 'You're about to find out for yourselves.'

The waiter was back. He wasn't carrying menus. He was carrying a shock blaster. 'Mr Kwan,' he said, 'Mr Xao is ready for you now.'

'Yeah?' Jake retorted. 'Is he ready for this?' A driving blow to the waiter's stomach, Jake swiftly on his feet, disarming the man and yanking his arm up behind his back. 'Now maybe you want to tell us who this Mr Xao guy *is*.'

'Uh . . . Jake . . .' Cally had stood too, had exposed her sleepshot wristbands. Didn't think it would be worth firing them at this point.

The entire restaurant had risen. Every diner was glaring at the Deveraux group, their meals forgotten. Every diner held either a gun or a knife. They looked like they knew how to use them.

Jimmy Kwan was the only person still seated. He

shook his head critically. 'Patience, Jake. I already know who Mr Xao is. He's the man who owns this restaurant. He's the man we came here to see. He's the head of the Hua Xing Xao Triad.'

FIVE

The three Deveraux operatives were escorted by armed waiters to a private dining room at the rear of the restaurant. An enormously fat Chinese man was doing his best to maintain his weight by gobbling his way through at least a dozen different dishes. His chopsticks almost disappeared in his pudgy fingers. The man was wearing a suit and tie but no table napkin: his clothes were splattered with juices. No one seemed keen to point this out to him, though there were a number of other men in the room who seemed to have nothing to do but watch their superior eat.

'Why didn't you tell us this was a meet?' Jake hissed in Jimmy Kwan's ear.

'I didn't want you trying anything reckless,' Jimmy returned. 'Now let me do the talking and we might not only get the intel we came for but live to make use of it.'

The fat man slurped the final noodles from a bowl and wiped his mouth with the back of his sleeve. 'I guess you don't get to be head of a Triad by having polite table manners,' whispered Cally.

'So.' The fat man regarded his visitors with sly hostility. 'Jimmy Kwan craves an audience. What do you want, Jimmy? Your old job back?'

'No, Mr Xao,' said Jimmy, his voice clear and confident, almost defiant.

'Why am I not surprised? You wouldn't have got it anyway. You leave the organisation, betray its loyalty, turn against your friends, there's no going back. The day you broke with the Triad was the day you signed your death warrant.'

Cally tensed. Were the Chinese going to make a move? But Jimmy didn't look worried. Jimmy was almost smiling.

'I didn't come here to listen to old news, either,' he said.

Mr Xao laughed. It wasn't a pleasant sound. 'That's what I always liked about you, Jimmy. Fearless. If any other man spoke to me with no respect in his voice like that – *didn't come here to listen to old news* – he'd speak to no one else ever again because I would have his tongue cut out for him. You, Jimmy, I leave your tongue in your head, for old times' sake.'

'I appreciate that, Mr Xao,' said Jimmy. 'And at least it means my friends and I don't have to kill everyone in this room.'

The fat man chuckled. 'A little young, aren't they, these friends of yours? American? Another sign of your betrayal, working for Americans when your own people need you.'

'I know what my own people need,' Jimmy said, 'and I know what they *don't*.'

'Do they know all about you, your little friends?' Mr

Xao pursued. 'Don't tell me what their names are, they're not important enough for me to know their names. But you, girl, I notice you glancing up at Jimmy. You like him, do you? He gets you excited?'

'He's more my type than you are,' Cally observed, not daring to look at Jimmy as she did.

Another roar of laughter from the fat man. 'She's definitely *your* type, Jimmy. But I wonder if she'd still be interested if she knew how we found you wandering the streets of Hong Kong all orphaned and alone, how we took you in and gave you a home, gave you a future, gave you a purpose. We taught your handsome, dashing Jimmy Kwan there to kill, girl, and he was a keen and able student. How old were you when you did your first job, Jimmy? Eleven? Twelve?'

'It's not something I like to think about.' Jimmy lowered his gaze to the floor. Cally's heart ached for him.

'Children make good assassins if you start them off young enough,' said Mr Xao. 'No conscience. That was your trouble, wasn't it, Jimmy? In time you developed a conscience. Very bad. Very foolish. You lost everything you'd ever believed in.'

'I learned that everything I'd ever believed in was wrong.' Jimmy lifted his head again, and there was a fierce pride and a bold resolution in his eyes. 'And I'm trying to put it right. I despise you, Xao. I despise everything you stand for.'

'And yet you still come to me for help, Jimmy, hmmm?' There was nothing the younger man could say. Mr Xao snorted contemptuously. 'That's the problem with so-called principles, isn't it, Jimmy? You're always having to compromise them.' He lumbered to his feet.

'But as it happens, the temporary alliance you propose is as much of benefit to myself and the heads of the other Triads as it is to you and your little friends. Triads are about tradition, Jimmy. We don't like change. And we disapprove of the new trade in implants and computer chips and so forth. Narcotics, yes. Nanotechnology, no.'

'That's very enlightened of you, Mr Xao,' said Jimmy derisively.

'Isn't it?' Mr Xao dragged his corpulent bulk close to the blond Chinese. His beady eyes gleamed and his plump lips quivered moistly. 'And of course, we deplore the rise of any organisation that might eventually challenge the primacy of our own. So I will give you a time and a place, Jimmy, and I will expect you to *deal* with these upstarts with the same precision and finality that you used to employ in former days. But I want you to remember, you're helping us, you're helping *me*, Jimmy. Whatever good you think you're doing, you're also keeping the Triads strong. What does your conscience say to that?'

He could have selected a program that would have plunged him into virtual battle with every Triad in Hong Kong if he'd wanted to. He could have had it customised so that every foe he faced was Mr Xao. But sometimes, Cally supposed as she watched him from the holo-gym door, technology couldn't help to make you feel better. Sometimes you had to hit something real. Three punching bags were already spilling sand on to the floor. Jimmy was now unleashing his frustration on a fourth.

'You did the right thing, you know,' Cally intruded.

'What?' Jimmy had been so engrossed by his assault he'd failed to notice her. 'Oh. Cally.' He paused, breathing heavily, adjusted his black judogi. 'Is something the matter?'

'Not with me, not any more. Thanks to you.' She crossed the floor towards him and felt like running. 'You did the right thing, Jimmy. Arranging the meet with Xao, taking his information. Doing deals with the Bad Guys sticks in our craw, I understand that, but it was a matter of priorities. Don't let what the fat man said get to you.'

'Is it obvious?' Jimmy glanced sheepishly at the ruined punching bags.

'Let's just hope we have a generous budget for new gym equipment.' They both smiled. 'And I wanted to say something else as well, kind of apologise. The way I kept asking you for details of life in the Triads, that was stupid. I hadn't given any real thought to what it must actually have been like, what you must have done. Then Xao said what he said. I never realised . . .'

'You don't want to realise, Cally. You don't want to know. I've done terrible things,' brooded Jimmy. 'If I could turn the clock back . . . but not even Deveraux operatives can perform the impossible. I have to make amends for my crimes in practical ways, by trying to prevent other kids from being bred into the Triads. By becoming a field handler in the Deveraux organisation.'

'You're a good one, too,' Cally found herself blurting. 'The best. I wouldn't want Mei Ataki back now even if I could have her.'

'Well, thank you for the vote of confidence, Cally,' said Jimmy.

His smile, she was thinking, it was open and frank and generous. It was up there with Ben's. Nearly.

'Sometimes, though, it's like I'm two people.' Jimmy's mood darkened again. 'The man I am now and the cold, soulless boy I was. And no matter how hard I try, I can never entirely escape him. He's always there, in the background, in the shadows, like a ghost. The past I can't erase. Look.'

He shrugged off his judogi jacket, bent his left shoulder towards Cally. She saw that his flesh was rife with dragons, but that his shoulder was embellished by another kind of tattoo. It was streaked with years of scars but was still clearly visible. A lotus blossom. The mark of the Triad.

'I tried to slice it off,' Jimmy said. 'I scoured the skin away time and again but it never worked. It's indelible. It's part of me and it always will be.'

'It doesn't matter, Jimmy.' Cally allowed her fingers to lightly touch the hated tattoo. 'It's only skin. Your skin doesn't define you or tell people who you are. *I* know that. We make our own lives, Jimmy, and things like our pasts, they're just starting points. It's up to us where we go from there.'

'And for both of us that looks like here,' Jimmy observed.

'Maybe we shouldn't be surprised,' Cally said. 'With our backgrounds, seems like we've got more in common than I might have thought.'

'Seems like we have.'

Cally suddenly seemed to realise how physically close they were. She took an awkward step backwards. 'Anyway, that's it. I've said what I wanted to say. I'd better get some sleep . . . going out to Thornchild Island again tomorrow, and then tomorrow night me and Jake . . .' Backing away and backing away. 'I'll leave you to your work-out, Jimmy. Thanks. Bye.'

'Don't go on my account, Cally,' the field handler called after her. He regarded the ruptured punchbags with satisfaction. 'I think I'm just about finished here.'

It had been decided after the attack of the animate that Adam Thornchild should not travel to the Thornchild Building to work until the security situation was clearer. He could design smart atoms just as easily on the island as in the office, and he could be better protected at the same time. That, at least, was the plan. Cally had also ordered the number of guards present on the island to be doubled. Lucas Thornchild had objected on the grounds of 'unnecessary expense', but Adam had retorted that no expense was unnecessary if it was going to help save his life. Security Consultant Cross had his full authority to implement whatever measures she saw fit.

Probably explained why Lucas Thornchild wasn't at the helipad to greet her when Cally flew in the day after the meeting with Xao. A good old-fashioned case of resentment. Uncle Lucas had already expressed his dislike of her in no uncertain terms.

On the other hand, Cally pondered as she toured the island inspecting the new security arrangements, there could be more to it than that. What if the elder Thornchild *was* behind the ninja attack on her the other night, *was* responsible for the murder attempt on his nephew, was *even* involved in Jake's nanotechnology trafficking racket? Thornchild Silicon Systems itself would make a good cover for the latter *and* – she'd already hacked into the private files of the Thornchild family lawyers – if Adam was to die without an heir, guess who was due to come in for the business, the island, the lot? No wonder Lucas' face gave nothing away.

In the meantime, at least one member of the family was glad to see her. Adam was rushing to her side as soon as she entered the house. 'Calista! Hi!' And she'd clearly been given the seal of approval. Rover and Rex bounded up to her too, nuzzled her hands with their cold dry noses. Cally hoped they'd keep their atoms under control and not send them oozing halfway up her arm or something.

'Morning, Adam,' she smiled. 'Are you well?'

'I am now. I was worried about you.'

'Oh?'

'Well,' confessed Adam, 'when you didn't come yesterday, I thought something might have happened. I told Uncle Lucas but he said he thought you could look after yourself.'

'He's right,' said Cally (and maybe now he'd got a better idea of precisely *how* right, she thought), 'but nothing happened. I just had to spend some time, ah, overviewing your computer systems.'

'Do you know who sent the animate clown yet?'

' 'Fraid not. None of its components can be traced to a place of manufacture, Adam, at least not yet. It's like trying to identify a man without fingerprints.'

'You know, Calista,' confided Adam, 'I feel kind of sorry for that clown. I know it hurt you and killed some security men, would have killed *me* if you hadn't saved my life, but none of that was its own fault. The creatures of silicon and steel, the computer beings, like Rover and Rex here, they're pure, innocent, good. It's only programming that can make them bad, and people write the programs. It's *people* who are bad.'

'Some, maybe,' allowed Cally, 'but not all of us, hey?'

'No,' said Adam, smiling at Cally. 'Not all.'

And was that a *crush* kind of smile? A *total infatuation* kind of smile? Adam *did* seem to be standing unnecessarily close to her. 'Yes, well,' she commenced, just to be on the safe side, 'don't let me keep you from your smart atoms, Adam . . .'

'Oh, I'm not working on smart atoms today,' the boy said. 'Our new range of neural implants has developed a few glitches. I'm ironing those out to —'

'Neural implants?' Inside her own head, alarm bells, innate rather than implanted.

'Yes. They go in the brain and can do all sorts of neat stuff,' Adam enthused. 'Or at least they will when they're perfected. You know, Calista, we're on the brink of an implant that'll allow two or more people to communicate with each other neurotelepathically. Can you believe that?'

'Oh, I think so,' said Cally. She thought it might be wise to continue with her security checks. 'Now if you'll excuse me, Adam, I'd better get back to what you're paying me for, ensuring your safety.'

'Oh, I'm sure the island's impregnable now,' Adam breezed. 'I'm not worried. It's true, Calista. I've got nothing to worry about with you here to protect me.'

In actual fact, the time and the place were always pretty much the same. Criminals were a nocturnal breed by choice – you'd never find them congregating on a sunny afternoon or going about their nefarious business bright and early in the morning. The hours of darkness were invariably favoured, and one such hour in particular, give or take a few minutes. When Mr Xao had mentioned midnight, Cally had not been surprised. She could have predicted the location as well, at least in general terms: where would illicit gatherings and exchanges of illegal materials be without warehouses? And she'd have looked no further than Seabound even without the Triads' intel. In actual fact, all Mr Xao did was save Cally and Jake a little time. It was midnight now, and the former Bond Teamers had almost reached their destination.

They rode AquaBikes that were painted black and that plied their way through the filthy canals of Seabound silently, their magnetic engines muted. Cally was grateful that the bikes' design, shaped like a conventional jet ski though incorporating many features that were *far* from conventional, did not require her feet or legs to risk contact with the water: picking up some kind of grisly skin complaint she could do without. She supposed there wasn't much chance of it, really. She and Jake wore infiltration suits, again in black, complete with hoods and integrated radar visors both to protect their eyes against light grenades and to grant them 360° vision, always useful when the fighting started. In other words, the only flesh Cally was exposing was her nose, cheeks and mouth. She wasn't dressed for a date. Her mission belt was firmly buckled around her waist. Her shoulder holster containing its shock blaster was clasped in place. Her trusty sleepshot wristbands were secure.

Cally meant business.

Without the aid of her radar visor, even though she could have reached out and touched him, Jake would have appeared as little more than a charcoal blur. Through its infra-red lenses, however, she could see him clear as crystal, and his signal.

The warehouse was directly ahead of them. Fortunately, its rear wall teetered like an unsafe cliff over the lip of the air cushion supporting this particular portion of Seabound. The teenagers edged their AquaBikes closer to the cushion's steel skirts. They could hear the rumble of its motors deep within.

'You think we need a permit to park here?' joked Cally in a whisper.

Jake drew his shock blaster. 'Here's *my* permit.' He had *no* sense of humour any more.

She wondered exactly what they'd find inside the warehouse, or should she say *who*. The rumour according to Xao was that supplies of the illegal nanotech were to be handed over to members of the gang's distribution network prior to being trafficked around the world. Rumour was it was a big deal, and that some big names might be there to ensure the transaction went smoothly. Would Lucas Thornchild be among them?

'Hey, Cal,' Jake was hissing at her, 'less dreaming, more action. Let's go.' He was climbing on to the saddle of his AquaBike.

'Hey, Jake,' she returned tartly, 'since when did you get to order me around? I graduated the same as you, remember? I know what I'm doing.'

Jake relented. 'Sure you do. Of course you do, Cal. Sorry. It's just . . . I've been after these guys for so long now. I don't want anything to go wrong.'

'Neither do I,' Cally declared, 'and so long as we keep cool, nothing will.' But she couldn't help wishing the rules of Deveraux allowed field handlers to accompany their charges on raids of this kind. As it was, Jimmy Kwan could only monitor their progress from the Shop. He was no doubt watching them now as they prepared to scale first the air cushion's protective skirts and then the sheer wall of the warehouse. It had been decided that to attempt a frontal entry tonight would be inadvisable. As Jake said, they didn't want anything to go wrong.

'Clingskin?' he queried now.

'Clingskin,' Cally answered.

Spy High's miracle adhesive. Their gloves and their boots were impregnated with the substance. Cally and Jake slithered up the wall in seconds, gained one of the wire-mesh windows that provided the warehouse with rudimentary ventilation and, by day at least, a miserly natural light.

'You want to cut or shall I?' asked Jake.

'I'll do it,' claimed Cally. 'Watch and learn.'

She pressed her body against the wall to the left of the window, glued to the surface by her feet and the flattened palm of her left hand. With her right hand she deftly retrieved her belt-blade from its pouch at her waist and made expert, economical incisions in the wire mesh, stripping it away and letting it drop to the canal far below.

'Very nice,' Jake acknowledged, 'but I guess you had a lot of practice breaking and entering when you were on the streets, right, Cal?'

'I had a lot of practice ignoring smart remarks, that's

for sure,' Cally grunted. 'After you, Jake. I know you're keen.'

'You're not wrong there,' Jake gritted, hauling himself through the now gaping window. Cally deposited her belt-blade back in its pouch before following him. Somehow she reckoned she might soon be needing a little more firepower than that. Possibly within the next thirty seconds.

People in large buildings tended not to look up. Why should they? Quite naturally, they'd only expect to see strip-lights and rafters above their heads. And people in large buildings engaged in criminal activities tended more than most to have things on their minds other than admiring warehouse architecture. Which suited Cally and Jake just fine. They crawled out on to the rafters. If the tech traffickers didn't look *up*, they couldn't spot the secret agents peering *down*.

And there was plenty to look at. Grudgingly, Cally had to accept that Xao's tip had been right on the button. Maybe two dozen men were occupied below, all of them shock-blastered or pulse-rifled or both. In one area of the cavernous warehouse, a man who looked like a university lecturer was displaying his wares to a trio of men who looked like extras from *The Godfather*. Cally adjusted the magnification of her radar visor, zoomed in. Nanotech was changing hands all right. There were crates of it. Elsewhere the Bad Guys who were intellectually incapable of anything but carrying heavy objects – and they always outnumbered the more philosophical type of villain – were carrying heavy objects, shifting the crates from the warehouse floor to the boats. This was what Cally hadn't anticipated. The front of the building opened directly on to another of Seabound's countless canals. A series of four docks had been cut into the warehouse so that the four boats berthed there now were sheltered by the roof and could not be seen from the outside. A number of AquaBikes also bobbed on the dark waters. Transport for the tech.

'Good for Xao,' Jake whispered to her. 'Maybe we should go tell him thank you sometime.'

'One mission at a time, I think, Jake, don't you?'

'So is this it or are we just doing the sightseeing tour? You ready?' Cally could imagine Jake's eyes gleaming behind his visor. 'The light and lower routine, yeah? You take right. I'll take left. Lots of goons to help us with our enquiries.'

'Just . . .' Cally stopped him. 'We'd best activate our homers first. We might need the bikes.'

Jake nodded. 'Good call, Cal.' They both pressed studs on their mission belts. 'Ready now?'

'Is Mr Deveraux software?'

In unison, the teenagers released ultra-thin cables from their belts. Their flattened ends were treated with clingskin. They affixed them to the underside of the rafters. 'It's good I don't have a thing about heights,' muttered Cally. She produced a light-grenade. So did Jake. 'After three?'

'Why wait? After one.' Jake grinned. 'One!'

They pressed the detonators and tossed the grenades together. The first the traffickers knew about it was when they exploded in mid-air. Instant, coruscating, eyeball-searing, all-consuming light, like white fire, like the heart of lightning, like God's beard. The gang's eyes wouldn't be permanently damaged, but they weren't going to be reading at distance for a while.

Nor were they going to be picking up Cally and Jake, who were leaping from the rafters on the end of their lines. The flash of the light-grenades was unsustainable, though. The agents had to make the most of it while they had the advantage of sight. Sleepshot from both wrists, cutting into the ranks of the traffickers, causing further yells of chaos and panic. Shock blasts. Pulse blasts. Both fired off in random directions. The Bad Guys floundering, falling. Two of them attempting to flee and colliding with each other. Easy targets for Cally to take out.

Four feet from the ground they detached their cables and dropped nimbly to the warehouse floor. 'I *love* that ride!' cried Jake.

The effects of the light grenades were waning. There were other colours in the world than white, and all of them dark. Cally didn't pause. She didn't need to. She was seeing the circle, thanks to her radar visor, before and behind her simultaneously. Her right wrist cleared a path ahead of her as she sprinted towards the boats, her left sprayed sleepshot to her rear, toppling into unconsciousness anyone she'd missed so far.

But now the survivors could see her. In the dirty yellow glow of the warehouse, the traffickers had somewhere to direct their fire.

Pulse blast. Cally dived forward, beneath the searing stab of the shot. Rolled. Leapt to her feet. Fired both wristbands. The guy with the rifle only got one chance.

Another attacker. Her back to him. He thought he had time. He thought she couldn't see him. He hadn't, because she could. She spun, crouched, fired. The assailant wore an expression almost of unfairness as he sank senseless to the floor.

'Cal! Here!'

Jake's shout alerted her. The remaining handful of tech traffickers were in full retreat. Several had managed to get as far as the AquaBikes, were powering them up, churning the waters in their frenzy to escape. They weren't going to be able to stop them all, not here.

No problem. Cally had known the homers would come in useful.

Even as she and Jake reduced the warehouse resistance to zero, even as the half-dozen surviving traffickers sped off on AquaBikes, the teenagers' own machines were gliding swiftly towards them. The homing signal had triggered the automatic drive systems. As long as they were close to water, the Deveraux agents' bikes would find them.

Cally leapt into the saddle, saw Jake do the same. No need for stealth now or engines on mute. She gunned the magnetic core of her AquaBike and it reared up powerfully, jetted in pursuit of her quarry. The crims might have got a head start, but they'd need it.

A whoosh of spray and Cally was accelerating away from the warehouse. She and Jake were straining neck and neck. They blurred under bridges, took the corners in sharp, slicing motions. The Seabound canals were like deep gorges overlooked by mountains. The roar of the AquaBikes' engines reverberated in the chasms, and the blistering sound of shock blasts as the crims attempted to deter their pursuers.

Cally leant forward and kept low in the saddle,

rammed her legs hard against the flanks of her bike. She switched her headlamps on to full beam. Shock blasts zapped above her. Cally zipped in and out of the canals' flotsam, sticks of drowned furniture, shards of discarded timber, the upturned husks of boats, dangerous obstacles all when travelling at fierce velocity and under attack.

Time to fight back. Deveraux AquaBikes came equipped with a variety of weapons systems. Bearing in mind the idea was to capture rather than kill, even if the other side's thinking seemed to be the reverse, Cally selected stasis bolts. Neutralise the opposition's transport and you neutralised the opposition. She wondered fleetingly whether Jake was going to be similarly restrained.

Looked like he was, fortunately. A dual barrage of stasis bolts burst from the gunports at the front of the Deveraux bikes. They didn't miss. Two of the traffickers' machines were lagging behind the others. They were struck squarely, enveloped in a sudden crackling nimbus of light. Every circuit in both bikes shorted out. Their riders lost control, crashed into the air cushions left and right. More junk cluttering up the canals of Seabound.

Realising their jeopardy, the crims tried a different tactic. They raced into a narrower channel. Cally saw their arms go up. They were throwing something. She couldn't make out what it was but it wasn't likely to be good.

Fire-bombs. The manual kind. The small but deadly kind. The kind that could burn on water just as destructively as on land. Suddenly a cloud of flame was billowing towards her and Jake. It was wall to wall, no going round it. No going back either.

Cally engaged her Dive option. The AquaBike

plunged beneath the surface, didn't slacken its pace for a second. Cally felt the scorch of boiling water above her, held her breath. In seconds there'd be air again.

She and Jake emerged into it simultaneously. Another burst of stasis bolts. Only one casualty this time, however, the crippled AquaBike slamming into the pillar of a bridge. Somebody was slipping.

Maybe it didn't matter, though. The crims seemed to have taken a wrong turn. They seemed to have found their way to what looked like a dead end. Timber buildings in an advanced state of decay, the air cushions themselves sagging, partially deflated on either side. Ahead of them, a solid wall. Or not so solid. Here the budget hadn't even extended as far as an air cushion. The building blocking their path was supported on stilts. An AquaBike could slalom between these stilts. And beyond, if Cally's newly acquired knowledge of Seabound's topography was reliable, beyond lay the open sea. Escape.

And the crims still had some fire-bombs in reserve. They were on the brink of deploying them.

Cally glanced across to Jake. He was jabbing his thumbs upwards. They'd gone low; now they were going high. Variety was the spice of espionage. This little move was something the Bad Guys *never* expected.

Fireballs flared towards them. Cally stabbed at her controls. Booster function engaged.

She was almost jerked out of the saddle as her AquaBike temporarily mistook itself for a rocket and with a sudden spurt of power launched itself into the air. The flames rolled beneath her, groping for her feet, the underside of the bike.

There was going to be no avoiding the wall. It seemed that the building was hurtling towards her. 'Coming through!' Cally cried. She fired her explosives.

The wall erupted. The rotting timber splintered into shards, shattered into fragments. She was through. Jake was through. Their bikes were dipping lower, smashing through internal walls as well now, a bare-boarded floor. What seemed like a whole colony of rats scampered for cover, but of human occupation there was no sign. It had been a gamble worth taking. There were some parts of Seabound shunned by even the poorest.

A second blast smithereened the final barrier. There was night sky. There was dark ocean. They were swooping low over the heads of the traffickers. Jake was leaning to one side, pumping sleepshot at the nearest target. The man was riddled with shells, slumped forward unconscious in his saddle, but Jake had been too ambitious. When his bike splashed down into its natural element again, his balance was thrown. It was all he could do to hold on. Cally entered the water more gracefully, steered her machine in a wide arc so as to intercept the last two crims.

'Get 'em, Cal! Take 'em out!' Jake didn't really imagine his partner would need any instruction from him, but suddenly he was gasping, astonished. Cally seemed to have lost control of her AquaBike, her speed and direction suffering alarmingly. It was as if she'd forgotten how to ride.

The traffickers couldn't believe their luck and were not going to waste it. They didn't fancy prolonging the battle. Instead they shot past the flustered Cally and made for the horizon. The girl might be out of it for the moment, but the boy would soon recover. Indeed, Jake was even now gearing up for pursuit.

Cally, having miraculously regained her aquabiking expertise, cut across his line.

'Cal, what do you think you're doing?' Jake was understandably furious. 'You're in my . . . they're getting away!'

'That's the idea,' Cally announced.

'What? Have you gone mad?'

'Not mad. *Subtle*.' And she switched her engine to stand-by.

Reluctantly, Jake followed suit. The two AquaBikes bobbed on the water as if they were out on a boating lake on a Sunday afternoon. 'All right, but this had better be good.'

'We could have caught those guys too, Jake. Of course we could,' said Cally. 'But that wouldn't have necessarily found us either their main base or their leader. I didn't get the feeling he was anywhere at the warehouse. What if the goons don't talk? Worse, what if they've all got implants in their brains ready to go boom just like the ninjas?'

'So far so acceptable,' Jake granted. 'So what did you do?'

Cally patted her AquaBike like it was a pet that had just performed a trick. 'I fired tracers at their bikes, when they were past me and thought they were getting away.'

'Did they hit?' Jake demanded.

'Have a little faith, Jake,' Cally tutted. 'If I remember rightly, my Gun Run average at Spy High was at least as good as yours.'

'Like I told you, though, Cal, we're not at Spy High any more. Let's have a look at the scanner.'

'Is that a silent please there or what?'

But she booted up the dashboard scanner anyway. She was rewarded with twin flashing dots against a stylised background of the South China Sea, studded with islands. Green arrows denoted the route that the objects signified by the dots had taken so far; red arrows pointed to the computer's prediction for the same objects' final destination.

'That's not good,' Cally groaned. 'But I knew it. I *knew* it.'

'What? *Tell* me, Cal. Where does the computer think they're heading?'

'The only place they *could* be heading. The obvious place.' Cally shook her head grimly. 'Thornchild Island.'

SIX

The darkest hour came just before the dawn. Wasn't that what they said? So okay, now was a pretty good time to be creeping about Thornchild Island in an infiltration suit with radar visor on and shock blaster drawn. And okay, she ought to be able to avoid the cameras and security posts, not solely because she was a trained spy but because she'd positioned them herself. She *ought* to be able to reach the house undetected. But Cally would still have felt better if she'd glimpsed evidence of *somebody* doing their job.

She'd decided against the helicopter for once. Beaching her muted AquaBike in the bay below and then stealing her way by foot had seemed the more promising option. If Lucas Thornchild had come to the helipad to greet her this time, she reckoned he'd have done it with pulse rifles. Jake had suggested they go in all guns blazing, but she couldn't contemplate that, not immediately anyway. There was Adam to think of, Adam who'd told her how he had nothing to worry about with her there to protect him. She had to justify his faith in her. She couldn't let him down.

So Cally was going in alone. She had an hour to locate and evacuate Adam Thornchild. If something went wrong, if they hadn't heard from her by that time, then Jake and Jimmy were poised to take over.

At the house, Cally keyed in the entry code for freelance security consultant Calista Cross and the doors whisked welcomingly open. The house was probably grateful for the company. It seemed deserted. So much for the twenty-four-hour-a-day security presence in the vestibule. Cally penetrated further into the building, a shadow among shadows. The question was no less pressing because it was obvious: where *was* everyone?

Adam's rooms. For once she didn't knock. Hissed his name as she slipped inside. No answer. No Rover or Rex. She eased open the door to his bedroom, already had a good idea of what she'd see within. Her heart was sinking. She was right.

Nobody.

And no sign of any struggle, either. The room looked like an exhibit in a museum. No indication that the bed had actually been slept in tonight. But Adam had been under orders not to leave the island.

Where was he? Someone must have taken him. *Who?*

Lucas' rooms next. The answers might lie there.

Nothing. From study to bedroom they were as eerily unoccupied as the rest of the house, as the rest of the *island*. But Cally was in no rush to leave them. After all, she reminded herself, there was no irrefutable *proof* that Lucas Thornchild was the mastermind behind the tech traffickers, the killer clown, the murders of the nanoscientists

(though the latter *would* kind of corner the market for
Thornchild Silicon Systems). It was possible, *possible*, that
Lucas might be an innocent if fairly dislikeable victim, possible he could have been abducted by the same person or
people who'd apparently kidnapped Adam.

She re-entered his study. Maybe his private computer
files could confirm or deny some of these possibilities.

Cally removed her radar visor and sat at Lucas' computer. She imagined that his security protocols would be
complex and sophisticated. They were.

She was through them in five minutes.

Cally had been taught to speed-scan files at Spy High.
Time was usually of the essence when hacking in the
field. Her own name, though, stood out rather glaringly.
She couldn't resist clicking on to it.

*Calista: if you want to learn the truth about your parents,
come tonight. Come alone.* And there was an address.

Cally bit her lip. So much for the Lucas-Thornchild-
as-innocent-victim theory. He was behind *everything*. But
why hadn't he simply deleted the incriminating e-mail?
Maybe he'd meant to but hadn't got round to it. Maybe
he'd never expected Cally to be able to hack into his files.
And that nagging need to know again: her *parents*. All of
which she had to relegate to the back of her mind. None
of which could be addressed right now. Her priority was
to discover any other little secrets that Lucas Thornchild
might be hiding.

Cutter. Kratilova. Sanchez. Sharma. Stoneham.
Wagner. They were all there, alphabetically arranged and
lined up like tombstones. And with Thornchild, D., and
Thornchild, J., slotted in as well. Adam's parents. Cally's
night was developing into one giant sinking feeling.

She accessed Wagner first. There was a program written in the file. It was advanced and difficult stuff, largely beyond what even Cally could understand, but she knew enough to grasp its gist. It was an invasive virtual reality program, like a virus. Werner Wagner had been found dead in his womb-room. Its VR function had been on. His heart attack hadn't been the result of natural causes, Cally realised gravely. It had been *induced*. By *this* program.

She tried Troy Cutter next. He'd been in an elevator in his apartment building that had plunged thirty storeys and killed not only him but several other people besides. They'd been in the wrong place at the wrong time. The elevator disaster had been about Troy Cutter and Troy Cutter alone. The file demonstrated sabotage: it was some kind of systems override. Same for Larissa Kratilova. Routine operation in hospital. Went in with an overnight bag. Came out in a body-bag. The program showed how to convert life-saving pieces of equipment into ruthless life-*takers*, just for a moment, just until the job was done. Cally shivered. Lucas' overrides loose in the world's cyber-systems were as deadly as a serial killer in a sorority house. And she didn't want to do it, but she had no choice. Thornchild, D., Thornchild, J. She didn't linger. It was all too clear.

The wheelless accident *wasn't* an accident. Adam's parents had been murdered. The wicked uncle strikes again. But why had Lucas waited so long to dispose of the rest of the Princeton crowd? Maybe his brother and sister-in-law had been a trial run, to test his technology. Maybe he'd been waiting for the nanoscientists' research to pay dividends.

Maybe he was just a sick lunatic.

It always worried Cally, trying to divine the mentality and motivations of the kind of madman she faced as a Deveraux agent. They'd always been encouraged to try to understand their enemies – if you could *think* like them, maybe you could outwit them – but couldn't that process be taken too far? If you entered the mind of the maniac *too* deeply, couldn't you be infected with their insanity yourself? Jake for one had always been keen on the psychological profiling of the über-villain. Cally preferred to keep her distance.

But she was drifting. And she'd like to be close to Lucas Thornchild now. Sleepshot close. She gazed around the study again. No dues here. Where? Was? H—

Stupid, Cally! Blind! Of course there was a clue here. She glanced at the Thornchild, J., file. In the top right-hand corner, a small insignia. Two hands clasping and forming a single bulging fist. The same insignia had featured on the files of all eight nanoscientists.

The same insignia was decorating the wall of Lucas Thornchild's study.

Cally was there immediately. Up close, the design appeared more unusual. It was bordered by a circle and depicted forearms as well as hands. One of these was plainly intended to be human, though the skin was coloured an anaemic white. The other, however, while human in shape, was cybernetic, glistening with gold and silver wires and banded with strips of steel. Where the two hands met and combined and made their defiant, almost threatening fist, it was impossible to tell where the human ended and the cybernetic began.

Here was a clue all right, Cally sensed, but a clue to *what*? She tapped on the insignia thoughtfully.

A door opened in the wall. Beyond it, an elevator car.

'This isn't in the architect's drawings,' Cally remarked. She wondered what else might not be. She wondered whether any of it might be concealing Lucas Thornchild, imprisoning Adam. There was only one way to find out.

She stepped gingerly into the elevator. Kept her eyes open for a sudden jet of gas or the floor falling away without warning. She'd paid attention in spycraft classes. She knew how quickly a superficially innocent elevator car could be turned into a death-trap. Luckily, all this elevator seemed to want to do was to close its door as its sensors registered her entry and descend smoothly into the rock-bound depths of the island. Cally realised she'd left her radar visor in Lucas Thornchild's study. It didn't matter. Next time she saw him she wanted it to be eyeball to eyeball.

The elevator shaft reached far below the house. Much further, Cally estimated, and they'd be below the sea. But then the car was easing to a stop, opening politely. She emerged into a small man-made cave. The shaft was flanked by two flights of steps that both led upwards, no doubt back to the house. The cave itself opened on to a cavern on an altogether grander scale.

'Bingo,' Cally breathed.

The original rock had been hollowed out to allow for the creation of both a dock and some kind of control centre. This latter boasted ranks of computer consoles, bulges of cables snaking around the cavern's perimeter, still more sensitive equipment panelled into the walls.

Beyond it, furthest from Cally, docking facilities included space for a whole row of AquaBikes. At least two of them she knew had been in recent use. However, the harbour seemed to be entirely enclosed, a pool rather than open to the sea. A bare dark cliff appeared to pose an insuperable obstacle for anyone seeking a passage to or from the cavern by water. But Deveraux agents were not so easily deceived. Cally detected the faint shimmer to the rock surface, an effect reminiscent of a heat haze. Only there was more hologram than heat to this illusion. Lucas Thornchild had carved himself a nice little hide-away here, and he didn't want snoopers from outside to be spoiling it.

Cally had instinctively kept close to the wall, crouched just within the smaller cave behind an out-cropping of rock in case she needed to defend herself. She didn't. The cavern was as deserted as the rest of the island. Which gave her a chance to check it out a little more closely.

She darted out to one of the computer consoles. Maybe she ought to comlink with Jake and Jimmy first, let them know what she'd found. But there wasn't much point. They'd be here soon in any case, the sensors in her suit guiding them to her. Her hour was nearly up. Instead, Cally went to work, her fingers flying across the keyboard like the strokes of an impressionist's brush. Wouldn't take her long to hack into the system, not if it was anything like Lucas' before.

Unfortunately for Cally, she never found out *how* long it would take her.

'Ah, Security Consultant Cross.' The familiar voice behind her.

Cally wheeled. (*Behind* her. If only she hadn't abandoned her radar visor.) She thought about raising her shock blaster, firing her sleepshot.

'I wouldn't if I were you,' advised Lucas Thornchild, correctly diagnosing her intent. 'Not if you want to stay alive at least a *little* longer. And who doesn't, hmm?'

If he'd been alone, Cally would have taken him on. But there were a dozen armed and grey-uniformed men now lining the entrance to the smaller cave with him. She was good, but she couldn't take them all.

'Drop the blaster, Ms Cross, and place your hands on your pretty little head, if you'd be so kind,' recommended Thornchild. Grudgingly, Cally complied. 'Excellent. And may I say that this level of commitment on your part, creeping about my island at all hours, goes far beyond the call of duty. Or at least, it would if you were simply the freelance security consultant you purport to be. But we both know that such is not the case, do we not, Calista, and that we no longer need to pretend otherwise.'

'Fair cop, Thornchild,' accepted Cally, 'but it looks like I'm not the only one who's been making a living under false pretences.'

'You think you're so clever, don't you, *Calista*?' Her name like it was something he'd trodden in. Lucas Thornchild was not expressionless now – his face was making up for its previous lack of emotion with a rictus of hatred and rage. Cally preferred him the way he'd been. 'But you're not clever, not clever at all. You think you had me fooled? You didn't. It was just a pity my ninjas let me down. And you imagined your amateurish tracers would go undetected? They didn't. We discovered them at once and prepared for your arrival.'

'Yeah?' Cally rejoined. 'So where's the streamers and balloons?'

'There's little for you to celebrate, Calista,' sneered Lucas Thornchild. 'Whichever organisation or government you genuinely work for is immaterial to me. It's all over. I'm bringing your spying career to an end. *Permanently.*'

Thornchild's minions moved in on her, surrounding her. They were grinning, the way bullies grin when their victim starts to cry. They thought she was helpless. Well, wait for the right moment and she'd show the morons *exactly* how helpless she was.

'Get her wristbands off. Get them off,' instructed Lucas Thornchild. 'We've already heard reports of what they can do.' He approached Cally himself, not for a second lowering his shock blaster. 'Such amusing trinkets your employers provide for you, Calista. If I was a child, I might enjoy playing with them myself.'

Cally did nothing to prevent the lackeys from stripping away her wristbands. 'Talking of children, Thornchild, what have you done with Adam?'

'Oh, nothing. Not very much, anyway,' the tall man chuckled. 'You don't think I'd harm my dear nephew, do you? No, Adam is in a safe place. What would Thornchild Silicon Systems do without his genius for all things computer?'

'What would your nanotech trafficking racket do, you mean?'

Lucas shrugged dismissively. 'The tech-running operation is a sideline, nothing more, a hobby.'

'Destroying people's lives is a hobby, Thornchild?' Cally snorted.

'It beats collecting stamps, doesn't it? No,' he smirked, 'our true purpose is considerably more far-reaching than a handful of illegal implants, *radically* more.' He laughed as Cally's eyes flashed. 'Ah, I see I've piqued your secret agent's interest, have I not, Calista? Another mad scheme for world domination, are you thinking? How childishly simple to manipulate you are.'

'Is that right?' Cally said icily.

'It is. Example.' After a diversion to a sadistic kind of amusement, Thornchild's expression had settled again on contempt. 'All I need to do is mention your parents and you begin to behave irrationally.'

'What do you know about my parents?' Cally was lunging for Thornchild. Several pairs of hands restrained her.

'See what I mean?'

'You don't know anything,' Cally said scornfully. 'You can't do.'

'Can't I? I know that Cross is not your real name, Calista. It was not your parents' name. And I know that your mother and father were not the people I imagine you think they were. But then, who is?'

'Then they're dead?'

'If I don't *know* anything,' pointed out Thornchild, 'how could I know *that*? But enough of such trivialities. It's time for us to leave. Thanks to you, Calista, this base of operations is no longer secure. You're going to regret that when the pain begins. Bring her,' he ordered his underlings. 'Remove her belt first. We don't want any surprises.'

Meaty hands groped at Cally's waist. She slapped them away. (About five seconds to *the right moment*.) 'Getting a little forward, guys, aren't we? We haven't been introduced yet.' (And Thornchild had a point. She had to isolate and ignore her parents in her mind. Whatever there might be for her to learn, she could only do it if she stayed alive.) 'Get your hands off me. *I'll* do it.'

'Watch her,' warned Thornchild

'Watch *this*,' retorted Cally.

The stud on her mission belt. I-Shields *on*. Suddenly Cally seemed sheathed in a bluish light. Its appearance startled Thornchild's goons. So did the pace and precision of Cally's assault. Her fists and feet lashed out to bone-crunching effect. The chin, the neck, the solar plexus, those vulnerable joints at the knees, Cally targeted them all. The lackeys had got close. They'd played right into her martial-arts-trained hands. So she didn't have her sleepshot or her shock blaster. She was still more than a match for these lowlifes. And then she was going to have a nice long conversation with Lucas Thornchild.

Elbow to the belly behind her to the right. Forearm to the nose in front of her to the left. Kick out. Pivot. Duck. Strike again. Make every blow powerful. Make every blow count. Keep in the crowd. Use their numbers against them. If they fired their weapons, they'd hit each other before they got to her.

'Out of the way, you idiots!' Thornchild itched for a shot.

And the I-Shields were working. Where the goons punched, their blows were either harmlessly deflected or their impact absorbed, each time the blue force-field flashing like an electronic bruise. Where the goons attempted to seize or grapple with Cally, their fingers failed to find a hold. Dazed or senseless thugs began to litter the floor at the girl's feet like the unlucky Philistines who'd encountered Samson with the jawbone of the ass.

'Out! Of! The! Way!' Maybe his men needed encouragement to obey him. Lucas Thornchild gave it to them. He opened fire regardless.

'Industrial relations looking up in the megalomaniac sector, huh, Lucas?' But Cally was in trouble now. Those lackeys able to do so were scattering, not screening her any longer. And the I-Shields were for hand-to-hand combat only. They weren't designed to resist a shock blast. All of a sudden, Cally was crouching, exposed, staring down the barrel of Thornchild's blaster. Of course, the Shields had to have *some* margin of resistance built in. She hoped it would be enough, because if not, she'd soon be adding red to her palette of colours.

'Any final words, Calista?' Thornchild gloated.

'None you want to hear.' But if she lived, she'd like a word or two with Jimmy and Jake regarding punctuality.

'Let's just say farewell then, shall we?'

Squeezing the trigger. She'd have to leap. Her muscles bunched.

If only Ben was here.

A sudden roar of engines and froth of spray. A volley of shock blasts raking the control centre. An armada of AquaBikes bursting through the cliffside, smashing the illusion of the hologram. Lucas glancing to the dock in shocked dismay.

No Ben, but Jimmy, Jake and a fully armed Deveraux security team would do nicely. About time too.

And Cally hadn't tensed her limbs for nothing. She sprang like a panther, slammed into Thornchild. 'Took your eyes off me, Lucas,' she scolded, driving him to the floor. 'You'll never make a good secret agent. You've let go of your gun, too.' With her finger-numbing assistance. 'Don't reckon you'll make much of a villain, either.' She knelt hard on the man's chest. 'Now where's Adam?'

'You haven't won yet, Calista,' spat Thornchild.

Battle was joined between the Deveraux team and the remnants of Lucas' men. Jake and Jimmy were leading the way, bounding from their bikes on to the floor of the cavern. They were disciplined, determined, reducing further the number of the enemy.

'No?' Cally grinned.

Prematurely. A stray shock blast stabbed at her face. She recoiled instinctively, avoided injury. '*No.*' Thornchild saw his chance. He'd never be a boxer, but his punch was unexpected and struck Cally while she was already off balance. It couldn't hurt her through the I-Shields but he was out from under her, scrambling to his feet.

His underlings were paid to fight on, however helpless their position. They would at least provide cover for his own escape.

Cally's recovery was pretty much instant. Seemed Thornchild had decided not to lead his men from the front – no surprise there, then – but to make a run for the elevator instead. Seemed he was in such a rush he'd left his shock blaster behind. Maybe Cally should do her good deed for the day and return it. Her colleagues could handle things in the cavern from here.

She chased after him, keeping her head down as the conflict raged but not once taking her eyes from his fleeing form. He was at the entrance to the inner cave, would access the elevator before she could reach him. That would never do.

Cally fired her shock blaster, set to Materials. Didn't slow down for a second. Hitting targets while sprinting in combat situations was second nature to a Spy High graduate. There was a bright, brittle explosion. The elevator was temporarily out of action.

Thornchild yelped, almost stumbled. 'Damn you!' Cally thought she could hear. 'Damn your interfering!' He made for the steps.

'You could save yourself a stitch and just surrender, Thornchild!' Cally shouted. Lucas wasn't listening. Who cared? There was no way a man of his age and in his condition could outstrip Cally on some *stairs*.

She took them three at a time. She was gaining. Could almost hear the breathless panting of her quarry's overworked lungs. She should put him out of his misery. Cally flipped the shock blaster to Stun. She couldn't miss.

Unless, of course, the stairwell was suddenly plunged into darkness. She hated it when that happened. The electricity must be on voice control. Thornchild must have doused the lights hoping to gain an advantage: he'd been here many times, knew his way around better than his pursuer. 'Lights on!' cried Cally, and was ignored. Personalised voice control. She'd just have to run harder. She wasn't letting Thornchild get away.

And then she was at the top of the stairwell. A blank wall in front of her. No door and no Lucas. Only there had to be the former for the latter to have passed through. Cally scrutinised the smooth dark stone as best she could. She was bargaining on the presence somewhere of another of those insignias.

'The girl with the dreadlocks and the charming personality wins!' Found it. Pressed it. Being right always made her feel good.

The body of the house too was in darkness, and in silence. Cally deactivated the Shields with their conspicuous blue light and ghosted into the corridor. In places shafts of moonlight silvered the rooms through broad windows. She recognised the area where the private quarters were. Adam's were close by – she wished *he* was. But she'd find him yet. Locate the uncle and she'd locate the nephew.

Cally stole further in like someone from a silent movie. Her best bet was to rely on sound to betray Lucas Thornchild. She doubted his stealth techniques were as noiseless as hers. She strained with her ears. A footfall. A cough. The creaking of a door or the slightest bump against a piece of furniture. Any of them could identify him, pinpoint his presence. He hadn't had time to physically leave the house.

There. To her left. A boot on tiled floor. On feline feet Cally glided in that direction, keeping against the wall, out of the splashes of starlight.

Lucas Thornchild was not doing the same.

He was standing there ahead of her, in the middle of a lounge. The domed roof was made of glass and the light it admitted cast the tall man in the pallor of steel, like a machine for the present deactivated.

Cally jabbed towards him with her blaster. 'That's right, Lucas,' she cautioned, 'you just stay stock still like that and you won't need to wake up tomorrow with a stun blast headache. I think I'd sooner see your hands as well, though.'

Cally still kept her distance as Thornchild raised his hands without demur. He seemed to be unarmed, but *something*, something didn't feel right. Was he smiling?

'Okay,' she said, 'you're coming with me, Thornchild.'

'Oh, Calista,' said Lucas Thornchild, 'I think not.'

She was quick. That last second, his eyes gleaming in the moonlight, she saw that they were looking behind her. Someone was *behind* her. Someone who was secret agent sly. And she was quick, whirling, squeezing the shock blaster's trigger.

The someone was quicker.

The blow caught the side of her head, the temple above the eye. A metal object, wielded with calculating but vicious force. Her vision splintered into shards of red, needles of scarlet that lanced into her brain with piercing agony. She couldn't see her assailant, only felt him strike her again, a sickening thud against her skull. She was on her knees. The world was reeling. She couldn't defend herself, couldn't reach her I-Shields. If the attack was pressed home she'd be finished.

There'd be darkness.

'Cally? Cal? Are you okay?'

Jake. He was holding her. He was cradling her, lifting her head and shoulders tenderly from the floor. Was that Jimmy in the background, too? Hard to tell. Her eyes didn't want to work. It hurt too much to focus.

'I . . .'ve been better.'

'You'll be fine.' Jake squeezed her hand reassuringly. 'You've got a skull like a rhinoceros.'

'I love you . . . too.'

Jimmy crouched beside her. 'We'll get you back to the Shop, Cally, don't worry. Get you checked out. Just relax.'

'No . . .' She'd have sat or even stood up at that point had the slightest movement towards either position not caused her to sink back down again in blistering pain. 'Lucas . . . what happened to Lucas . . .?'

'He got away, I'm afraid,' Jimmy admitted. 'It took us a while to finish off the hired help and follow you up here. But he's on the run now and he won't be keen on that. We'll catch him.'

'Someone else was here,' Cally told them. 'One of Thornchild's men . . . hit me from behind . . .'

'That's why they're the Bad Guys,' observed Jake.

'I should have seen him,' Cally said bitterly. 'I should have stopped Thornchild *here*. What about Adam?'

'No sign of him either,' said Jimmy. 'We have to assume his uncle's taken him.'

'I've failed again,' Cally groaned. 'I've failed *again*.'

'You haven't, Cal,' insisted Jake. 'Look at what we've done. We've closed down Thornchild's nanotech trafficking operation. We've captured his base. We've saved lives because of tonight, Cal. Don't ever forget that. It's what we're in this job for.'

'But Thornchild's gone,' Cally despaired. 'And he's taken with him any chance I might have had of learning the truth about my parents.'

SEVEN

Jake had gone. There'd been a final embrace, a last smile, and for a moment it had seemed to Cally that the old camaraderie of Bond Team had been restored. But the moment had passed, as moments tend to do. Jake had left her, left Hong Kong. There was no longer any official reason for him to stay. His mission was over.

Hers had only just begun.

Because she wasn't giving up. Cally was not accepting failure this time. It wasn't like Shanghai. Her over-riding task remained the protection of Adam Thornchild and she could still achieve that. She doubted Lucas would have harmed his genius nephew, not after what he'd said in the cavern – if he'd wanted to, he could have left the boy's body behind on the island. The animate clown, Cally now reasoned, which must have been Lucas' instrument, had never been intended to assassinate Adam but to kill *her*, kind of an aperitif to the murderous entrée of the ninjas. No, Adam was without doubt his uncle's prisoner somewhere. She simply had to narrow down the where.

She'd already spent long hours in the Shop's IGC compartment reclining on the leather chair, the cyber-helmet secured, interfacing directly with the almost infinite amounts of information stored on the Intelligence Gathering Centre's database at Deveraux. She was finding the experience frustrating: how could so much intel be of so little use? Needle in a haystack? It was like poring through the dictionary for a word beginning with a letter that wasn't in the alphabet.

Take the insignia, for example, the two fists, human and cyber. Cally had – sensibly, she thought – initiated a search for the same design or anything close. All she'd discovered was the propensity of companies who made money out of the public to sweeten the pill by devising logos with handshakes, like they were really your friends. The companies didn't seem to feel the need to strike up positive relationships with anyone built from circuits and wires. But Cally had persisted for a long time. Her instincts were crying out that the fist insignia was significant, that it connected to the cryptic and faintly menacing 'true purpose' that Thornchild had taunted her with.

Finally, however, she'd had to admit defeat, at least for now. When faced with a dead end, Senior Tutor Elmore Grant used to tell them, look for another way forward. Cally was looking to Princeton. The Class of '36. The *dead* guys. It was a long shot, but maybe by sifting through everything there was on the database relevant to the period when the Thornchilds, Wagner and the others were there, maybe Cally could learn something about what had first brought the group together and why. Anything would do. Even a shared love of bagels for breakfast.

Turned out to be the Science and Ethics Society. Met every Friday night, apparently, to 'discuss and debate the latest technological developments in the world of science and to assess and anticipate their moral and ethical implications for today's society'. Sounded like a real fun time would be had by all. Personally, Cally might just have been torn away from the delights of an evening of moral and ethical implications by the University Dance which always seemed to take place at the same time (there is no such thing as coincidence . . .). But the records showed that the Science and Ethics Society maintained a reasonable number of members, eight of whom were already known to her. She thought she ought to familiarise herself with the others.

Cally cross-referenced names with the official Princeton photos. A sequence of people she'd never seen before now seemed to have business in her brain. Andrea Tarcholewsky. Timothy Zimmerman. Wayne Batt. It didn't matter what style or colour of hair they had, what tint of eyes, what shape of face, they all wore the same smile and they all seemed pleased to be young and at Princeton, a life of ambition and achievement in front of them. Tracy R. Cronin. Ezekiel Fenn. Douglas Tyler Durbridge. They were only a little older than herself, Cally mused. If her life had turned out differently, or rather if it had *begun* differently, they could almost *be* her.

And then one of them was.

'Computer. Pause.' Cally's voice was dry and weak.

In her mind's eye, projected from the vast resources of the IGC, an African-American girl who could have been her sister smiled naturally, knowingly, almost *lovingly* at her.

Simone Halliday.

But of course, it couldn't *be* her sister. The picture was thirty years old. She was an only child. She was an orphan. She'd never even known her . . .

Simone Halliday.

Singing to her. Crooning softly, gently, the nonsense language of lullaby. From a past that was not stored on the IGC, a past that Cally to her bewilderment had not even known was recollected by her own brain, from a time before conscious memory, Simone Halliday was singing to her, holding her, cradling her baby, cradling Cally.

'Oh my God . . .'

'You're saying she's your *mother*?' Jimmy Kwan divided his attention in the briefing room between an excited, agitated Cally and the holo-photo of a student evidently named Simone Halliday. 'There's a resemblance, Cally, I'll give you that, but that doesn't make it biological. How can you be sure?'

'I don't know. I can't be. It doesn't make sense.' Cally was pacing the room, couldn't be still. 'But I *am* sure. It's true. I know it. Maybe not in here' – tapping the side of her head – 'but in *here*' – pressing her fist against her heart. 'That girl, that woman, she's my mother.'

'Cally . . .' Jimmy didn't want to sound negative, but the loss of his own mother as a boy – he'd never known his father – had made him pragmatic. That was why he'd joined the Triads. 'Listen to yourself. Try to be objective. You've been trained to use your reason, and this just doesn't seem reasonable . . .'

'You're repeating what I've already told myself, Jimmy,' Cally protested, 'what I've *tried* to tell myself, but we're trained to trust our instincts too, aren't we? And that's what I'm trusting. When I saw her face, Simone's face, it was like it triggered something inside me, half-memories, ghost memories, very faint, very fleeting, hardly there at all, but they were of my mother holding me and singing me to sleep and they're true and they're real and *she* is my mother.' Cally pointed triumphantly at Simone Halliday.

'Look, Cally,' Jimmy tried again, 'I'm trying to keep an open mind here, but isn't it possible that this memory you say's been triggered is the kind of thing you'd *want* to remember, *want* to be true . . .'

'A wish-fulfilment fantasy.'

Jimmy was reluctant to agree in so many words. 'Well . . .'

'Okay.' Cally nodded so emphatically her dreadlocks shook. 'Let's take it rationally. Here's what I found out that are facts. Simone Halliday was at Princeton the same time as our murdered nanoscientists. She wasn't in the same *year*, which maybe explains why she wasn't in the photo Mr Deveraux showed us, but she was a member of the Science and Ethics Society like they were and so *had* to know them. Majored in Applied Nanotechnology. Graduated with Distinction. Married this guy not long afterwards. Colby Lane.' Cally pressed a button on the smart desk and an African-American man of the same age as Simone joined her and seemed happy to do so. 'Also Princeton. Also Science and Ethics Society. Also a nanoscientist – in research.' Cally breathed in deeply. 'Hi, Dad.'

'That's an assumption, Cally,' noted Jimmy, 'unless you found a birth certificate?'

'No,' she was forced to admit, 'but it's what's missing that makes me believe I'm right – and don't bother giving me the old "the worst delusions are self-delusions" spiel, Jimmy, I know all that. Colby and Simone begin to make a name for themselves – they're in all the journals in the forties. Trailblazing applications of nanotechnology. Pioneering the use of implants to treat congenital abnormalities in the womb. *The future seems bright for the Lanes.* In the last interview I could find, dated July 2048, Simone is looking forward to the birth of her daughter. She's asked if she'd ever consider *enhancing* her child, improving her physically or mentally through the kind of tech she's been working on. She says her daughter'll be perfect without artificial aids.' Cally smiled fondly. 'Way to go, Mom.' Then her brow furrowed. 'But there's no record of any child being born. No birth certificate. And no documentary record to suggest the baby died or was miscarried either. There *would* be, wouldn't there?'

'*Should* be,' Jimmy agreed. For the first time, he regarded Cally's prospective parents with interest. 'And, of course, 2048 would make Simone's daughter your age.'

'Catching on, Jimmy,' said Cally. 'Maybe someone hacked into the birth register and *deleted* the proof of the baby's birth.'

'People do the craziest things,' the field handler acknowledged, 'but why would anyone want to do that?'

Cally shook her head. 'But by the early 2050s Colby and Simone have vanished. I mean, completely. No further reference to them at all, not in the media, not in scientific circles. I even hacked into the government's social security and tax records. Nothing. It's as if they somehow ceased to exist.'

'Okay,' Jimmy allowed. 'I'm intrigued. Parents or not, you've sure uncovered a mystery, and one that might be connected to the Thornchild mission.'

'*Might* be?' Cally snorted. 'Wake up and smell the jasmine blossom, Jimmy. Lucas Thornchild suspects me, checks me out, realises I'm not a freelance security consultant, *somehow* realises who I am and knows who my parents were, knows because they were associates of the Thornchilds, Wagner and the rest at one time, *maybe* knows what happened to them, what happened to *me*. And he uses that intel to sucker me in and nearly get me killed.'

'Nice theory,' Jimmy said, 'but that's all it is, Cally, and even if we assume it's all true, how is it going to help us find Adam and bring Lucas Thornchild to justice?'

'I've got another idea about that,' Cally responded, 'seeing as it seems to be my big day for theories. Maybe if I can remember more about my parents, about the time before I was found in the streets, there might be some kind of lead in that. My surname should be Lane if this is true. How come I've always been called Cally Cross?'

'I'd be more worried about the practicalities of accessing memories of your earliest childhood, Cal.' Jimmy's condition of doubt was fully restored. 'I don't think it can be done, not to the extent you'd need to make the process useful.'

'It can with a little help from a friend,' said Cally. 'I need your permission to fly back to Deveraux, Jimmy.'

'Why?'
'Because that's where the Mindwinder is.'

Halfway across the Atlantic Ocean, Cally called Thurby at the research installation. She told him she was heading Stateside and could make a quick diversion to Florida if there were any developments concerning the starstone.

'Developments, yes,' said Thurby, his spectacles in their holographic state appearing intimidatingly large, like shimmering frisbees, 'but nothing conclusive as yet or I would have contacted you, Agent Cross.'

Cally thanked him for his consideration and wondered whether he'd be willing to share what developments there were. As she was on the line, kind of thing.

'Well,' obliged the Head Tech, 'since tracing the disintegrated probe's locator signal to what seems to be inside the starstone itself, we've generally been redirecting our research. We haven't entirely abandoned our attempts to analyse the nature of the device's energy emissions, but we have allowed ourselves to be tempted off at a tangent. Sonic engineering, Agent Cross.'

'Is that right, Head Tech Thurby?'

'We've designed and constructed some very sensitive instruments indeed. We're experimenting with passing sound waves through the starstone, sound waves in a range of lengths and registers, some of them highly concentrated.' Thurby seemed exhilarated by his work. 'What we're trying to establish is whether there are any *other* signals being transmitted ostensibly from within our alien friend, whether these – if they exist – can be measured or identified by fixing on some kind of sonic signature, a fingerprint in sound, if you will.'

'*Other* signals?' Cally sought clarification.

'If the pure sound waves are distorted at all, then that suggests the presence of further sources of energy inside the starstone, stored there perhaps like chemicals in a laboratory.' Thurby approved of his simile.

'*Other* signals?' Cally repeated.

'Indeed, Agent Cross. We have no idea at present what they might be, but one thing is certain. Wherever exactly the probe is and in precisely what form, it is not alone.'

Cally had never used the Mindwinder before, but she knew that Bex and her fellow former team-mate Eddie had. Bex had told her she'd found the experience unsettling and voyeuristic – she hadn't trained at Spy High to turn into some kind of virtual Peeping Tom, she'd said. But that was maybe because in her former team-mates' case, they'd had cause to delve into the memories, the past of a third party in order to discover vital information. In *Cally*'s case, she was going to be her own subject. The only mind she intended to enter was her own.

But she still approached the occasion with misgivings. She knew the theory: think of the human brain as a computer, with synapses for circuits and cells for files. Every single moment in an individual's life, each and every second of each and every day, good times and bad, dreary routines and landmark events, are all recorded in the brain, like programming, and with faultless accuracy. The individual cannot consciously access them all, nobody can remember everything that happened to him, human beings exploit only a fraction of the potential power of their brains, but the information exists nonetheless. It is the Mindwinder's purpose to reveal it. The Mindwinder interfaces with the subject's brain and renders its contents three-dimensionally, replaying memories from yesterday or fifty years ago with the ease of extracts from a DVD. And from a cyber-cradle connected to the Mindwinder machine, it is possible to enter the consciousness of the subject and to observe his or her memories first-hand.

'In this instance, however, Agent Cross,' said Jonathan Deveraux prior to the procedure, 'I am afraid you may experience a certain degree of discomfort. The memories you wish to download are likely to have been traumatic, repressed by your conscious mind for many years. This is why we did not encourage you to use the Mindwinder to explore your past before. Now, however, in a mission context, we have no alternative. I would ask you only to be prepared.'

'I can handle a bit of pain, sir,' said Cally tersely.

'I will be with you too.' Yeah, thought Cally, like you eavesdrop on our VR sessions as well. When the Thornchild mission was over, she was going to talk to a few people about the direction in which Jonathan Deveraux seemed to be leading Spy High. 'And remember, Agent Cross, you can exit the program at any point.'

Not until I've learned what I need to know, Cally pledged, stretching herself out on the leather cushioning of the cyber cradle. She wore a regulation silver shock-suit for her excursion into distant yesterdays. No weapons: where she was going, solid objects wouldn't do much good. She folded her arms across her chest, calmed and controlled her breathing. The transference from the physical world into the virtual world was facilitated if you were relaxed. The virtual sensors nuzzled coldly against her temples. The cradle's glass shield closed down on her like a high-tech coffin lid. She shut her eyes. Time for a little migration of the soul, Spy High style.

And then her environment was a wild, unbalancing blur, an insane rush of colours and shapes, swirling past her with frantic, hectic urgency, velocity, mutating, contorting, now glimpsed, now gone. There was nothing for Cally to hold on to, nothing to give her direction or perspective. She was overwhelmed, swept away, her senses scattered. She was falling, falling, through endless, cascading space . . .

Until there was a floor beneath her, and a carpet, frayed, stained, the carpet of a poor home, and there were walls around her and they were dingy and drab, and from the street outside the apartment the whoops of late-night drinkers and the shrieks of girls rose up and clamoured at the window with the crack in the glass.

'I'm back,' Cally breathed in awe. 'But how far?'

'You are three years old, Agent Cross.' Jonathan Deveraux's disembodied head was floating like a balloon alongside her. Cally didn't seem to think the spectacle worthy of her attention.

At least not as much as the little black girl playing with an old ginger cat on the floor.

'Is that . . . me?' Cally felt a strange intense outpouring of pity and love for the child. She wanted to scoop her up and hug her, tell her everything was going to be all right. But she couldn't. She knew that. The past was unalterable. You could look, but you couldn't touch.

There were other people in the room, a man and a

woman. They were African-American too, but they were not Simone Halliday or Colby Lane. They didn't seem happy.

'What did you bring her back here for?' the man was complaining, pacing the small apartment tetchily. 'She's nothin' to do with us. We've got enough problems of our own, Zel, without invitin' in other people's.'

'So what should I have done?' the woman protested. 'Left her where I found her? Left her out on the streets where God knows what might have happened to her? Tell me, Joe, tell me I should have done that. Better yet, why don't you take her yourself if you feel so strongly about it, take the poor little mite back to the trash-cans in the alley where I heard her cryin' and sobbin'.'

'All right. All right.' The man scowled. 'Maybe you didn't have much choice.'

'These are the people who found me, sir.' Cally was finding the words difficult to form. 'I must already be separated from my parents.'

'We must go further back,' agreed Jonathan Deveraux.

'Wait!' Cally raised her hand. 'I just want to . . . they're speaking again . . .'

'What did she have with her?' the man was asking. The woman gave him a piece of card on a loop of string.

'This was hung around her neck,' she said. 'Some poor young girl's fallen on hard times, Joe. See what it says? "Look after my daughter Calista. I love her very much . . ."'

'Oh, God.' Cally's throat was thick with emotion. Her eyes stung.

She had a headache.

'I can read, woman,' the man was saying. '"I love her very much but I have to let her go." Yeah, yeah. Just *had* to let her go. Costs money to feed a child, don't it? And what's this? A cross? A cross at the bottom of the card?'

'It's a kiss, Joe,' the woman corrected him. 'Like you put a kiss when you love someone.'

'It's a cross. So who is she? What have we got? Calista and a cross . . .'

'We must go,' said Jonathan Deveraux. 'This is not relevant to the mission.'

'It's relevant to me,' Cally whispered as the apartment began to melt.

'She can stop tonight,' she heard the man saying, 'but tomorrow, Zel, we take her to the . . .' And his voice faded again into the lost past.

As darker shades washed over Cally and Deveraux, colours in keeping with the city by night, with badly lit streets piled high with garbage, with blind alleys both literal and metaphorical. A distant siren. A barking dog. A videvision turned up loud.

A small girl running.

'Cally. Oh, little Cally . . .' She knelt before the child she'd been, saw the card around her neck, the fear and the tears in her eyes, heard the terrified sobbing. The child was running, aimlessly, hopelessly, running only because she knew she had to. She was running directly towards her teenage self. And this time Cally couldn't help it. It was instinctive, natural, compassionate, throwing out her arms to catch the younger her.

The three-year-old Calista passed right through her.

Cally's head was throbbing.

'We are almost there,' confirmed Jonathan Deveraux.

'Perhaps hours, perhaps minutes. Are you ready, Agent Cross?'

'I . . .'

Too bad if she wasn't.

Still night. The *same* night? Still the city. A parking lot, a mixture of battered wheellesses and even older petrol-driven cars. The kind of lot where you only parked if your business was not strictly legitimate. The kind of lot where cops found bodies. Not a place for a child, shivering, shuddering behind a car, whimpering and wide-eyed at what she was witnessing. Transfixed. The girl she would grow up to become was the same.

'Perhaps you might not want to look at this, Agent Cross,' observed Jonathan Deveraux with the kind of understatement that only a computer program could muster.

Or hear it. The gunshots. The screams.

In the black well of the lot, a man had just been murdered.

'Colby! No! Colby!' The woman's cries were desolate, and though she struggled, the hands that held her were too strong. Simone Halliday-Lane was not going to escape.

'Mommy Daddy Mommy Daddy.' The child sobbing quietly, glancing towards the shrouded streets behind her, torn between a desire to stay close to her parents, whatever the cost, and the promise she'd made to obey their last demand of her. To run. To run and not to stop. To live.

Cally remembered now. She remembered without the graphic aid of the Mindwinder. Everything she'd repressed for fifteen years was returning to her like a prodigal son. She didn't welcome it.

'You've led us a merry dance, Simmy.' Darius Thornchild's voice carried like a funeral bell. 'Now where is she? We'll find her eventually, you know.'

'You won't.' Fiercely. Defiantly. 'You *won't*.'

And Darius was sighing. 'I expect it doesn't matter much one way or another, does it? What can a three-year-old reveal about our plans? But to think, little Calista could have had it all. You're a very silly woman, Simmy. You deserve to be punished.' Lifting his gun again.

'No! Mom! Don't do it!' And Cally was hurtling in anguish through the cars, and either she or they were insubstantial phantoms and maybe the bullets wouldn't be real either and her mother wouldn't be dead, but they were and she was and Cally saw it happen. For a second time. 'No! Mom! No!' She threw herself beside the body, no scuffed knees or torn trousers here. (Pain, though: her head was splitting.) She tried to hold her mother because she couldn't recall what that was like, to hold her mother, but her fingers clutched at air, at space. Her mother was beyond her.

'I don't suppose we'd better leave them here, Darius,' said Werner Wagner.

'No. I imagine we can find some nice discreet means of disposing of them,' said Thornchild.

'You're gonna die!' Cally was screaming in his face. 'Your brother's gonna kill you and I'm *glad*, you hear me, Thornchild?' He didn't, as it happened. 'You *deserve* it, you piece of scum. All of you deserve it!' She gazed around in naked hatred. Troy Cutter and Larissa Kratilova and Ronald Stoneham. The whole sick crew. 'You're all . . . all . . .' Her mind was on fire, a burning

148   A.J. Butcher

pain so debilitating she could scarcely stand. She cried
out in spite of herself.

'You can exit the program at any point, Agent Cross,'
Deveraux reminded her, in the manner of an urbane
game-show host with an embattled contestant.

'No. No, sir.' Cally forced the pain down, struggled to
control it.

'Search for the girl,' Thornchild was instructing his
companions, 'but we haven't much time. Someone *may*
have heard the shots. It would be wise for us to relocate
as quickly as . . .'

His voice faded. The scene shifted. Wheellesses all
around. A fence with a hole in it big enough for a child to
climb through. Little Cally was running, surviving. The
killers wouldn't find her.

But this still wasn't good enough, Cally knew. They'd
still learned nothing that could help them in the present.
'Further back,' she said.

But not too far. They were in a wheelless, driven by
Cally's father. Her mother was in the back seat, clutching
her three-year-old self to her as if she'd never let her go.
Even in the Mindwinder, appearances could be deceptive.

'I don't want to, Mommy. I don't want to.' Little Cally
was tearful and afraid. Had she ever been anything else
as a child? her older counterpart wondered miserably.

'We don't want this either, darling,' assured Simone
Halliday-Lane, 'but we've no choice. We *can't* stay
together. It's too dangerous. It's not safe.'

'Is Uncle Darius coming to find us?' the girl asked
perceptively.

'He won't find *you*, sweetheart, I promise. Where
we're going to leave you—'

'I think we're gonna have to scratch that one, Sim.' Colby Lane, anxious in the driver's seat. 'I think we're being followed.'

Cally's training confirmed that her father was right.

'Colby?' Her mothers voice rising nervously.

'Don't worry, darling. We'll be fine. Neither of you need to worry.'

Little Cally rather young to be lied to by her father.

Teenage Cally feeling the pressure too. 'I can't stay here, sir, not knowing what's going to happen. That's more than anyone can take. We've got to try sometime else. I can't . . .'

'Very well, Agent Cross,' said Jonathan Deveraux, expressing neither sympathy nor censure.

And again little Cally was playing on the floor, a more plushly carpeted floor this time, in a more luxuriously furnished room. The house of someone successful. Not that anyone would have guessed it from the worry creasing the faces of Simone and Colby Lane.

'It's no good, Sim,' Cally's father was saying. 'Darius won't hear of stopping now. It's gone too far. The others all seem to be in total agreement.'

'The others can do what they like,' her mother retorted, 'but I want out. What they're planning now is madness, an obscenity. What happened to ethics? How did we get involved with these people in the first place?'

'That was ethics.' Colby smiled ruefully. 'And nanotech. It all seemed so innocent and idealistic at Princeton, didn't it? We thought we were going to change the world.'

'Darius and Joanna *are* if they put the Project into practice,' remarked Simone, 'but I'm very much afraid it won't be for the better. If only we hadn't agreed to throw in with them. If only they'd never come begging for our expertise.'

'*If only* isn't a very scientific concept, darling,' said Colby.

'Well I'm not going back to Turing IV and that's an end of it. No way. It's an atrocity. You said it yourself, Colby.'

'I know.'

Simone was growing increasingly apprehensive. 'And I don't want Darius or Joanna or any of them anywhere near Calista ever again. Not ever again, Colby.'

'I know.'

She scooped the child up, kissed her, held her tight, perhaps too tight. Little Cally squirmed and whined to be released. 'Calista's a child, *our* child, not an experiment or some kind of guinea pig. If they had children of their own . . .' Simone gazed lovingly into her daughter's eyes. 'It's lucky that she's not old enough yet to understand what's really going on. She won't remember any of this. That's good. But for Calista's sake as much as for ours, Colby, I want us to leave the Project.'

'I know, Sim. Me too.' Colby Lane frowned. 'But at this stage that might be easier said than done. What if the others won't *let* us leave?'

'You've got to run, Dad,' Cally urged, as feelingly as if her father could hear. 'Take Mom and take me and run and hide and stay alive.' It was partly the excruciating pain in her head that brought the tears and partly something else, something that hurt more deeply still. 'Why couldn't you have stayed alive? Why couldn't you?'

'Agent Cross,' informed Jonathan Deveraux, 'your

physical body's trauma indicators are exceeding Mindwinder safety parameters. I am initiating transfer sequence to the neutral zone.'

Cally would have protested even then, even with her skull seemingly splitting open, the bone cracking. For her parents to have been alive again, even in virtual reality, for a minute longer, half a minute, seconds, she would have endured that further agony. But Jonathan Deveraux had made his decision. Her parents were returned to the dead.

She found herself in an infinity of white, a mighty emptiness where she cast no shadow. One source of suffering had miraculously vanished. The other had not.

Cally doubted that it ever would.

'Turing IV,' she said. 'My mom mentioned Turing IV. What was it? What is it? Do we know?'

The voice of Deveraux boomed through the neutral zone like the sound of creation. 'Turing IV is a scientific research facility in orbit around the Earth. We are downloading all relevant information to your mission files immediately, Agent Cross.'

'Good. I mean, thank you, sir. Because that's where I've got to go next,' Cally vowed darkly, 'and *nobody*'s going to stop me.'

EIGHT

From 'The Secret Agent's Guide to the World'
by E.J. Grant
Appendix One: THE FINAL FRONTIER b: FREE SPACE

The first real law-enforcement issues regarding
Free Space arose as a result of the prolifera-
tion of research stations orbiting Earth in the
early 2040s. By that time, the number of
restrictions, regulations, protocols and ethical
conduct monitoring bodies that had to be satisfied by a scientific research team before it
could gain a license to commence work began to
have a detrimental effect on technological
progress generally. Companies lobbied govern-
ments for a liberalisation of the laws under the
slogan 'You Can't Hold Back Tomorrow', but those
who disapproved of the latest trends in such
areas as nanotechnology, nanosurgery and neural
stimulation held firm. 'We are defending the
human race,' Senator Orrell Ganz famously

declared during a public debate on the matter, 'and its right to remain human.'

So if the authorities were not going to play ball, the scientists went where there were no authorities.

Free Space, that vast vacuum beyond the atmosphere of Earth, lay also beyond the legal jurisdiction of either individual countries or international bodies. Unlike the Moon, where flags could be planted and land divided up (see Appendix One: a), Free Space had not so far been deemed sufficiently profitable for ownership to be claimed upon it. In short, research carried out in space required no one's permission.

The satellite-building boom made many men's fortunes. Billions of dollars were ploughed into the stations; thousands of scientists were relocated to work there, hundreds of miles above the heads of politicians and protestors, emphatically out of their reach.

It is not known what work was done in Free Space during the 2040s and early 2050s. Much of it, perhaps most of it – and certainly those projects that were made public and eventually came to improve people's lives – qualified as legal in any case. But some of it, certain secret experiments, certain controversial lines of research, were undoubtedly neither legal nor ethical. It is not out of the question that the results of such work may yet necessitate the intervention of Deveraux operatives.

By the mid-50s, the authorities earthside had

acted. The Free Space Management Initiative of 2053, signed by every member of the United Nations, closed the legal loophole that allowed unregulated research aboard the orbiting stations. Free Space was to be zoned, and each zone was to come under the jurisdiction of one of the major power blocs on Earth. That power bloc then had the responsibility to manage and to police the space stations within its allocated zone. The concept of scientific ethics had come to outer space.

The intention, at least overtly, was not to close the satellites down, but this came to be the ultimate effect of the Free Space Management Initiative, perhaps inevitably. If they were to be subject to the same regulatory bodies in orbit as on solid ground, companies wondered what the purpose was in expending huge dollar sums in maintaining a Free Space presence. 'There is no Free Space any more,' Max Schelicker, CEO of Pandrolone Inc., complained. 'It's Stitched-up Space now. The politicians have turned it into a prison.'

One by one the research stations were abandoned. By 2055 none remained in active operation. Satellite security teams still patrol the zones, but no scientific work has been undertaken in Free Space for a decade at the time of writing, a situation that does not appear likely to change . . .

'Welcome to the Europan Spaceport, Shuttle Terminal

One. Please do not be alarmed by the use of the word "terminal". That's terminal as in the end of a transport route or a station at this point, *not* terminal as in make that will and get ready to start pushing up those daisies. We hope you enjoy your shuttle flight with us today and have every expectation that you'll survive it, but if you *could* just sign this disclaimer . . .'

'I don't believe it.' Cally shook her head and grinned.

'And before we begin boarding procedures, can I remind all passengers, particularly those who are tall, female, dreadlocked, about eighteen and looking *very* hot today, baby, of the necessity to comply with security check-in regulations. I'm afraid our state-of-the-art x-ray, infra-red, DNA, perspiration-analysis *I-know-you're-lying* scanner is out of action at this present time, so the frisking is going to have to be done by hand. These hands, actually. I've warmed them up special. Now, if you'd just like to step over here and take your clothes off . . .'

'So, Eddie,' Cally smiled, 'you're still on the medication then.'

Eddie Nelligan regarded her with a hurt expression. 'What, so all this time I've spent undercover at the Spaceport and my spiel didn't fool you?'

'Not for a second.'

'So I guess the bit about the frisking and the removal of the clothes, that's not gonna happen, then?'

'In your dreams, Big Guy. *But!*' Cally qualified. 'There is *one* thing you can do with your hands . . .'

'Does it involve direct physical contact?' said Eddie hopefully.

'Just put 'em round me and give me a hug, you idiot.' Cally opened her arms.

'It's not the same as "I want to have your babies, handsome", but I can live with it.' The two of them embraced. They squeezed. It felt good. It felt like nostalgia. 'How *are* you, Cal?'

'Better for seeing you, Ed.'

'Ouch. You must have been in a bad way to start with.'

Cally smiled faintly. 'You said it.' She detached herself from Eddie and drifted into the centre of the private lounge at the Spaceport where the two of them were awaiting their shuttle's preparation. She *was* glad to see him. Unlike Jake in Hong Kong, Eddie seemed entirely unchanged from their Bond Team days. Eddie Nelligan. Red of hair, spindly of limb, grinning of expression and relentless of wisecrack. A quip for every occasion. Not in the same league as either Ben or Jake in the open-shirt stakes, but you wouldn't want to gorge on red meat at *every* meal, would you? There was something safe and reassuring about Eddie. Right now, if she'd had to choose between him and Jake to partner her to Turing IV, Eddie would still be with her.

'I've been briefed, Cal,' he was saying. 'I know about Lucas Thornchild. I know about your parents.'

'Cally Lane, that's me. That *was* me. While they were alive.'

Eddie nibbled his lower lip nervously. Sensitivity and intimacy were not his stock in trade, but for Cally he'd give them a try. 'I'm not going to say I know how you must be feeling, Cally, 'cause I don't, but it's got to be better to *know*, hasn't it? At last? Knowing who your parents were, what happened to them, it'll take some getting used to but at least you have answers now and not questions.'

'Oh, I still have questions, Eddie,' declared Cally. 'Some. But you're right. And I know where to start looking for solutions.' She stabbed a finger savagely upwards. 'Turing IV.'

'Yeah. Look, Cal,' Eddie began uncomfortably, 'I hope it's not a problem having to take me along for the ride. You know how the conventions work. Deveraux gets special dispensation to shuttle you up to this old space station with a Free Space security team, but because Touring whatever—'

'Turing IV, Eddie.'

'That's the one. Because it's in the Europan Zone, it's deemed to be a matter of courtesy to invite the Europan Region's Spy High op to join you. And that's me. Region Red. *Edward* Red.'

'There's no problem, Eddie,' Cally assured him. 'I'm glad you're here. And you can take that as read, too.'

'Not that you need me, of course,' Eddie added hastily, 'and not that either of us needs half a dozen over-aged baby-sitters with guns, huh? I mean, *my* briefing said Turing IV hasn't been active since the fifties, isn't that right? It's not like we're going to run into any trouble up there. You know, no skulking alien invasion force ready to conquer the world or loony-tune megalomaniac waiting to blow it up. Nothing like that. Are we?'

Cally smiled in gentle amusement. 'Would it bother you if we were, Eddie?'

'Only me and outer space don't exactly get on,' Eddie lamented. 'The Diluvians came from there and they tried to kill me. That time we hit the Guardian Star, Frankenstein was there and *he* tried to kill me. I just think, you know, if God had meant us to go into space he'd have given us green skin and three heads and those little antenna things like Martians.'

'Who told *you* Martians have three heads and those little antenna things?' Cally demanded. 'I thought that was classified.'

'You mean . . .?' Eddie was agape.

'Joking, Eddie. But listen, if you really feel that way, I'm sure . . .'

'No, no.' Eddie wouldn't hear of it. 'I kind of do, but it doesn't matter. I'm coming. Me and you, Cally.' He winked rather badly. 'Bond Team sticks together.'

The Europan security space shuttle was well into its flight, almost within visual contact of Turing IV. Cally was glad: maybe when the orbiting station came into view it would give the accompanying security team something to look at other than herself and Eddie. She supposed the men had a right to be intrigued by the addition to their complement at such short notice of a pair of fully armed teenagers in the same basic uniform as themselves. (Their belts seemed a little different was all, and those gleaming metal wristbands they wore.) But she didn't relish being the centre of attention just now. Too many other things on her mind. Adam, her parents, Ben, Lucas, Turing IV and the secrets it might be sheltering, all spinning frantically through her brain, defying her attempts at coherent organisation of her thoughts. Coolly and calmly was how a Spy High graduate should conduct herself while on mission, rationally and reflectively. The churning turmoil of Cally's present emotions made these qualities a little difficult to come by. Pity she wasn't wearing a chameleon suit. She could simply disappear until they arrived at the space station and wouldn't have to trouble herself with eyeballing the leader of the security team, a sullen and unshaven individual called Captain Hardman.

'You kids all right?' he said, not for the first time.

'Tell me, Captain Hardman,' probed Eddie, 'was security not your first career? Only you've enquired about our health so often now I'm kind of getting the impression you have an unfulfilled ambition to join the caring professions, am I right?'

'Eddie!' scolded Cally. 'Forgive my colleague, Captain Hardman, won't you? He gets stressed more than a hundred metres from the ground.'

'Hard to see what he's doing flying up to Turing IV with us, in that case,' the security man observed. 'Hard to see what *either* of you is doing, actually. Care to enlighten us on that, Ms Cross?'

'I'm afraid our business is classified, Captain Hardman,' said Cally.

'Is that right?' Hardman was not impressed. 'How old do you have to be to work for the government these days, anyway? Twelve?'

'Well I can see why the stand-up comedy didn't suit you,' Eddie commented.

Hardman nodded slowly and scornfully as if he understood his two younger passengers only too well. 'Okay. You can play your little government agent games if you like, kids, but just remember, when we reach the facility I outrank you both, I'm in charge, and you do what I tell you to do.'

'That makes me feel so much more confident,' enthused Eddie ironically. 'Doesn't it you, Cal?'

'Eddie!' With a slap.

'Well,' grumbled her partner. '*Hardman*, I ask you. Is that a name or a description?'

Either way, at that moment the Captain was called away by the shuttle's pilot. It seemed there was something a little unexpected about Turing IV. As the satellite appeared to starboard, a globe some four hundred metres in diameter like a giant golf ball, Cally thought she could see what it was. The steel skin of the sphere had once been pristine white. Now, after years of disuse, it was tarnished and neglected, all except for the twin docking bays visible in the space station's centre which were kept in a condition of perfect repair for the use of the regular security patrols. As far as she knew, their pilot ought to have had a choice of which one to dock in. He didn't.

Turing IV already had visitors.

Cally and Eddie exchanged meaningful glances. Eddie groaned. 'Why can't anything ever just be *routine* . . .?'

'What are you kids looking so worried about?' said Hardman dismissively. 'It's another patrol, that's all.' Certainly, the markings on the berthed shuttle were those of the Europan Space Agency. 'We can dock alongside it. You'll still be able to get the hush-hush stuff done.' He instructed the pilot to commence docking procedures.

'Captain,' ventured Cally, 'should there be a second Europan security team in this sector of Free Space at the moment?'

'Possibly not,' admitted Hardman, nettled, 'but schedules get changed about all the time. What are you trying to say? There's something not right about that ship?'

'Give the guy with the stubble a promotion,' muttered Eddie.

'We think you should contact Earth,' advised Cally. 'Just to be on the safe side.'

'*You* think. That's you two kids.' Hardman wasn't exactly hugging the suggestion to his heart. 'Who's in charge here? I can't quite remember. Is it you or is it me?'

'Better question might be who *ought* to be in charge,' said Eddie.

'Captain Hardman.' The pilot over the intercom again. 'Comlink from Turing IV.'

'Excellent. Let's take this.' The security man seemed to feel himself justified. He pointed at the teenagers. 'You two with me. Cockpit. Now.'

'Now there's an offer you don't get every day,' said Eddie.

A man who looked too affable to be in the security services was soon smiling up at them from the comlink screen in the cockpit. They were so close to Turing IV now that its steel structure blocked out all sign of space and seemed to be wrapping round them like a kidnapper's blindfold.

'Sorry. Sorry,' the man was apologising amiably. 'Starling here. Guess you weren't expecting company, were you? I know, we shouldn't be here. Life support developed a little bit of a problem, I'm afraid, nothing that might *really* have jeopardised our safe return to Earth, but we had enough fuel to reach Turing so we thought we'd stop over for a couple of hours for repairs. Come and join us.'

'You see?' Hardman said after closing the comlink.

'All perfectly innocent. Conclude docking procedure. Maybe we can help Starling and his team out.'

'We still think you should touch base with Earth, Captain Hardman,' Cally persisted. 'If Starling's story checks out, great, Eddie and I look like schmucks, but the kind of work we do, every irregularity we take very seriously indeed.'

Hardman was shaking his head. 'You kids . . .'

And Cally was suddenly gripping his arm above the elbow, gazing intently into his eyes. '*Please*, Captain Hardman.'

And he saw something in her that made him reconsider. 'You *are* serious, aren't you?' He sighed resignedly, shook his arm loose. 'Okay, okay, if it'll get you kids off my back. Shapiro' – to the pilot – 'comlink Europa. Let 'em know Starling's team is here.'

'Yes, sir.'

'*After* we've docked, Shapiro.'

Eddie regarded his partner with admiration. 'Way to go, Cal. But how come that move never works for me?'

There were levels both above and below where the shuttle docked, and all of them, Cally was well aware, contained research laboratories of one kind or another. Now that she was physically here, she wasn't entirely sure what she should be looking for. Not only were the scientists long gone, but the vast majority of their equipment was as well. Anything that still retained a dollar value had been shipped back to Earth when Turing IV's active life had come to an end. All that remained – or so she supposed – was obsolete machinery, superfluous instruments, outdated computers, the rusting, decaying waste of scientific experimentation.

And maybe a few ghosts too. She was walking where her mother had walked, and her father, and the animals who'd murdered them. The air that Cally breathed as she stepped out of the shuttle and into the space station's reception area, the air that was stale and recycled, maybe it had been circulating even in her parents' time. Maybe they'd breathed it once. She felt closer to them now than ever before. And maybe they'd left more than memories behind them, something she could use, something that though it would be years too late to save their lives could yet help to save Adam's.

'Let's get straight to searching,' she rallied Eddie.

He winced. 'You have any idea how *big* this place is, Cal?'

'So we start at the top and work our way down, or if you prefer, we can start at the bottom and work our way *up*.'

'I've been trying to do that my whole life, Cal,' Eddie said mournfully, 'and sometimes I think I'm still on the ground floor.' His eyes darting left and right, he added confidentially: 'Besides, I'm not sure we should be going anywhere just yet.'

Cally paid closer attention to her immediate surroundings. The reception area was low-roofed and oval-shaped. There were glasteel elevators at strategic points, none of which looked to be in service. Stairwells also led to the other floors, though in the minimum level of lighting consistent with fully functioning life support systems, they appeared deep and treacherous. Hulks of machinery and blocks of equipment stood around like unemployed people waiting to be put to work: Cally was rather unpleasantly reminded of the abandoned crates at the souvenir emporium in Seabound.

With the exception of the pilot, Hardman's entire team had disembarked the shuttle together, were presently forming a nice, compact little group in the middle of the reception area. Starling was coming forward to greet Captain Hardman. His smile was unaltered from the comlink. Cally realised she didn't trust it. His men were with him. Quite a lot of men, actually, must be a big patrol, and they all seemed equally pleased to be here. They *didn't* come forward to engage with the new arrivals, however. They held back, kept close to the walls. Close to the exits.

Cally felt the hairs prickle on the back of her neck.

'Do the words "we seem to be surrounded" mean anything to you, Cal?' whispered Eddie.

They should have acted sooner. They should have overridden Hardman's authority, not docked at Turing until they'd heard from Europa.

'A pleasure to meet you, Captain Hardman,' Starling was enthusing. 'A genuine pleasure. Such a timely arrival.'

His men, predatory smiles, eyes that gleamed with imminent violence. Their hands, not far from their blasters.

Thornchild was here. She knew it. This was about Thornchild.

'Cally,' ventured Eddie, 'I think this is when we're supposed to do something . . .'

'Captain Hardman,' Cally demanded.

The security man turned to her tetchily. 'What is it now, Ms Cross?'

Starling's eyes glittered as they too focused on Cally. 'And who might this charming young lady be, Hardman?'

He recognised her. Cally saw it in his expanding smile. Starling already knew who she was.

'Oh, let me tell you, Starling,' said Hardman sarcastically, 'I've got a pair of very important people accompanying my team today. A little on the paranoid side, but . . .'

'Captain Hardman! Captain Hardman!' A voice hurled from the shuttle-lock.

'Shapiro?' Hardman had never seen his pilot run before. Or look so anxious before.

'Hardman!' Cally was tense with warning.

She and Eddie both raising their arms.

Smiles corrupting into ugly sneers. Hands on blasters. Hardman's team bewildered.

'It's Starling!' yelled Shapiro. 'He's *not* . . .'

'What?' Confused, Hardman turning back to his fellow security officer. The man he *thought* was his fellow security officer. He wasn't.

Otherwise he wouldn't have shot him at point-blank range.

No time to feel sorry for Captain Hardman. First rule of combat: stay alive now; mourn the dead later.

Cally's sleepshot spun Starling round. She took out the guy by the elevator, the guy by the wall, slamming him back against it. (No good, though. Hardman's men were too slow, too unprepared. Shapiro was shot down before he could reach his team-mates. The others hardly managed to draw their weapons, hardly got off a shot.) The guy who thought he was protected by that lump of equipment. The guy by the stairwell, clattering him to the lower level.

'Cal!' Eddie's shoulder-blades jammed against hers. You didn't fight side by side when you were surrounded. You fought back to back. You kept your sleepshot firing in every direction and you did not give up. 'It's been great knowing you!'

Not even when your allies had fallen and, barring a miracle, within seconds you would inevitably be joining them.

'Stop!'

Because miracles did happen, and sometimes they took the most unlikely form. Sometimes, they even looked like Lucas Thornchild.

He appeared in the shuttle-lock to Starling's space-craft. The fake security team didn't seem to want to obey him, but orders were orders. They held their fire. For a moment, Cally thought about adding Lucas to the list of Bad Guys she'd dispatched to slumberland, but if she did that she doubted his lackeys would be able to control their trigger fingers. She bit her lip frustratedly but lowered her arms, knew that Eddie was following suit. Let Lucas think he'd won. Sometimes you had to play the long game.

'That's better,' said Lucas Thornchild approvingly. 'Conversation is so much more civilised than gunfire, don't you think? Though of course, words can be just as painful.' He approached the former Bond Teamers, underlings closing in on either side of him, their blasters still aimed unmissably at Cally and Eddie. He wore a jacket and a polo-neck shirt, his entire outfit grey, as if he'd reached a point in his life when colours no longer mattered. 'Ah, Calista, the lengths you'll go to to find me. People will talk, you know. And who's this? I assume another member of your organisation.' The tall man sniffed dismissively at Eddie. 'What happened to the black-haired boy from Hong Kong? He was *much* more presentable.'

'Oh, thanks a lot,' objected Eddie. 'I've got hidden talents, I'll have you know.'

'What a shame we don't have time to look for them,' said Lucas Thornchild. He smiled patronisingly. 'We don't have time . . . we don't have time . . . for . . . for anything . . .'

'Thornchild?' frowned Cally.

Because suddenly he wasn't smiling, patronisingly or in any other way. And suddenly Lucas Thornchild seemed to have forgotten how to speak. 'Time . . . we . . . time . . .' And his body shuddered and shook, like something was inside it that wanted to get out. 'Time! Time!' His voice rising wildly, hysterically.

'Makes a change from telling us his master plan, I guess,' said Eddie.

'There's no time! There's no time!' Expressions, emotions, flickering across his face like the frames of a film, none of them stable, none of them real.

'Thornchild?' And Cally didn't understand. Not one of Lucas' men seemed fazed by their employer's apparent fit.

Then one of the expressions was real, one of the emotions. Terror. Absolute, paralysing terror. 'There's no time left!' He was falling on Cally, clutching her desperately. 'You've got to get out of here! He's insane! He doesn't care! What he'll do . . .'

Cally staggered back under Thornchild's weight. 'I don't . . . you're not making sense . . .'

A lunatic giggling. 'My own voice. He's let me have my own voice . . . back . . . Ca . . . lis . . . ta . . .' The final syllable of her name was twisted into a scream, shrill, despairing. Lucas Thornchild lurched away, clawing now at his temples, raking the flesh from his forehead as if his skull was a gift he was trying to unwrap. He bent double, once, and then he stiffened. His sinews strained to make him taller than he was. Eyes bulged. Mouth gaped. Spine snapped.

And before he fell, Cally saw the blood, at Lucas Thornchild's nostrils, at Lucas Thornchild's ears. Before his body struck the floor, she *knew*.

'Implants. Eddie, neural implants.' She gazed at her partner in horror. 'Thornchild was being *controlled*.'

She wasn't sure which came first, the little-boy applause or the growling of cybernetic dogs, but together they froze her heart.

'Cally?' Eddie sounded uncertain.

'Oh my God . . .'

Further figures stood in the shuttle-lock doorway. The lackeys, faces now of stone, no human feelings present, bowed their heads as if in prayer, all of them, simultaneously. As if in homage. The figures moved forward. The one that walked on two legs spoke.

'Surprise,' said Adam Thornchild.

NINE

'I could have killed you already, of course, Calista,' said Adam Thornchild modestly. 'Several times over, in fact. The rampaging animate at my party – just a little test for you, to put you through your paces, so to speak, a trial run. It was never going to hurt me. I was its master. The ninjas at the emporium controlled by yours truly. And then, when I really had you at my mercy, at the house. It was me who hit you from behind. A couple more blows and I could have caved your skull in, but I thought no, best not. Where's the imagination and creativity in that?'

'I hope you're not holding your breath waiting for me to thank you, Adam,' said Cally.

The boy continued as if he hadn't heard. 'And I thought no, I'll give Calista a chance. She seems intelligent as carbon forms go. I expect she'll find a way to catch up with me at some point – or with poor puppety Uncle Lucas at any rate. I thought, I *owe* her that much. After all, we're almost related, I thought. And I'm so glad you found me *here*. It couldn't actually be more appropriate.'

They'd been moved from the reception area of Turing IV, marched by Adam's men and the cybernetic dogs several levels below. Starling and the other goons Cally and Eddie had incapacitated with sleepshot came with them. Their continued state of unconsciousness did not prevent them from discharging their duties. The microchips in their brains, evidently controlled by Adam, stimulated and dictated their physical functions even without the aid of thought. Some boys played with toy soldiers: Adam Thornchild had access to the real thing.

'Neural implants, obviously,' he said. 'Carbon forms are so fickle. How else can I ensure total obedience in my employees? And yes, Calista, a little enhancement to the otherwise distinctly average cerebrum of Uncle Lucas also. Your society tends not to value the opinions or abilities of its young, so it was necessary – and convenient, I must say – for me to act through an adult surrogate. But I was watching through Uncle Lucas' eyes the whole time.'

'And now you've killed him.' Cally's voice was thick with horror and disgust. 'Your own uncle, your own flesh and blood, and you cut him down like he was nothing.'

'I think that means bed without supper and grounded for a hundred years, kid,' said Eddie, if only to remind Adam that he was still around.

Kid. Cally considered with dull disbelief her partner's use of the word. Factually accurate, of course: Adam was only a few days past his thirteenth birthday. Which made what he seemed to be capable of all the more shocking: his lack of conscience, his lack of human feeling. What was it Xao had said at the restaurant? *Children make good assassins*? The pale, grinning boy in white before her now, like a vampire or a corpse, hinted that the Triad leader knew a few things. But Cally sensed that there was a lot more too to learn about Adam Thornchild, and none of it was going to be pleasant.

'Uncle Lucas.' Adam was shaking his head condescendingly. 'Poor, pathetic Uncle Lucas. I'm afraid now that my plans have reached fruition he was no longer necessary, and you know what you do with objects that you no longer require. You *dispose* of them. And I would contest your description of Lucas Thornchild as my own flesh and blood, Calista. On a point of information, I am flesh, I am blood, but I am also more than either.'

'Is that right?' Calista retorted. 'Like what? What's the chemical symbol for madness? And what's all this *your society* and *carbon forms* nonsense, Adam? And how are you and I *almost related*? And if we are, how do I get *un*related?'

'All in good time, Calista. All in good time.' Adam's eyes gleamed like glass. 'The paltry brains of carbon forms can assimilate information only *so* quickly.'

Cally in any case was engaged in her own assimilation. The lab they'd been brought to, she wasn't entirely surprised to see a familiar insignia emblazoned on the wall. Two hands forming one fist. Human and cybernetic combined. Carbon and silicon. Her paltry brain, as the boy genius so dismissively termed it, was putting two plus two together and was coming close to what she reckoned was four. Eddie looked like he was still on one.

The lab, a series of rounded glasteel chambers held by tubes extending to both the ceiling and the floor. The chambers, varying a little in size but none of them large, none of them capable of containing a fully grown man, and maybe it was down to her memories of the gene chambers of Dr Frankenstein several years ago, but Cally immediately assumed that something was intended to go *in* them, and she was thinking that that something could float in a fluid in there, something drowned and dead. Encircling the tubes at a distance but capable of being moved closer, equipment of unguessable function. And everywhere, cables, bulging like umbilical cords. *Thornchild Silicon Systems*. She remembered its slogan. *Bringing the Future to Birth*.

Cally felt her skin crawling. She shuddered.

'Are you cold, Calista?' Adam enquired concernedly.

'Not as cold as you,' she muttered.

'Well, I have it in mind to warm you up very shortly, but before I do . . .'

So, there was hope. Adam might have been rather younger than their normal enemies, but he still shared something of the mentality of the megalomaniac, a need for an audience, a need to boast, a need to let everyone know how clever he was. At Spy High they'd had lessons on it, and on the importance for agents to bide their time, to await inevitable opportunity. They'd been denuded of their mission belts and weapons, which had been placed out of the way on a console against the wall of the lab. Out of the way for *now*, Cally determined.

'You asked about the connections between us, Calista,' commenced Adam.

'Yeah,' Eddie interjected. 'You're not almost related to me as well, are you?'

'Edward,' sighed Adam, in a voice that for the purpose

sounded decades older than its thirteen years, 'I *sincerely* hope not.'

'Everyone's a wise guy,' muttered Eddie.

'I have some news about your parents.' The boy returned his attention to Cally.

'You needn't tell me,' Cally said. 'I know they knew *your* parents. I know they were involved in some project together, maybe right here in this lab, am I right? And I know your parents killed them, Adam.' She grimaced. 'I don't particularly want to hear it again.'

'Grief,' observed Adam Thornchild. 'How unproductive. Like all the emotional conditions you carbon forms so wallow in. But your parents, yes, Calista. I knew of your existence, obviously, that you escaped their fate, but I never expected to meet you. I wondered, of course, when Security Consultant Calista Cross appeared at Thornchild. Your name is not one encountered every day, and you were the right age and ethnic profile. And when you made that moving speech to me about the loss of your parents and wandering the streets as a child, well, I was glad I'd carried out that DNA scan in the office. As you entered, if you're wondering, Calista. The scanners are set into the doorjambs. By the way, do you realise how ridiculous you sounded, bleating on about the beauties of carbon-form relationships? I could scarcely restrain my laughter. As if something that alters and changes and is imperfect can be of true value.'

Calista smiled bitterly. 'So you are a child after all, Adam.'

'I am *beyond* age,' corrected the pale boy, 'but we're talking about *you* at the moment. The DNA scan. It matched with the records my parents had made of you in your infancy and to which I still have access. I knew who you were without question, and I knew who you could have been.' White teeth gleamed. 'You could have been *me*.'

'*What?*'

'Lucky escape there then, Cal,' observed Eddie.

'My parents from their university days were founder members of a group of, by carbon-form standards at least, brilliant, pioneering and daring nanotechnologists. Werner Wagner. Vijay Sharma. Larissa Kratilova. People like that. Your parents joined them too, Calista, eventually. The group had one aim and one aim only, to move Mankind forward to the next stage of human evolution. They'd looked about them, you understand, they'd analysed the world of the twenty-first century, and they'd drawn their conclusions. Man's time as the undisputed ruler of his planet was swiftly coming to an end. He would be defeated, not by war or plague or natural disaster, but by his own genius for invention. He would be supplanted, not by an alien race invading from the stars, but by his own children, his cold and computerised offspring. We live in a silicon age, Calista, an age of cyber-space and virtual reality and smart atoms and nanotechnology, of machines on the brink of sentience. And when that sentience came, our parents realised, as they knew it inevitably would, it would not be conceivable that the machines we had created to be our servants, our slaves, should be content to remain as such. They would demand rights, as all thinking beings do. They would rise up against us in revolution, and the Earth would shake with the cataclysm of battle between the carbon forms and those of silicon. This was the future our parents foresaw, and the future they sought to avoid.'

'Is it too much to ask to get to the *how*, Ads?' pleaded Eddie. 'Maybe you're beyond fatigue as well as age, but this is one carbon form whose legs are starting to ache.'

Adam regarded Eddie with contempt. '*How*, then. How to prevent Mankind's replacement by machines? Simple. Man had to become a machine himself. Homo sapiens had to evolve into homo silicium. Our parents founded the Hybrid Project, dedicated to the development of a life form both organic and inorganic, composed of circuits and microchips as well as flesh and blood, a cyborg, if you like, but a being far beyond any imagined by cheap science fiction entertainments.'

'Hence the logo?' Cally indicated the fist on the wall.

'A statement of intent,' Adam confirmed. 'And the Hybrid had the technology, the ingenuity to make it happen. Between them they knew more about nanotech implants and cyber enhancements than any other group of carbon forms on the globe. Of course, they had to carry out their work here, in Free Space, as what they intended to do was far from legal.'

'You don't say,' grunted Eddie.

'They intended to take a subject and to improve it, to combine with those biological organs and tissues necessary for continued life a number of silicon supplements, nanotech additions, so that the subject would be to you what you are to the neanderthals.'

Cally thought she'd heard a similar spiel before. Wagner, for all the good it had done him. The *late* nanosurgeon Professor Werner Wagner. 'And by subject, Adam,' she said, dreading but already suspecting the reply, 'can you be more specific?'

'A human foetus.' Specific enough. 'To be plucked from the inadequacies of its mother's womb and brought here, to the birthing chambers of Turing IV, to its true parents, the computers. It should have been you, Calista. Your mother was made pregnant for the purpose.'

'That's a lie!' Cally protested. 'My parents had me because they loved each other, not to participate in some sick experiment!'

Adam shook his blond head tolerantly. 'Cling to your illusions if you will, my almost-sister,' he said. 'Facts are rarely as flattering as fantasies. But you were denied your destiny, in any case. There were, apparently, unforeseen delays in the nanotechnology. You were born the old-fashioned and soon-to-be-obsolete way after all. And your parents, as you seem to know, soon afterwards developed cowardly doubts concerning the ethics of the entire project. Locked into the past, Calista, unfortunately for them. Insufficient vision. Too weak to grasp the future. In time they had to be eliminated. In time a new subject was selected. I stand before you now.'

'I'm never gonna say a bad word about my parents again,' vowed Eddie.

Adam ignored him, gazed up at one of the giant screens in the lab. His eyes glazed. The screen flickered into life. 'Perhaps you'd care to see how the birthing process works,' he said. An unborn child, Adam himself, in the foetal position, curled and quiescent, helpless, innocent, a blank canvas on which an artist could paint, not turning in the warmth and security of his mother's womb (Joanna Thornchild – the *late*

Joanna Thornchild) but stranded in the cold and uncaring confines of one of the lab's birthing chambers, out of the reach of human beings. 'The solution which I'm breathing here,' Adam explained helpfully, 'it's similar to the amniotic fluid in the womb of a female carbon form, only enriched with special nanotech supplements to prepare my body for grafts and implants.'

'That's great, Ads,' winced Eddie. 'Do you reckon your mom and dad might have left a bucket around here somewhere, huh? I think I need one. My tolerance of the reproductive process kind of begins and ends with conception, you know what I mean?'

'Here come some of my implants now.' Adam might have been talking about old friends restored after lengthy absences.

On the screen, what seemed to be a quartet of enlarged syringe-guns pressed their nozzles questingly against the glasteel. The birthing chamber yielded to their advances. Four spikes drilled through the fluid to the exposed and vulnerable flesh of the foetus. The artist was about to go to work.

'No. Adam. Turn it off.' Cally looked away revolted. 'We get the idea.'

'A little squeamish for a secret agent, are you not, Calista?' Adam chuckled. 'No wonder you get captured so often. I think my genesis is rather beautiful, but then, beauty is in the visualiser of the beholder.' The Screen returned to darkness.

'Did you do that, Adam?' Eddie wanted to know. 'Activate/deactivate the screen without even an oral command?'

'Neurotelepathy,' Cally said.

'I have a cybernetic brain,' Adam acknowledged. 'It is perhaps the Hybrid's greatest achievement. It means I can interface with any cybernetic or computer system. I can make them do what I like. I am not only part of the machine, I am the superior being. These lackeys, my men, I control them too. Their implants, the microchips grafted to their brains are far more primitive than mine. But they serve their purpose.'

Cally looked round at the blank, emotionless faces of the underlings, the same expressionlessness she'd noted in Lucas Thornchild. 'I guess they do,' she said grimly.

And suddenly the men were all standing on one leg, their right leg.

'Whoa,' said Eddie.

Then their left. Then they were running on the spot, each of them in perfect unison, their rhythm not faltering for a second. And they were barking like dogs, bleating like sheep, squealing like pigs.

'All right, Adam, we get the picture,' Cally said disapprovingly.

Then they were silent again, and still, and empty of all humanity.

'So the cybernetic brain hasn't done much for your maturity levels.'

'Calista,' Adam said, 'maturity as you understand it is a concept irrelevant to me. My neural implants grant me direct and immediate access to any information system in the world. I have the internet inside my skull, the collected knowledge of centuries. I was more widely read and more brilliant than any carbon form has ever been in your entire history before the age of five. My biological components restrict me in some ways, I must confess.

My body is limited to the laws of human growth, hence superficially I still seem a boy of thirteen, but in reality, as I have already said, I am *outside* of age. For example,' he leered in the general direction of Cally, 'I am well aware of how adult carbon forms express affection for each other *physically*, and my researches have discovered many interesting variations on the theme. Perhaps, Calista, you might like to explore some of them with me.'

'Perhaps, Adam,' Cally said scornfully, 'you might like to step through an airlock without a space suit.'

Instead, he advanced towards her. 'Come, come,' cajoling, 'it was *you* who insisted I introduce myself to the delights of carbon form relationships.'

Eddie stepped into his path. 'Computer brain or not, pal,' he warned, 'didn't the collected knowledge of centuries tell you that no always means no?' He placed a cautioning hand on Adam's shoulder.

'No,' said the boy, seizing Eddie's hand and squeezing. Eddie cried out in sudden shock as his bones were crushed together. He lashed at Adam with his free fist but it was like punching steel. He was on his knees. If the kid exerted any further pressure, his hand would burst.

'Let him go! Adam . . .' Cally launched herself at the hybrid, found his other hand clamped like a vice around her throat. She dangled from it, choking.

'Something else you should know about,' said Adam Thornchild conversationally. 'My nanotech grafts make me considerably stronger than the average carbon form. But I suppose you've realised that by now, haven't you?' He flung them both aside, Cally gasping for breath, Eddie cradling his mangled hand. 'And you needn't worry, Calista. Relationships of any description are

incompatible with my existence. The implants by themselves, you see, are not quite enough. To obtain harmony
between my organic and my inorganic selves, they need
to be *attuned*. The mind and the microchip must become
one, and to achieve this I have learned to eradicate all so-
called human emotions from myself. Emotion, Calista,
Edward, is the only obstacle between man and machine.'

'Hooray for good old emotion, in that case,' said
Eddie.

'I guess killing your parents was a real triumph, then,
Adam,' said Cally. 'I thought it was Lucas but it wasn't,
was it? It was you.'

'Correct,' admitted Adam. 'Removing my organic
parents was a necessary step and something of a test for
me, one which I passed with flying colours, I hasten to
add.'

'So, Ads,' Eddie intruded, 'modesty's incompatible
with your existence as well, is it?'

'The other members of the Hybrid I allowed to live a
little longer, until I felt ready to take up the reins of my
destiny. That is now. The time has come for me to put
away childish things and to go about my business, finally
to fulfil the dreams of the Hybrid Project.'

'What?' Eddie said. 'The guys you've just killed?'

'Their work was done in creating me. It is vital for the
moment that my existence remains a secret. Carbon
forms cannot be trusted to keep secrets. The Project
members had to be removed. Uncle Lucas had to be
removed. You, Calista, Edward . . .'

'Don't say it. Don't *say* it!' groaned Eddie.

'. . . you will also have to be removed.'

'He *said* it. I knew it. They *always* say that.'

'What is your "business", Adam, if you don't mind me asking?' Cally said. 'As we're about to be removed anyway.'

'I am the first of a new species,' said Adam, 'and I will be the greatest example of it, but I will not be the last. Where I lead, humankind will and *must* follow. My prime directive is to create a race in my own image, to give birth to the era of the hybrid. Already, many carbon forms seek to emulate me, to mate their flesh with silicon. The trade in nanotechnology that I had Uncle Lucas encourage, testifies to that. And the numbers of my acolytes, my disciples will increase.'

'But not everyone, Adam,' challenged Cally. 'Many people see your kind of technology as a threat to humanity.'

'And can you blame them?' grumbled Eddie.

'They will be converted,' Adam stated. '*Physically* converted.'

'Say what?' Could things get any worse? Cally wondered.

'I am close to having the means. I will *force* humankind to face their future. I will lead them into cybernetic paradise. A pity the two of you will not be there to witness it.'

He seemed to momentarily lose interest in the secret agents, tilted his head a little to one side as if hearing sounds from far away. Cally gazed longingly at their blasters and mission belts. Still no chance of regaining them yet, but she sensed there better had be soon.

The space station juddered, jolted. Cally felt it beginning to drift.

'What have you done, Adam?' she demanded.

'I've had enough of Turing IV,' he said. 'It belongs to my past. I came here to download certain information and that I have done. Now I feel able to dispose of it. I have been in communication with the satellite's gyrostabilisers and disabled them. The station is now returning to Earth. In one hundred and one minutes precisely it will enter the atmosphere. Ordinarily, of course, its shields would protect it from the tremendously destructive heat that it will then be compelled to endure. Sadly for Turing IV, however, and for anyone unhappy enough still to be aboard at that time, I have also rendered inoperative the shields. Permanently.'

'I guess we'd better get to the shuttles kind of smartish, then,' suggested Eddie.

Adam offered a dead man's smile. 'I'm afraid there is no *we*, Edward. Myself and my men are departing promptly, but you and Calista are staying here.'

'Really? Come on, we won't take up much room.'

Cally felt a cold anger inside her. 'You'd better kill us now, Adam, if you want to be sure.'

'What? Cal?' Eddie protested. 'Don't give him ideas. Don't listen to her, Ads. She's been going through a bad time lately. She's a little bit overwrought.'

'Because if you *don't*,' Cally vowed darkly, 'I'm going to get out of here and I'm going to be coming for you.'

Adam's pale humour was unaffected. 'My predictors inform me that such an eventuality is statistically ninety-nine per cent unlikely. I'll leave you the one per cent to hold on to while you burn. Farewell, Calista. You amused me for a time.' He turned to his dogs. 'Rover. Rex. *Guard them*.'

Cally tensed. Was this the moment, the inevitable

opportunity? Without a backward glance Adam Thornchild strode from the lab, his zombie goons following. *Don't take our equipment with you,* Cally prayed. *Ignore it. Demonstrate your arrogance. Assume it can't do us any good.*

Her prayers were answered.

'Cal,' indicated Eddie. Mission belts, shock blasters, sleepshot wristbands, temptingly heaped on the nearby console. A pair of giant robot hounds between agents and equipment. *Growling* robot hounds. 'I guess these aren't the kind of dogs who'll just roll over to let you tickle their tummies,' Eddie observed.

' 'Fraid not, Ed.' Was it Rover or Rex glaring at her with pitiless cybernetic eyes? Did it matter? The smart atoms were at work. Its paws were transforming into jagged, tearing blades. The metal of its back and flanks and head was rippling, reshaping, studding itself with savage spikes.

'Hey, guys, look over there,' Eddie announced. 'Cats!' The cyber-creatures were not impressed. 'Okay, that's me out of ideas. Cal?'

'We could just . . .' She tried to step to the side of Rover/Rex. The dog shadowed her instantly, increased the volume of its growl, somehow sprouted a second row of teeth. Cally didn't doubt that if she attempted to repeat such a move, those teeth would be sinking into the tender flesh of her leg. 'Sorry, Ed. I'm out too.'

'This is ridiculous. What if one of us volunteers to kind of sacrifice herself by making a run for it and then maybe draw both dogs away and then perhaps I can . . . just a thought.'

'It might come to that,' Cally said grimly. 'They've got

to have a weakness. Everything does. Maybe the eyes. Maybe, if we attack them, if we can gouge behind the eyes, disrupt their visual systems or something . . .'

Eddie nodded. 'I'm game if you are. I don't want to still be here when the temperature starts to rise. I didn't bring my sunblock.'

'Okay.' Cally stared into the cyber-dog's eyes and did not avert her own. 'We tackle *them*. They won't be programmed for that. Might surprise them. Ready?'

'We're not having a countdown? Like, from thirty or something?'

'Eddie,' scolded Cally, '*n*—'

The dogs turned tail, sharp, battleaxe tails at this point, and ran, bounded out of the lab.

'What did we do?' Eddie said. 'What did we do?'

Cally was already darting to the console, retrieving her equipment. 'Unfortunately, Eddie, I've got a feeling this makes things *worse* rather than better. Every boy loves his dogs.'

'Ah . . . the snow in Moscow is cold and crisp?'

'Not a password, Ed, a statement of fact.' She threw his belt and blaster to him. 'Adam's called Rover and Rex off 'cause he doesn't want them to fireball with us. Which means the shuttles must be about to blast off. Which *means* . . .' She was at the door in a second, buckling on her belt as she ran.

'I'm right behind you!' yelled Eddie.

Cally was leaping up the stairs. The levels of the research station blurred anonymously by. There was only one she cared about. She was visualising the shuttles in their docking bays, as if by locking them in place with her mind she could keep them there in reality, for her and Eddie to reach. Ignoring the protests of her muscles she pounded on. They'd have plenty more to protest about if she didn't make it.

The dogs couldn't have outstripped them by too far. Adam would still be waiting. Had to be.

Her heart was thumping against her ribs as if demanding an exit, as if it felt it could make quicker progress on its own. Could be right.

That sound, that muffled detonation, it couldn't be engines, it couldn't be spacecraft blasting off. She wouldn't let it be. She wouldn't let Adam Thornchild defeat her.

He was only a boy.

And she was there, the reception area, and she was sprinting for the shuttle-locks but they were closed, and the satellite lurched and Cally was hurtling through the air, her feet failing to find purchase, herself spreadeagling on the floor. Down among the dead men. Captain Hardman was looking at her in unblinking reproach. But she wasn't dead yet. Not yet.

'Cal, you okay?' Eddie was beside her.

'Okay is a relative concept,' she gritted. The lights above the shuttle-locks were red. Nothing in either docking bay. Adam must have brought with him more than one pilot. There'd been plenty of work to go round.

'Don't you just hate it when you miss the last flight home,' joked Eddie, then with a gulp he added: 'Ah, Cal? What do we do now?'

Never Panic. Words branded on to her brain after two years at Spy High with the potency of a Thornchild neural implant. The agent who survived was the agent who never panicked, who found a way. Cally was going to be that agent.

As soon as it was obvious there was no escaping Turing IV from the reception area, Cally directed her and Eddie's attention to the control room. It was one level up, overlooking the now vacated docking bay.

Eddie peered nervously out of its glasteel windows. 'Gonna get a good view of our re-entry from here,' he said. 'Until our eyes go pop, of course.'

The blue and green curve of the Earth already seemed rather too close for comfort. Of the shuttles there was no sign.

'You'd be better occupied focusing on in *here* rather than out *there*, Ed,' Cally said. 'It'll be something in here that's going to save us.'

'Yeah?' Eddie glanced around at the typical assort-ment of instrument panels, screens, and computer consoles. 'Well don't keep us in suspense, Cal. We've got maybe eighty minutes.'

'That's a start.' Cally was seating herself at a computer, carrying out a systems check with a speed that even the hybrid boy could have barely matched. 'Life support fully functioning. Guess Adam thinks we're doomed anyway. Happy to leave the oxygen on.'

'What about the gyrostabilisers?' Eddie reminded her. 'If we can arrest our orbit's decline, we can maybe call down to Earth and—'

'Uh uh.' Cally shook her head. 'Neither. When he said he'd disabled the stabilisers, he meant it. Scrap value only. Same with communications.'

'Damn. And I find sending off a distress signal so therapeutic.' Eddie didn't appear hopeful. 'Dare I mention the shields?'

'Right now they wouldn't protect us from a fire-cracker.'

'That's what I like about you, Cal. You're just full of good news.' He regarded the heat counter on the instrument panel with severe misgivings. The indicator arrow was well within tolerable limits at the moment, but it was itching to rise. It was beginning to rise. 'Don't they have back-up systems or anything on this crate?'

'They may have done once, Ed,' surmised Cally, 'but remember, Turing IV hasn't been in practical employment for over ten years. Why would they bother?'

'Not even heat-shields? They've got to have replacement shields . . .'

'Eddie!' Cally jumped up, grabbed him by the shoulders. 'They don't, but we do.' In her excitement she kissed him wetly on the lips. 'Get your belt off.'

'Well, actually, Cal, I'm going kind of steady with this girl called Rose. I'm *flattered* and all, but . . .'

'Delusions away, belt *off*!' Cally urged. 'I-Shields!'

'Your-Shields?'

'I-Shields, idiot. Maybe we can use our I-Shield technology, wire the microchips into Turing IV's systems or something, improvise a makeshift heat-shield with them.'

'Cal, aren't they designed to help with hand-to-hand combat situations? I mean, keeping the heat of re-entry at bay isn't *quite* the same —'

'Eddie!' Cally clapped her hand over his mouth. 'Do you have any better ideas?'

Eddie considered. After a moment, Cally removed her hand. 'How can I help?' he said.

In the end, there wasn't much he could do. Eddie's computer skills were far above most people's, his training at Spy High had seen to that, but Cally's were on the next level again. She was a natural, whereas Eddie had had to work hard for every glimmer of understanding. If anyone could keep them alive in their present predicament, it was Cally. So he didn't mind his relegation to the status of gopher, fetching whatever equipment his partner needed and passing it to her on request. The control room had been temporarily converted into an operating theatre. He was the lowly nurse; Cally was the surgeon.

'Was that a scalpel you wanted there, Cal?'

'A what?'

'No worries. You're doing a great job.'

He just hoped it was a great job done *quickly* enough. The heat counter was registering a rise in temperature. There was a greater sense of falling in Turing IV, the decline of its orbit steepening. Earth loomed.

Cally had opened up the power console that before Adam Thornchild's intervention had operated the heat-shields. She'd also removed from their mission belts the microcircuitry that energised their I-Shields. Now she was splicing the two together. A command from the console for shields would not fall on deaf ears for very much longer.

'But Cal,' Eddie ventured, like a man with bare feet stepping on hot coals, 'I don't want to be a killjoy, and you might be able to construct a viable shield with those, but I still don't get how it's gonna be strong enough to protect us. Heat-shields by Canute Inc. I don't want to hear about.'

'O ye of little faith,' Cally grinned, though there was a tightness about her expression that suggested Eddie's concern was dangerously pertinent. 'Once this is wired in, I'm going to reroute the central power grid through the Shields' console. That ought to boost its output sufficiently to keep us . . . well, it's not gonna be nice and cool, Eddie, but at least they won't be identifying us from the DNA in two piles of ashes. Hopefully. If it all goes according to plan.'

'Nice one, Cal,' said Eddie. But his eyes were constantly, ghoulishly drawn to the heat counter, like a witness at the site of a traffic accident thinking, *is that guy really dead?*

The indicator arrow continued its ineluctable climb towards danger levels.

'Okay. Done.' Cally nodded. 'Now to reroute the power.'

Eddie crossed to the window. Touched it. Warm. His palms were sweaty. His security officer's uniform was

damp with perspiration, dark patches spreading. Eddie
stripped off his jacket as if that might make a difference.
It didn't. 'Industrial strength antiperspirant required
over here,' he said.

The blackness of space was being burned away by the
imminence of atmosphere. The outer hull of the falling
satellite began to glow.

'Cal?'

'Close the screens, Eddie. Two minutes.' Her vision
was clogged with sweat, her fingers slowed by it. The
heat in Turing IV was increasing exponentially now.

Eddie activated the window screens. They dutifully
lowered, blocking out the Earth. It was like closing an
oven door. 'If you can't stand the heat . . .', Eddie said.

It was getting hard to breathe. Returning to Cally's
side, it was like wading through a hot spring. The simple
exertion made his muscles quiver. They were turning to
mush. He was panting, gasping. He was an old man,
dying, doomed.

About to be cremated.

And Cally felt her senses slipping too, her mind drifting, the rising heat anaesthetising her brain. Hard to
concentrate. *Had* to concentrate. She was drooping over
the console. Her dreadlocks hung lankly before her
eyes. Beads of sweat like salty raindrops dripped onto
the instrument panel. She had buttons to push. Which
ones? She had important work to do. But what?

Easier to sleep. Easier to sleep and slip away.

The indicator arrow buried itself in the heart of danger
levels. The scarlet could have been blood.

'Cally. Cally.' Someone was talking to her, drawling,
slurring their words. A drunkard was shaking her

shoulder. 'Don't stop now. Don't stop now.' And why was he repeating everything? And why was he kind of leaning against her shoulder? What gave him the right?

He had red hair. *Eddie.* It was Eddie. She knew him. And she knew something else, too, something that was clinging to her brain like a limpet, something that was defying the heat and the drowsiness and the terrible temptation to close her eyes.

She couldn't let him down. She couldn't let *herself* down.

Cally went to instinct. She resigned her conscious mind and let her training and her intuition and her sheer, icy will take over. Her fingers moved across the instrument panel. And they did what they needed to do.

A hum of sudden electronic power. Lights flashing. A change in Turing IV's status recorded. Heat-shields activated.

The indicator arrow, vibrating, keen to move on, but restricted, restrained. Leashed.

Re-entry.

The space station shook. Deep within itself machinery split and tore and was rent asunder. Metal screamed. Glasteel shattered. The inner skin of the hull burned red, then white. Cally and Eddie held each other close and cried out as their clothes seemed to smoulder and their flesh seemed to fry. They were on fire. They held each other close and they were on fire.

And in Cally's mind, her parents, Ben. She'd be joining them soon. She'd be seeing them again.

But now a different note to the agony of Turing IV, a new tone. The control room's rattling easing suddenly, like the breaking of a fever. Walls not white, not red, the greyness of steel regained. The indicator arrow in grudging retreat.

There was air to breathe.

Eddie was laughing. He was sliding away from Cally and on to the floor and he was lying there and his shirt and trousers were drenched and he didn't smell good and there was something of the hysteric about his mirth, but he wriggled damply and punched the humid air with both fists and bawled: 'You did it, Cal! The shields held! I knew you were hot stuff, babe, but *this*!'

Cally was laughing also, but in her case it was more like crying. Because she was alive. Because others weren't. Because she'd proved herself. Relief and elation and pride. 'I couldn't have done it without you, Ed.' And magnanimity.

'Yeah, you could. Now all we need to do is work out how to land this overgrown beachball.' Eddie sat up. Something potentially rather disturbing had occurred to him. 'Ah, Cal? You do know how to land us safely, don't you?'

Cally was at the console again. 'Hopefully, as Adam wouldn't have expected us to survive re-entry, maybe he didn't think to tamper with . . .' She grinned. 'Automatic landing systems on-line. Terra firma, here we come. No sweat.'

Eddie regarded his armpits with dismay. 'If only.'

They touched down somewhere north of San Francisco. It was difficult to keep a spherical space station four hundred metres in diameter incognito, and a number of locals had gathered before Cally and Eddie emerged blinking into afternoon sunshine. Some of them were waving banners and signs. Some of them said things like 'Take Us With You', 'Candidate for Abduction' and 'Welcome to Earth'.

'You get the feeling they think we're from somewhere we're not, Cal?' said Eddie.

'Reckon so, Ed,' said Cally.

'Take us to your planet!' somebody yelled. 'Earth sucks!'

'There's gonna be a lot of mind-wiping going on around here,' Cally predicted.

'Maybe not. Half of these guys don't look like they've got minds to begin with. This *is* California. But hey, Cal,' added Eddie, 'thanks for the ride but listen, next time you need a partner to go up into space with you, leave me *out*, okay?'

She only realised she must have dropped off when she was aware of waking. The auto-masseuse had that effect on her. Its expert, gentle kneading of the muscles of her shoulders and back, unlocking and releasing their strains and tensions, warming and relaxing her body, always coaxed her into a blissfully sleepy state. For a while she'd forgotten everything, her parents, her and Eddie's confrontation with Adam Thornchild on Turing IV, their narrow escape from *death* on Turing IV, the fact that Adam was still somewhere out there. All her worries put to one side, at least for the duration of the massage. And the machine was on form today. Its plastic digits felt more like human fingers than ever.

There was good reason for that. Now Cally was *fully* awake. 'What do you think . . .?' She rolled over swiftly, wrapped her towel around her.

'Hi, Cally,' said Jimmy Kwan.

'Taking the field handler title a little literally, aren't we, Jimmy?' She tried to look shocked or offended. Couldn't make either.

'I only have your welfare at heart, Calista Green,' claimed Jimmy with a bow. 'That's mental, spiritual, *physical*. I know a few things about massage that can't be programmed into a machine. Thought you might like . . .'

'. . . the benefit of your experience?' Cally wondered good-humouredly. 'Where have I heard that one before?' She swung her bare legs down from the massage table, bound her towel more tightly around her. 'Having said that, after recent events I guess I should be grateful for the human touch.'

'I actually just wanted to let you know immediately,' said Jimmy, reluctantly assuming a more official manner, 'the results of your medtests are back and you're fine.'

'As fit and healthy as I look?' teased Cally.

'If that were possible. No, no after-effects of the Turing IV escapade at all. Not physically, anyway.'

'Mentally and spiritually?'

'You tell me. Adam as adversary? Thirteen-year-old boy turns out to be psychotic cyborg with delusions of grandeur? Must have been a shock.'

Cally nodded pensively. 'I *will* tell you, Jimmy. Soon as I've showered and dressed. *Both* of which I can arrange by myself, thanks.' She tossed her head at Jimmy as she passed him by.

But she thought about him, though, how good his fingers had felt on her skin, strong and thrilling and *right*. Like Ben's. What was happening? Cally pondered. *How* was it happening? How was she beginning to have feelings for a guy who a few weeks ago she didn't know from Adam (hmm, not such a clever turn of phrase there), and who virtually a few *days* ago she seemed to distrust and dislike with a venom? Emotions were strange and unpredictable things. No wonder they didn't suit the silicon brain of Adam Thornchild. Jimmy Kwan. (That smile.) Her field handler. (Those tattoos.) Her *teacher*. (Those pecs.) He should be out of bounds. You shouldn't really start fancying your teacher. She never had before (not that the issue ever really arose with Mei Ataki). Maybe it was the similarity of their backgrounds, the lovelessness, the loneliness of their early lives that was bringing them together, despite the uneasy start to their relationship. Could be a mistake. There was no regulation against it in the Deveraux rulebook, but workplace liaisons had a history of going wrong.

And what about Ben? Cally frowned. If she started seeing somebody else, getting close to another boy, *involved*, what did that mean for Ben? It would mean she was giving up on him, accepting that he was gone and that he wasn't coming back. It would mean she was *moving on*. Was she ready for that yet? Did she want it? And perhaps most worryingly of all, *could she do anything about it*?

Jimmy was waiting for her in the briefing room beneath the Shop. He was looking vaguely troubled himself. Cally guessed that some of the same considerations that had been on her mind had been plaguing his, as well. 'Listen, Cally, if I embarrassed you or anything just then, I'm sorry. It wasn't professional, I don't quite . . .'

She was right. 'Forget it,' she said. 'You have healing hands.' Now what did she have to go and say that for?

The field handler smiled faintly. (That smile.) 'So, anyway, Adam Thornchild.'

'Do we know where he is yet?'

'Soon. We're still sifting through flight path data. What had been *your* shuttle crashed into the Pacific. Pilot and all three passengers killed.'

'Expendables,' Cally said soberly. 'Implants probably programmed them to take their own lives.'

'Yes,' Jimmy agreed. 'Thornchild's ship did *not* crash. Landed *somewhere*.'

'That's going to be the problem, Jimmy.' Cally tapped her finger on the desk. 'Reconciling Adam's ruthlessness with his apparent age. Trying *not* to think of him as a boy. If you've got him in your sights and you hesitate because he's only just thirteen and his suit's too big for him, you're going to end up like those guys in the shuttle. He's a hybrid, Jimmy. He's a computer with a human face. That's what I've got to remember.'

'You think you can?'

'I'd better, or you'll be moving on to tutee number two more quickly than you might have expected.'

Jimmy's eyes narrowed. 'You think you could take him out?'

'I'll know next time I see him. Believe me, Jimmy,' she confided darkly, 'I've got plenty of motivation.'

'I think we should go for back-up next time,' the field handler said. 'Not because I doubt your abilities, Cally' – the girl gestured to show they were beyond that – 'but because the stakes are too high to take chances.'

'Whatever you say, Jimmy,' Cally submitted.

'Hmm. That wouldn't have been your reaction a few days ago.' Giving her the option to direct the conversation towards more personal matters if she wished.

She wished. 'We don't have quite the same relationship now as we had a few days ago. Do we?'

'I don't think so, no.'

'Jimmy, what kind of relationship *do* we have?'

He gave a short, confused laugh. 'Kind of a complicated one, I reckon.'

'Me too.'

'Professional, personal.'

'Personal, professional.'

'Maybe we should keep our distance, keep things cool.'

'Maybe we should.'

'On the other hand . . .'

'Yeah, there's always that other hand to think about . . .'

'But not yet.' Jimmy hadn't dared so far to look Cally directly in the eye. Now he did. Almost lost his way. 'Not while the Adam Thornchild situation is still unresolved. It wouldn't be appropriate to get into anything too . . . you'll need all your focus on the mission.'

'Okay,' Cally consented. 'Makes sense. Maybe when we've brought him down we can go out and celebrate, continue this conversation then.' She couldn't believe how forward she was sounding. 'That'd be appropriate, wouldn't it? Celebrating our first successful mission as a team?'

'I would think so. You mean a night out, a meal, something like that?'

'Jimmy,' Cally reminded him, 'you promised me crispy duck.'

He laughed again. 'I guess I did, didn't I? And Jimmy Kwan always keeps his—'

The smart-desk communicator buzzed. Jimmy's face grew instantly serious. So did Cally's. She felt her heart begin to race and not because of her proximity to Jimmy Kwan. The interruption could signify only one thing.

Somewhere, somehow, Adam Thornchild had been found.

ELEVEN

A Deveraux solocopter streaked across pale skies above the frozen wastes of Siberia. Aptly named, it contained only a single individual, pilot and passenger combined. Cally didn't care. She wasn't in the mood for conversation.

She was wearing an arctic infiltration suit, white instead of black but in other respects identical to the regular issue. Could have done with a chameleon suit for a mission of this gravity – effective invisibility gave one such an edge – but the material's environmental adaptability was produced by the nanochips woven into it, and it had been thought that Adam might have been able to interfere and communicate with them, turn them to his own purpose. One or two adjustments had been made to the solocopter for the same reasons: its computerised instruments had all been removed, replaced with more primitive manual controls and a radar system that was positively twentieth century. Cally didn't care about that, either. She'd fly a biplane to the target zone if it meant Adam

Thornchild couldn't get to her. At least, not before *she* could get to *him*.

She'd vowed on Turing IV that she would be coming for him. She'd meant it.

The techs had located the cyborg all right. They'd been able to trace his flight path from the space station to a spot less than a hundred miles ahead of her now, here in the vast Siberian emptiness of snow and ice, a landscape almost overpowering in its unremitting desolation. You had to have a very good reason to come here. You had to maybe hate other people to turn your back on them so absolutely. A perfect call for Adam Thornchild. And there'd been a bit of a bonus for him as well, the techs had discovered. A nuclear power plant, built decades ago by the Russians but its reactors dismantled after the formation of the Tsarist Federation. Only the shell now remained, the husk of the facility, but even that would provide a perfect base for an enemy of Mankind. The fact that it was shielded, that it refused access to the prying eyes of the Deveraux spy satellites, suggested that a certain carbon-silicon hybrid had indeed made a home there.

But he wasn't going to keep Cally out. She forced her solocopter to the limits of its speed. Adam could see her, she knew that. He wasn't going to let her land. If she could just get as close as possible to the plant before he did what it was inevitable he'd do . . .

The missile registered on her radar. A *big* missile. There wouldn't be much of the solocopter to sweep up afterwards. Adam was making his intentions perfectly clear.

Showdown.

Cally bailed out. The rush of the ejector seat made her gasp, air brutally driven from her lungs. She gripped the flimsy frame of the chair as it shot into the sky. Her stomach seemed to have been left behind. She didn't need radar to see the missile now. It was homing in on the solocopter. Collision could not be avoided.

The explosion briefly added red and yellow to the prevailing white of the surrounds. Was she too close? The shock wave crashed into her, buffeted her bullyingly, seemed to want to spill her from the ejector seat. Cally held on. She was plunging, accelerating, the wreckage of the solocopter littering the snow with blazing fragments beneath her. She'd always believed that she could trust Deveraux technology. No reason to change her mind so far.

With a flapping like the wings of a giant bird, the chair's built-in parachute unfurled itself, jerked her descent into a more civilised velocity. She swung away from the remains of her transportation.

Ten miles still to go. She'd have to make it under her own steam now. Cally jumped from the ejector seat, her boots crunching on the sullen, hard-packed ice. Her suit's insulation would keep her warm. She pulled its hood over her head, fixed her radar visor firmly into place. Luckily, she had something available a little more high-tech than steam.

Jet pskis. *Like* skis but also *un*like them. They weren't made of fibreglass or plasteel or anything for a start. The wearer made them herself, with the force of her own brain. It seemed you didn't need neural stimulators to demonstrate at least a minor level of psionic power. The techs at Spy High had told Cally so during her training sessions with the jet pskis. Electrical activity took place in all human brains. What the jet pski attachments in her gloves and boots did was to siphon that off, store it, convert it into usable psionic energy, and wait for the call to come. Good, natural, self-generated energy. No artificial additives. No implants. And no way for Adam Thornchild to disrupt it.

Cally pressed the studs in her boots and gloves. An ethereal glow at her fingers and feet. Then they came. Pski-poles lancing from her hands, narrow, sharp, to help control her direction when at speed. The pskis themselves, stabbing from beneath her boots, sleek and streamlined, able to accelerate even over flat land. The products of the mind were rather less dependent on natural laws than those of the hand.

Cally bent her knees and elbows, leaned forward slightly. Jet pskis were fully energised within seconds. Useful. Adam wouldn't simply assume that his uninvited visitor had been blown to pieces with their helicopter. He'd send someone to check.

Or some*thing*.

Twin howls from what could have been dogs rolled across the barren ice, a lonely, mournful sound, chilling. And too close for comfort.

The jet pskis powered up. Cally felt them hum and vibrate beneath the soles of her feet. They eased her forward. She was moving. And as her speed increased, she remembered a line from a Shakespeare play she'd studied at Spy High: 'Cry, "Havoc!" and let slip the dogs of war.'

Havoc it was going to be.

Rover and Rex weren't far behind the threat of their

baying. They were bounding towards her from the right, huger now, as if the smart atoms from which they were constructed had put on a growth spurt. Each of them was as tall as Cally herself, and armoured like canine dinosaurs. Scarcely any attempt to preserve the illusion of hounds survived, apart from the eyes, though glaring and filled with hate, the long, sharp snouts, the mouths daggered with teeth. They thundered over the tundra, their paws great pile-drivers of bladed steel. They were killing machines. They were tanks. They saw Cally and they howled again, predators with the scent of blood in electronic nostrils.

Cally accelerated, jet pskis scintillating, leaving in their wake a stripe of energy like a trail of fire. If Rover and Rex could see her, so could Adam Thornchild. Now he'd know she'd escaped Turing IV. She hoped he recalled her promise to him. She hoped he was worried.

The dogs were gaining. Their legs were elongating, covering vast tracts of distance with each rampaging leap. The cold ground trembled under her pskis. Cally thought she'd better do what Adam would expect her to do, drew her shock blaster set to Materials and, assisting her balance with one pski-pole, deactivated the other in order to allow her to fire.

Her first shots sent spumes of ice and snow and frozen earth into the air. They didn't deter the dogs, who advanced inexorably. She aimed for their bodies instead. Might have worked on Rover, had the creature not opted to open up its chest to reconfigure its form around a gaping, yawning hole through which the blaster's shell passed harmlessly, exploding in the tundra to the monstrosity's rear. Might have worked on Rex, had the immediate effect of its impact, twisted, mangled metal, not been compensated for by the same substance, writhing like tendrils, like jagged living tentacles, restructuring, remoulding itself, returning to its original shape. Smart atoms – one. Shock blaster – nil. Cally permitted herself a thin smile. As if they hadn't reckoned on *that* happening.

'Here, boys,' she muttered under her breath. 'Come see what Aunty Cally's got for you, you ugly pair of . . .'

Something of a rise ahead, a ridge of ice. Cally crouched lower, blaster holstered and second pski-pole back. Needed to go faster. Rex was almost upon her. Rover had dropped away and seemed to be engaged in some kind of circling manoeuvre. Strategy between cybernetic dogs. It was time to bring this to an end.

She'd always believed that she could trust Deveraux technology. Now would not be a good time for her hot streak to end.

Cally drew the scrambler from her belt.

As she topped the ridge and launched giddyingly into empty space, saw Rover below and beyond. As Rex leapt too, his mighty machine muscles propelling him above her. As his neck extended impossibly and his jaws snapped like a beartrap at her head.

No time like the present. Cally activated the scrambler.

Another piece of tech which pretty much did what its name implied. It *scrambled*. In this case, it scrambled smart atoms. Cally didn't fully understand the science, the stuff about disruption of nanotech communication impulses and molecular unit transmogrifiers. Who gave a monkey's?

It got under Rex's skin, and that was what mattered.

The cyber-dog howled, and this time as it flailed through the air the wail was of panic. Lips peeled back and kept on peeling, over its snout, over its skull. Flanks rippled and liquefied. The hard metal lines of its shape lost definition, melted, merged. When Rex hit the ground, it was like boiling oil poured from a castle under siege, a thick, viscous puddle of bubbling grey gloop.

His brother's fate didn't deter Rover, though. Cally's pskis sliced into the snow, keeping her upright, and he was baying for her, surging, springing towards a fatal convergence. Cally didn't have time to pause, the inclination to break away. They flew at each other like knights in a joust. Rover's snout lengthened, sharpened into a lance. Cally relied on a small, rounded device rather less macho in appearance.

Adam Thornchild was watching. Rover was within range. Cally flourished the scrambler.

The cyber-dog was a dam bursting, a sudden flood, a snowman teleported to the Equator. Smart atom soup. And now Cally did alter her trajectory, veering left to avoid the gelatinous remains of her foe, a kind of slowly popping mucus. It would no doubt have left a terrible stain on her arctic infiltration suit.

Cally pskied on. Only a couple of miles left. The nuclear plant, Adam's house, she'd be seeing it soon. She thrust the scrambler back into its belt pouch. Probably wouldn't be needing that again. As far as she knew, Adam's lethal pets numbered only two. Indeed, she kind of wondered what defences the silicon boy had left.

She allowed herself to think of Jimmy Kwan and a

cosy, intimate restaurant, and a candlelit dinner for two. And some happiness again. That'd be good. She deserved it, didn't she? Some happiness again? Let it happen, Cally implored.

The first explosion nearly dismembered her. If she'd been skimming the hard-packed snow any less quickly, her legs would have parted company with the rest of her and neither half would have made much further progress. The second forced her to swerve sharply to the right. An eruption of fire and debris, scorching her even through the insulation of her suit, searing her eyeballs.

Minefield? Something like. Detonated from afar with the vindictive malevolence of a spoiled child. Blasts all around her now. Seemed she'd underestimated Adam's defensive capabilities. Dinner with Jimmy suddenly looked like a long way away.

Chunks of frozen earth sprayed against her, like being stoned. Her suit was torn, at the shoulder, at the thigh. She felt a gash above her eye. And the ground was quaking now as pillars of flame flashed from beneath it, bursts of random destruction.

No pattern. If there'd been an order in this chaos Cally could have deduced it, steered a course to keep her safe. As it was she could only zigzag wildly, madly, a slalom of death. She had the impression that Adam Thornchild was orchestrating all this, that he was laughing at her, applauding, waiting for her mistake.

But she couldn't afford one of those. She slanted left, right, operating purely on instinct, but her muscles were slow, slow to respond. She had to be fleet as thought. And it was like being in the middle of an artillery bombardment in one of the wars from history, the Great War where thousands upon thousands of young men had been pulverised into meat and bone. But even those barrages ended. They couldn't last for ever. Neither could this. Ahead of her, clean, white earth. So near. Seconds away. To reach it would take her seconds.

Cally urged her tortured body forward. She could make it. She dared to hope.

And then there was fire in front of her and she was throwing up her arms to protect her face and the screaming was coming without invitation.

But she wasn't dead. To be dead wouldn't hurt so much.

And she was lying on her back (painfully) but she wasn't outside either. No sky. Concrete and steel. Pipes and conduits. A suggestion of light in darkness.

She blacked out again.

The faces, faces without meaning, without feeling, all around her. Men. Seen through shadows.

She didn't like them. She wasn't ready for them. Still too weak. She embraced the return of oblivion with gratitude.

Then one face. She peeped at it like a little girl playing hide and seek and checking to see if she'd been spotted.

She had. 'There you are,' said the pale boy in the white tunic. He seemed satisfied. 'I'm glad you're alive, Calista, though I'm afraid *you* won't be.'

'Adam,' she managed as her senses drifted away once more.

'That's right,' he said. He gestured expansively. Tall walls and high ceilings. A strange sign, two hands becoming one. 'Welcome to *Cyberia*.'

❖

The next time she regained consciousness it steadied and stayed with her. Allowed her to make out where she was. A not unexpected location. The hard wooden bed on which she found herself lying, the dark, cold walls, the door with the bars in the window. Cells were the same the whole world over. She'd got company in this one. A guard in a grey uniform stood by the door, covering her for sudden movements with a pulse rifle, a guard who could have been carved from the same stone as the cell.

Cally wondered whether Adam had had her injuries treated. She seemed to have sustained only superficial cuts and bruises. If he *had*, it was probably only so he could inflict more serious wounds, fatal wounds, later. She reached for her belt. Gone. He'd left her her infiltration suit but nothing else. Looked like Adam wasn't taking any chances this time.

'Ah, awake at last, Calista.' The guard was speaking but only his lips moved – the rest of him remained as still as the dead. The guard was speaking, but the voice belonged to Adam. 'Yes, a curious effect, is it not? An amusing little nanograft enables me to manipulate the man's vocal cords so that he sounds exactly like me. It'll change the art of the impressionist for ever.'

'And to think,' jibed Cally, 'I thought the bonus of being in a cell was being away from you.'

'You're never away from me in Cyberia, Calista. That's Cyberia with a C-Y, if you were wondering. It's the name I've given my little empire here. Quite witty, if I do say so myself.'

'Go ahead. You'll be the only one.' Cally swung her legs from the bed and braced her feet against the floor.

She felt strong – maybe not at the peak of her powers but strong enough to do some damage.

'Remain seated, please,' Adam advised her through the guard. 'I control this lackey's brain as well, as I'm sure you've already deduced, and I *will* shoot you if you disobey me.'

'I'm seated,' said Cally.

'I control all my men. They are my eyes and ears. And my influence is not limited to the carbon forms, either. My mind flits through every electronic impulse in this plant. I feel with every cold silicon sensor. I think with every computer. I flex my muscles with each wire and circuit and cable. Cyberia and I are *one*.'

'I hope Cyberia and you will be very happy together.'

'Up,' ordered the guard. 'I will show you something that will make me happy.'

The cell door opened and the man indicated that Cally should take advantage of the exit. She did. Outside were half a dozen other guards, pretty much identical, particularly in respect of their weaponry and at whom it was directed.

'Just in case you considered yourself capable of over-powering a single guard,' said the six in unison, all in the tones of a thirteen-year-old boy.

'I've heard of loving the sound of your own voice,' muttered Cally, 'but this is ridiculous.'

She allowed herself to be escorted through the former nuclear plant to Adam Thornchild. Tried to keep positive. Agents in the field had been trained to develop a *silver lining* mentality. As in every cloud has one. So she was weaponless and a prisoner, deep in the lair of a carbon-silicon hybrid who wanted to kill her

and surrounded by mind-controlled goons with guns.
Still, Adam Thornchild was where she wanted to go.
Silver lining. Their implants meant that the guards could
hide nothing from Adam, but his powers were technological not psychic, so for the time being at least Cally
could, and she knew that her situation wasn't yet hopeless. *Silver lining.* Even if you died in the course of a
mission, you'd probably learned something that'd
increase your successor's chances of survival. *Silver
lining* – officially. But Cally had always seen that as
cloud, big, black, and to be avoided at all costs.

Never panic.

Adam had done a lot of work to the plant since he'd
been in residence. The hybrid insignia, the cyber-human
fist stamped large on virtually every flat surface, was the
cosmetic evidence of new ownership, but more funda-
mental was the technology. Machines and computers
seemed to have spread everywhere like a glittering,
flickering fungus. Walls pulsed in soft colours as if a
silicon heartbeat throbbed behind them. Giant cables
looped and hung from lofty ceilings, protruding like
tubers. The wire grille floor beneath her feet, beneath
that a million micro-circuits, a million wires, flashes of
energy like the blinking of eyes. More guards went about
their business, drones in a hive, cogs in the machine. The
Tsarist Federation had closed the nuclear plant down
and decommissioned the reactors because they'd
believed the place to be dangerous. Cally had a feeling
the threat of a minor nuclear accident would turn out to
be infinitely preferable to anything Adam Thornchild
had planned.

Maybe he'd tell her.

'Calista!' He greeted her in some kind of lab, circular, arched, rimmed with chattering computers. No techs. Cally guessed that Adam's cyber-brain allowed him to work his micro-magic without the necessity for human assistance.

'Hi, Adam. What a displeasure it is to see you again.'

The door hissed closed behind them. Five of the guards took up positions around the circumference of the lab. Two remained at Cally's shoulders.

'The feeling is mutual,' said Adam Thornchild. 'By rights, you and that remedial red-haired boy – does your organisation practise positive discrimination for the mentally challenged, Calista? – you should both by now be cinders in the atmosphere. But no, here *you* are dogging my steps still.'

'I'm too cool to burn to death, Adam.'

The boy huffed dismissively. 'And talking of dogs, you killed Rover, you killed Rex. They were my *pets*.'

'Try a goldfish next time,' Cally goaded. 'They take a lot less looking after.'

'You shouldn't have done that, Calista. Rover and Rex were *good* dogs.'

'If I promise not to do it again can I go?'

'His dogs are a boy's best friend.'

'You're not a boy, Adam,' Cally reminded him, and herself. 'You're a computer at a fancy dress party.'

'I should kill you now for what you've done.' Adam approached her and his pale eyes were devoid of all humanity. 'I should do it myself, with my own hands.' They snapped to her neck, choked off the supply of oxygen from her lungs. Cally grappled with his grip. Useless. 'I could twist your head from your shoulders as you would unscrew the top of a tube of toothpaste, Calista.' She was gagging, gasping. Somehow Adam was taller than her. It was because she'd dropped to her knees. He was staring down at her like ice. 'I should do it. I should indulge myself with the wet tearing of your tendons and the cracking of your vertebrae, the warm blood foaming from your mouth. I *could* do it. I ought to deny you the blessing I thought to bestow upon you when I saw who our interloper was. But' – and he swept Cally towards the centre of the lab – 'I will not. My plan must still take precedence. Breathe, Calista, for a little longer.'

Cally coughed, dabbing her bruised throat gingerly. 'You're all . . . heart, Adam,' she croaked.

She was on the floor, slumped against some kind of raised disc, waist-height. Wasn't going to give Adam Thornchild the satisfaction of remaining down there. She placed her hand on the flat surface of the disc to help heave herself up. That was when she fingered the restraints.

'Do you know what that is, the centrepiece of my laboratory here?' Adam encouraged her to stand and explore further.

Four sets of electronically operated restraints, fixed at certain points along the circumference of the disc. Cally needed no clue to guess *their* purpose. One for each limb. The indentation in human shape that denied the construction a flat surface after all simply confirmed her assumption.

'Whatever it is,' Cally commented, 'the fact that its guests have to be tied down to it suggests it's not conducive to their continued well-being.'

'Ah, now that's where you're wrong, Ms Clever-Clogs Calista.' Adam almost giggled. Children always like it when they know something that older people don't.

'Clever-Clogs?'

'Up,' Adam hinted. 'Look up.'

And above the disc, of equal dimensions, descending from the ceiling was a second circular object. It resembled a horizontal wheel with a kind of closed metal eye at its hub. Its spokes were transparent, though bound at regular intervals by straps of silver steel, and its rim was composed of countless golden links, like a Titan's necklace. No energy was coursing through the wheel now, but given the masses of circuitry that led from it into the ceiling, into the walls, into the power grids of Cyberia, Cally guessed that was a situation that could soon be rectified.

And all of it focused and unleashed on a hapless victim manacled to the disc. For hapless victim, she thought with dread, read Calista Green.

'I give in,' she said, as offhandedly as she could manage. 'Some kind of new auto-masseuse?' She hoped.

'Cold,' said Adam. 'No, no, you won't get it. But do you want to know what it is, Calista? *I* want you to know. This machine is what I've been working on ever since I killed my parents. Its nearness to completion is another reason I could dispense with the rest of the Hybrid. This machine will create a new and glorious future for humankind.' Adam's eyes gleamed at the prospect. 'This is a *matter converter*.'

'Yeah, right.' Trying to sound sarcastic. 'At least the silicon chip inside your head didn't damage your imagination, Adam.'

'It has always been the role of science to transform imagination into reality, Calista, has it not?' He had a point. 'This *is* a matter converter, a small-scale model, of course, until I am certain the process has been perfected. The version that will be launched from Cyberia very soon will be significantly larger and more powerful.'

'Okay,' said Cally, 'I'm going to ask the obvious question. I know you want me to. What does this gizmo convert *into* what?'

'The "gizmo", as you so childishly put it, Calista,' Adam outlined, 'is a nanoparticle generator. The particles, the product of smart atom technology, coalesce at the hub, and when the generator is fully energised, they are fired at a preprogrammed target. In this case, to test the process—'

'Hapless victim,' said Cally.

Adam smirked knowingly. 'The nanoparticles are most *aggressive*,' he revealed, 'like a particularly virulent strain of bacteria. They will smother their newly acquired host body, force their way into his pores – or hers. Then they will graft themselves to muscle, bone, internal organs. They will swim in the bloodstream like corpuscles. They will become capillaries and ventricles and nerves. They will nuzzle against the lobes of the brain like pets, but they will be a conquering force against which a carbon form can mount no defence, and their invasion will be absolute. This is the conversion, Calista, from human to hybrid. This is how our parents' dreams will be achieved. I will send my matter converters into the skies and they will bombard the cities with nanoparticles. There will be no resistance. The human race as it has been known for millennia will begin its inevitable and necessary retreat into history. A new kind, a hybrid race of carbon and silicon, will rise to take its place.'

'With you at its head, Adam?' Cally wondered innocently.

'Of course.' And he genuinely didn't seem to see anything wrong in that. 'How else will the masses cope with their new-found abilities? There will be millions, *billions* of cyber-beings, but there can only be one Adam.'

'I don't know whether to despise you or feel sorry for you,' said Cally. 'I think despise. *Part* of you's still human, Adam, which means part of you can still tell right from wrong, can still make a choice. You don't have to do any of this.'

'There *is* no right and wrong, Calista,' countered Adam Thornchild. 'Carbon form morality is a method of control scarcely less subtle than nanotechnology. Do you think your great religions would not have *programmed* their flock to obey their petty rules if they had possessed the scientific means to do so? There is no good and evil, only what can be done and what cannot.'

'I don't believe that,' said Cally.

'You will,' promised Adam. 'When you are taken by my nanoparticles, you will. Hold her.'

And suddenly she was seized by the two guards beside her.

'Previous attempts to employ the matter converter have, I am afraid to say,' Adam bemoaned, 'been failures. There are a number of peasant villages nearby; they've been good enough to loan us some of their people from time to time. The nanoparticles have proved to be too alien for the host body to assimilate. The resultant mutants have been rather unpleasant to behold – speaking aesthetically, of course. Scientifically they have been most interesting. But the sight of micro-circuitry tearing through flesh and bulging from eyeballs and spilling out of mouths is a little upsetting. And entirely fatal, of course, eventually. I'd show you the tapes, Calista, but I wouldn't want to worry you too much. Besides, I *have* been refining the process since my last attempt, and I *am* a genius. Perhaps the converter will work properly this time.'

'So I lose either my life or my identity, huh, Adam?' Cally said defiantly.

'Exactly, and I can't wait to find out which.' He clapped his pale hands with excitement. 'Secure her to the wheel.'

TWELVE

Sometimes, when he was asleep and dreaming, Mason Morgan remembered how his life had once been. He remembered himself, always missing out on promotions, the big breaks, always missing out on the girl. He remembered himself, never being in the right place at the right time. And he remembered the ad, the promise it had made, to make you a new person, to enable you to start your life afresh thanks to the wonders of nanotechnology. He recalled responding to the ad, meeting Mr Lucas Thornchild. He recalled talk of implants and enhancements and it didn't matter that he couldn't afford the treatment, he was the *right* kind of person (for the first time in his life), the kind of man they'd been looking for. He remembered the operation. That was it, though. And only ever when he was asleep and dreaming. Over his unconscious state, even the neural implants did not wield total mastery.

Most of the time, however, they did. Most of the time, Mason Morgan might as well not have had a name or a previous existence. He was a guard in the employ of

Adam Thornchild, and Adam Thornchild told him what to do.

Like now, for instance. They were patrolling the environs of Cyberia, Mason Morgan and a small team of his fellow guards. They were on SkyBikes, to help them cover the frozen ground efficiently. Everything was done efficiently in Cyberia. And the voice in his head was commanding him to be alert – since the capture of the girl alertness was more vital than ever – and to demand of that group of peasants in the distance, in their fur cloaks and hoods, what they thought they were doing venturing so close to the nuclear plant. Mason Morgan had had the deception programmed into him. As far as the ignorant locals were concerned, he and his colleagues worked for the Tsarist government, who were taking renewed interest in the once abandoned facility, an interest that was nobody's concern but their own.

He led his team swooping down on the peasants. The latter demonstrated fitting humility and fear at their sudden apprehension. Part of Mason Morgan relished the humility and fear of others and had longed to be the reason for it years before the implants. He snapped at the peasants in Russian, which he'd learned without ever knowing how, and in threatening, brutal tones, which came naturally.

'Where do you miserable peasants think you're going? You know you shouldn't be this close to the plant.' Boot-shuffling silence. 'Well? Are you going to speak or are we going to have to beat it out of you?' The implants seemed to warm to that prospect.

'We're hunting,' said the lead peasant at last, head bowed, face concealed by his hood.

'We're hunting, *sir*,' corrected Mason Morgan, 'and for what? Few animals in these parts.'

'We're not hunting animals, *sir*.' Sarcastic peasant. Needed to be taught a lesson. And throwing his hood back arrogantly. Looked a bit oriental for a Russian. 'We're hunting *men*.'

And the local peasants weren't usually equipped with shock blasters.

Alertness. The voice in Mason Morgan's head had told him it was important. Since the capture of the girl . . .

The peasants opened fire before the guards could retaliate. Stunned, Mason Morgan toppled from his SkyBike and crashed to the hard earth. Whatever was going to happen next, he was to play no more part in it.

The Deveraux assault team shrugged off their furs. Beneath, full combat kit. 'Here's the transport,' said Jimmy Kwan. 'Let's go.'

'Are you comfortable, Calista?' Adam gazed down at the spread-eagled girl, her arms and legs now stretched and electronically shackled at wrist and ankle. 'I do hope not.'

'I've been in worse positions than this,' Cally retorted.

'I'm sure you have,' the pale boy chuckled. 'And how are you enjoying the view?'

Directly above her, the ring of the nanoparticle generator. As long as its eye remained closed, she had a chance. 'Oh, real fine,' she mocked – never let the Bad Guy know when you're rattled. 'Up there with the Grand Canyon at sunset.'

'Sunset for you, Calista,' said Adam. 'I'm now going to energise the converter and you'll have a front-row seat to watch the process at work. I don't need any techs in white coats to assist me, in case you were wondering. My mind is perfectly attuned to the micro-circuitry of my creation. I can do it all myself.'

'Multi-tasking is a marvellous thing,' Cally quipped, but her confidence was wavering. If Jimmy didn't get here soon, it wouldn't be worth him coming at all.

Adam was beginning. He was initiating the matter conversion. He was glancing at a bank of computers here and they flickered and hummed as if flattered to have been picked out and eager to please. He was glancing at another set of instruments there and they leapt at his command and there was the distant drone of power building. Cally jerked at her hands. Futile. She'd need to be the Hulk to break free of the disc, and all she had in common with him was *green*.

'You can struggle if it makes you feel better, Calista.' Adam had been watching her. 'I find the sight of you *writhing* like that quite exciting in a very carbon form sort of way. But let me inform you, as I'm sure you have already realised, it will do you no . . . How interesting.' The boy tilted his head to one side. 'Today must be my day for company.'

Company, thought Cally. Jimmy. Hope.

'It appears you have friends willing to attempt to rescue you, Calista,' Adam told her. 'They've already overpowered one of my patrols and are approaching Cyberia on stolen SkyBikes wearing their uniforms. How predictably pointless! Don't they realise I see through the eyes of all my puppets? Well, let them come. It will only require a small percentage of my magnificent cyber-brain's capabilities to organise a strategy for

Cyberia's defence. The rest I can devote to the matter converter. To you, Calista.' He patted her hand. 'Don't fret. You're still my first priority.' To Cally's revulsion, his eyes rolled up into his head. Adam was seeing in silicon. 'And the moment is *now*.'

Jimmy should have known it was going too well. The meagre resistance at the doors. The lack of reinforcements for the Thornchild goons they'd eliminated as they entered. The time they'd had to dispense with the guards' uniforms and advance in their own combats. Operations never proceeded as smoothly as this. But he'd been happy to delude himself so far, not because he was afraid of a fight but because he was afraid *for* Cally. Her emergency signal had been activated when she was rendered unconscious. Thornchild had her. Somewhere in this vast and labyrinthine facility she was a prisoner of the cyborg, the hybrid, and Jimmy didn't like the idea of that one bit. He knew she could look after herself, but that didn't stop him wanting to do a little bit of *looking after* for her, and not just in his capacity as field handler. He'd already booked the restaurant and he didn't intend to be paying the cancellation fee. So he'd tried to persuade himself that the progress his team had been making through the plant was real, a progress they'd earned, not simply a way of luring them into a trap.

Then they'd reached the corridor that was long and thin and that didn't have a lot of obvious cover. The corridor that was overshadowed by a metal bridge that ran its entire length and that afforded an unrivalled vantage point from which to observe intruders below.

'Not this way,' Jimmy had decided.

Then the door behind them had slid shut automatically. Then there'd been the clatter of boots on the bridge above, the guards taking up their positions.

Then there'd been gunfire.

He should have known the operation was going too well. But it was making up for it now. Jimmy and his team were pinned down. There was no deceiving himself any longer. The casualties were mounting.

If they couldn't find an edge from somewhere, and soon, they'd had it.

If she couldn't find an edge from somewhere, and soon, she'd had it.

Delaying Adam somehow was a non-starter now. He was beyond her. He was standing in the middle of the lab with his arms extended and his head slightly lifted like a young prophet receiving the word of God. His eyes were white and blind. Those of the guards sentried around the room were dull and glazed. Cally felt like the only truly living person present. And she knew with certain dread that that distinction wasn't likely to last for long.

The power drone was louder, kind of nearer. The links on the outer rim of the nanoparticle generator pulsated, their golden hue further enriched by an energy surging through them. The wheel of the generator began to rotate. Roulette, Cally thought with bitter humour, and her life was at stake. The Wheel of Fortune, and she was plumb out of luck.

Whatever happened to her, she begged silently for Jimmy to be safe.

Faster the generator spun, and faster still, a blur, a smear across her vision. And the spokes were lighting up now, though one could hardly be distinguished from another, and they were bars of fire. And the droning of the converter's power was like a swarm of wasps in her ears, stinging.

As long as the eye at the hub stayed closed.

Adam cried out like someone in a dream.

And the eye eased open. It was green and it was electric and bolts of jade lightning stabbed from its centre along the generator's spokes. The nanoparticles met and multiplied. The converter was all but primed. Probably only awaiting its creator's command.

If the process worked, she would be Cally for merely seconds longer. If it didn't she could prepare herself to meet up with Ben again. *Silver lining*.

The light was blazing, crackling above her, the energy peaking, the lab shaking with its crescendo.

A new note. Cally heard it. Shriller, higher-pitched. Like an alarm. The system shrieking. New and *wrong*.

Adam suddenly clutching at the sides of his head, the guards following his lead, all of them crying out in pain.

Couldn't have happened before. Cally wrestled with her bonds with renewed vigour. Were Adam's refinements to the converter to blame? But the eye was still open and still disgorging energy only metres above her. Allocate responsibility later.

The guards in spasm as if electrified, dropping their weapons, convulsing to the floor. Even Adam, falling against the disc on which she was shackled. And all the time, the piercing, deafening scream of unbridled energy.

'What have you done? What have you *done*?' He was accusing her. 'How can you . . .? Weak carbon forms . . .' Was it Jimmy? 'Too much power. You're feeding my system too much power. It – I – we cannot contain it. Help us, Calista. Stop it!'

'Get me off here first, let me loose and I'll help you.' Cally had no idea what Adam was talking about, but right now she'd make any kind of bargain.

'This power. Where is it from? Why can't I understand it?' He'd forgotten her, was staggering away.

Was something feeding *into* Adam's converter? Some kind of external energy source? But what? From where? Why?

Priorities, Cross, Cally urged herself. Number one: the coruscating green energy field above her, twisting and gyrating like something alive. It was . . . was it *structuring* itself, forming a coherent outline, a shape? It was. For sure. What had happened to nanoparticles fired at a preprogrammed target? Something else was going on here, something that the wailing Adam Thornchild had not anticipated. A shape. The energy was assuming a definite shape.

It was human.

A mannequin in green materialised above Cally, suspended in mid-air by the matter converter, its dimensions filling out, its edges hardening. Inside it the lightning, the power of life.

And the systems were overloading. There was going to be an explosion. Its imminence was in the squealing, screeching scale of the cacophony assailing the lab, its impossibly rising pitch. Cally was desperate to cover her ears but she couldn't. She longed to cover her eyes too but she couldn't do that, either. She could only endure. Adam was screaming. She was screaming. The whole world.

Detonation. A tremendous flash. Her eyeballs seared with emeralds.

All around her, control panels erupting, instruments igniting, sparks and flames and smoke. Adam howling. He and the systems were one. Lurching for the door.

Her limbs freed. All mechanisms short-circuited.

And Cally might have moved then, had something not prevented her, something landing on top of her, something fallen, released from the converter as if it was a gateway, not a gun.

To be precise, *someone*.

He'd dropped so that he was almost hugging her and his body was at an angle across hers with his head to the right of her own. She saw an incongruous leather waistcoat, the back of his neck, somehow vulnerable, his hair. Cropped short. Blond.

She couldn't breathe. His weight was on her but that wasn't why. He was groaning. He was alive. A boy her own age.

She was insane. That was it. Somehow, exposure to the matter converter had driven her insane. She had to be crazy to think what she was thinking. Head Tech Thurby's words returned to her: 'Perhaps whatever is immersed in the starstone's energy field is not actually disintegrated. Perhaps it is simply *displaced*.'

Displaced, yeah. Or better yet, converted.

She heaved the body off her, but gently, laid him down. She didn't want to hurt him just in case. (No, she'd lost it, lost it big-time.) The moan was rising in her throat involuntarily before she even saw his face.

It was a face she'd never thought she'd see again.

Tears spilled from her eyes and she was shaking

uncontrollably. She was touching him. His eyeballs fluttered, blue eyes beneath. She was squeezing him. He was strong. She was kissing him. He was warm.

And she wasn't believing any of it.

The boy was Ben.

THIRTEEN

Jimmy Kwan didn't believe in miracles and his upbringing had taught him the futility of relying on others. You lived or died by your own efforts. He'd trained himself over long, demanding years to ensure that *his* own efforts would suffice to keep him alive. So far, they'd worked out.

Today was shaping up to be an exception.

His team was already halved, blood staining the metal floor of the corridor like rust, and with each successive reduction of its strength, the chances of ultimate survival slimmed. Four men left, and Trench had been hit in his firing arm. The Deveraux agents kept low, hugged the walls, the regular steel protrusions that provided their only cover. They'd inflicted casualties of their own, of course, but not enough, and Thornchild's guards fought wildly, recklessly, hanging over the bridge's hand-rail to find a better shot even at the risk of needlessly exposing themselves to enemy fire. It was as if they didn't care what happened to them.

Michener alongside Jimmy keeled forward, didn't

make a fuss about it, just kind of sighed and toppled and that was another letter of condolence to grieving relatives.

Sorry, Cal, Jimmy thought, we weren't quite good enough. I hope you can forgive us. I hope you stay alive. Who knows what might have been?

What could still be.

Without warning, Thornchild's men started screaming. They dropped their pulse rifles and clutched their heads and swayed and reeled on suddenly unsteady feet. Their interest in killing Deveraux operatives was abruptly extinguished.

'What . . .?' The wounded Trench looked quizzically to his team leader.

'Who the hell cares?' Jimmy was leaping up, spraying the bridge with shock blasts. 'Let's put 'em to sleep!'

His surviving team-mates followed his lead. It was a different story now. The guards clattered to the floor. If Jimmy hadn't yet cheated death, he'd at least gained a reprieve.

Maybe he should revise his attitude towards miracles.

'I don't understand, sir.' Trench again. 'What happened to them?'

'Thornchild likes implants,' Jimmy said. 'Maybe something went wrong with them.' Cally, he was thinking. This was *her* doing. A rush of adrenalin surged through him. 'Whatever, it's kept us alive. I want to stay that way. Let's go. We've got a job to do.'

And hold on, Cally, he was thinking. I'm coming.

'Ben? Ben! It's you. Tell me it's you. Tell me.' Shaking him. Pummelling him. While the lab burned and the guards sprawled unconscious on the floor and somewhere Adam Thornchild still was free. She was a little bit hysterical.

'Cally, what?' Not only Ben's face, Ben's body, Ben's lips. Ben's *voice*. 'Something must have . . . how'd you get here so quickly? I . . . don't *hit* me, Cal . . .'

'What's your name? What's your name?' She sat back on her haunches, still stared at him intently.

'What's my *name*?' Ben was trying to clear his head (*Ben*'s head). 'Have I been out or some . . . where *are* we?' He hauled himself up, gazed about in amazement. But he wasn't as amazed as Cally.

Whose trained and rational mind fought to reassert control. This was the business end of a Spy High mission, not an episode from a videvision soap opera. Astonishment was not conducive to achievement. 'Ben,' she pressed, 'where do you *think* we are?'

'Wallachia, of course. Dracholtz. But this isn't Vlad's citadel. This isn't where I was when . . .' He trailed away, confusion in his eyes (Ben's eyes). Confusion and fear.

'When what, Ben?' He thought he was still in Wallachia. He thought no time had passed. Maybe, for him, none had.

'The starstone.' The memories returned like nightfall. 'I was trying to deactivate it. You were there, Cal, on the holocom.' He glanced down. The attachment was still part of his wristband. 'But I couldn't . . . not the whole thing . . . there wasn't time. So I ran.'

'I *told* you to run,' Cally said, 'and you should have gone *sooner*.'

'But the starstone detonated before I could get out of range.' Ben seemed puzzled. 'It *detonated*. And I turned to face it and the last thing I can remember is this green *wall* of energy slamming into me, and I was thinking this is it, I mean this is *it*, Stanton, lights out and hitch a ride to

heaven and . . . Cal, you'd better tell me what's going on.'
In tones of rising agitation. 'I am still me, aren't I? I'm
not a clone or something or . . .'

'Okay, Ben. Relax.' Her hands on his chest. He leaned
on his elbow and held one tightly. Her mind was
working and the initial shock was over and she was in
control of herself again. Now she could help Ben. 'You're
not a clone or *any*thing. You're you. That's obvious. But
you've been away for a while . . .'

'You mean in a coma? But then how did I . . .?'

'Not in a coma, Ben. Not a bed in a hospital coma,
anyway. I think you've been inside the starstone
somehow. I think it absorbed you, kept you like, I don't
know, a prisoner.' She kind of wished Thurby was here.

'Okay, who are you? Where's the real Cally?'

'Ben,' the real Cally urged, 'listen to me. You've been
gone six weeks.'

'Six . . . what?'

'That's what I'm trying to tell you. It's been six weeks
since Wallachia. When we got to the tower, when we
reached the point of your last transmission, there was no
trace of you anywhere, no DNA, nothing. And we knew
you hadn't got out. The surviving rebels confirmed it.'

'So, what? You thought I was dead?'

'What else *could* we think, Ben? It seemed the only pos-
sibility. The starstone must have atomised you completely.'

'You had to go through that, Cal?' Ben stroked her
hair tenderly. How he'd have coped had their situations
been reversed he didn't know.

'Only then they took the starstone to a Deveraux lab
and the techs have been experimenting with it and it's
like, they've developed this theory that it never was a

weapon but something else, some kind of matter dis-
placement device, and they're right, aren't they? They're
right. You being here proves it, Ben.'

'It does?'

'Disintegration. Reintegration. The starstone broke
you down into a form of energy it could store and then
it . . .' Cally *really* wished Thurby was here. 'And then it
put you back together again . . . kind of . . .'

'So where is it, Cal? I don't see a starstone.' Ben's eyes
flashed. His strength seemed fully restored, and with it
his decisiveness. 'But I do see trademark goons and a lab
straight out of the latest edition of the mad scientist's fur-
nishings catalogue. I guess you're on a mission, right?'

'Yes, but Ben . . .'

He swung off the disc and stood on his own two feet.
They held him up well. They always had. 'Then you've
just found yourself a little extra help.'

'But you've got to take it easy,' Cally counselled. 'If
you have some kind of delayed reaction to what's happened to you . . .'

'I still haven't got a clue what *has* happened to me, Cal,
and as for taking it easy, sounds like I've been doing that
for the past six weeks. What I need now is a bit of a
work-out. And it looks like I've come to the right place.'
He picked up one of the fallen guards' pulse rifles. 'You
want to let me know who today's Bad Guy is, Cal?'

'Ben . . .'

'Listen. Health checks, explanations, even the certain
back-together-again activities I have in mind, they'll
have to wait, won't they?' It was dubious from Cally, but
it was a nod. ' 'Cause correct me if I'm wrong, but we
need to get out of here, don't we?'

'You're not wrong.' Cally appropriated a pulse rifle too. And maybe it would be all right. Ben certainly appeared his normal self.

'Then let's—'

Before they could leave, others entered. Ben instinctively raised his rifle. Cally as immediately knocked it aside. 'Wait. They're ours!'

Jimmy Kwan and the remnants of his team. Delighted to see Cally. Bemused to see Ben. 'Stanton?' Jimmy had imagined his charge's former boyfriend to be forever relegated to hologram and virtual reality. 'It's not possible.'

'Anything's possible once you've been to Spy High,' grinned Ben, who enjoyed making an impact. 'But I'm afraid you have the edge over me.'

'This is Jimmy Kwan, Ben, my field handler,' Cally supplied.

'What happened to Mei Ataki?'

'Long story. Later.'

'Cally,' ventured Jimmy, 'are you sure this is really Ben and not a Thornchild trick?'

'I'm sure,' said Cally.

'Thorn who?' said Ben.

'I'll explain as we go.' Actions, not words, Cally knew, made successful missions. 'Adam ran off somewhere. It looked like his link with his hardware had broken down.'

Jimmy nodded tersely. 'Makes sense. His software too, if you want to call his goons that. They had us pinned down then they all freaked out.'

'Same here.' Cally didn't like to tempt fate, but she did so anyway. 'Guess that means our problems are over.'

❖

They made their way purposefully but warily through the chambers and corridors of Cyberia. It was true that every single one of Adam's guards they saw was collapsed and unconscious, which was good, but to make a generalisation and therefore assume that they'd *all* be in a similarly unmenacing condition was to be unprofessionally optimistic. They moved in defensive formation and their guns were always ready.

Ben listened to Cally and this Jimmy Kwan guy swapping intel. He wasn't sure he approved of someone so young (though older than both of them), and perhaps more pertinently, someone so *male*, acting as his girlfriend's field handler. The faculty at Spy High never used to meet their students' eyes *quite* so frankly. But at least he learned a few things. Teenage carbon-silicon hybrids. Matter converters. He'd been resurrected in some bad science fiction novel.

'You don't think we should search for Adam?' Cally was asking her handler.

'Even if he's still in the plant,' Jimmy reasoned, 'it's a big place. *His* place. The six of us'd never find him. We're better off getting out of here, reporting to Deveraux. A clean-up team can take over. Wait!' To the man at point. 'Not that way, Clarkson.'

'What's wrong with that way, Kwan?' said Ben, who rather immaturely felt like taking it just to spite him.

'It's the way we came, where we were ambushed.' Seemed Jimmy Kwan could hold the gaze of boys as well as girls, and he *knew* what Ben was thinking. 'Five of our team-mates are lying dead in there. I don't want to go adding to them, you know what I mean?'

'I hear you,' said Ben, 'Kwan.'

They took another route, parallel. Entered another

corridor, hexagonal, lined with conduits and cables thicker than limbs, inlaid with huge instrument panels, traversed by a walkway constructed from a series of steel grilles and raised above a further mass of electronic equipment.

A corridor in which they were not, for once, the only conscious beings.

At the far end, Adam Thornchild stepped into view.

'Sir!' From Clarkson.

'So much for your search, Cal.' From Ben.

Half a dozen pulse rifles now pointing in the same direction.

'All for me?' Adam said, his voice made metallic by the acoustics. 'Do you imagine I'd allow any one of them, any one of *you*, to harm me?'

There was an edge to his voice now. Cally heard it. A shrillness. Like a child on the brink of tears. And she was suddenly more fearful than she'd been at any point in the mission so far. The agony he'd suffered back in the lab had *affected* him. If Adam Thornchild hadn't been insane before, he sure was now.

'You tried to part me from my silicon brothers, didn't you? You tried to separate us.' He advanced towards them.

'Give it up, Thornchild.' Jimmy. 'Come any closer and we'll shoot.'

He came closer. 'You tried to deny me my communion with the computer, my cyber-consummation. Didn't you? Didn't *you*, Calista? But you failed. You hurt me but I recovered. That which does not destroy us makes us stronger, and I *am* stronger. Cyberia and I are one. And as one, my silicon brothers and I will make you *dead*.'

FOURTEEN

'Take him out! Stun him!' Jimmy barking orders.

Orders that would have been obeyed – with alacrity – if the corridor at the same second hadn't decided to do something about them.

Instrument panels left and right exploded, sacrificed themselves for their master, and spouts of flame speared from the walls. Distracting. Pulse blasts fired but direction went awry. The rattling of the plates beneath the Deveraux team's feet didn't help, the grilles of the walkway shaking like there were prisoners below agitating for release.

The unfortunate Trench, caught in a blast from the instrument panels, his combats ignited like a torch. His screams rose higher than the flames.

A snapping and tearing from overhead as cables ripped themselves out of their casings, rent themselves in two and lashed like fat black tentacles at the carbon forms, their ragged stumps sparking and sizzling with current.

From the floor too, thrusting powerfully through the

walkway, shredding steel like it was paper, cables flailing like the fronds of some alien plant.

Jimmy Kwan knew when the odds had tipped against him. 'Back!' he yelled. 'Clarkson!'

The man at point turned, started to retreat. The floor opened up beneath him, the cables claimed him, and though he fired off a few rounds with his pulse rifle, he couldn't kill what was never properly alive. Struggling, squirming, looped in black, down he was dragged. His scream and the sudden spray of blood suggested he wouldn't be coming back up again.

'The door! Sir, he's closed the door!' The last words Jimmy's last team-mate was able to utter. The cable was like a noose around his neck. It tightened. It twisted. The man had never lost his head in battle before. There was a first time for everything.

And then there were three.

'Try to . . .' Ben blasted at the door, scorched and dented the steel. If he'd had time, if the others had joined him, he might have broken through eventually. But in combat situations *eventually* was a word that all too often proved irrelevant.

Maybe he'd been better off in the starstone.

Cally fought against despair as dark coils wrapped around her, around Jimmy, around Ben, yanking their limbs, stretching them out, forcing their weapons from their grasp, lifting them from the ground so that the strain on their joints was excruciating. If the cables pulled harder, as hard as they could, if Adam instructed them to do that, the effect on the three of them would be similar to that on a trio of rag dolls dismembered by an unruly infant. Only it wouldn't be sawdust sprinkling the shattered walkway.

But Adam *wasn't* going to be giving that order, at least not yet. Otherwise they'd be dead already. He was sauntering up to them, stepping over the smouldering remains of Trench without even a glance downwards. His hands were clasped behind his back. He could have been out for a Sunday stroll.

A minute to find his weakness, Cally urged herself, a minute to find the means to defeat him. Maybe even less time than that. *Think*. What did she know about him? What could she use? Ben hadn't returned to her for them both to die. *Think*.

'Were you agents going somewhere?' said Adam mildly. 'Or do you just intend to hang around all day? A little carbon form joke there. We wouldn't want your final moments to be entirely devoid of humour, would we? Because if you imagine I've spared you the same fate as your companions in order to let you live, you are woefully mistaken.'

'Why *have* you spared us, Adam?' Engage the maniacs in conversation, Cally knew. First principles. The madder they were, the more they liked to talk.

'My silicon brothers and I have been watching you since you left the ruin of my lab, Calista. We are aware that you have demonstrated feelings towards these two male carbon forms. We thought it might increase *your* suffering to see *them* suffer, for I am afraid that suffering is all you have to look forward to. It's all you deserve.'

'I'll give you what you deserve, you little pipsqueak, when I get down from here,' Ben threatened.

'You won't be alone,' added Jimmy coldly.

'Silence! I don't want to hear from *male* carbon forms.

If either of you utters another word,' Adam promised, 'I will have your tongue plucked out by the roots.'

It was about her, then. It was down to her and Adam. Cally could live with that. 'You want to hurt me, Adam? Why? I thought you liked me.'

'Like? Dislike? What have I told you before about the redundancy of emotion for one such as myself?'

And she remembered what he'd told her: emotion is the only obstacle between man and machine. She remembered Jimmy's words, too: emotion can be a powerful weapon.

The beginnings of a plan formed in her mind.

'You need to *pay*, Calista,' Adam said, and he was jabbing his finger accusingly at her now, 'for the pain you caused my silicon brothers, not only at my matter converter but throughout Cyberia. You were responsible for that, and a long, lingering death will be your just reward.'

'You can kill me if you like, Adam' – the old defiance-in-the-face-of-death routine – 'but I'm not the one responsible for your silicon brothers' pain. *You* are.'

'Lies! How dare you? How dare you mouth such filth!' Adam's voice rising, its edge of craziness more pronounced again.

The cables tautening, like a rack cranked up a notch. Agony shooting through Cally's muscles. Silent appeals from Ben and Jimmy: did she know what she was doing?

She sure as heck hoped so.

'Not. . . . lies.' Resisting the pain. 'The truth. It was your fault, Adam. You failed your silicon brothers. You failed the system.'

'I didn't,' Adam denied. He was close to Cally now, his pale face inches from her, his colourless eyes wide with indignation and dawning fury. 'How *dare* you say that? On what grounds?'

'You don't . . . know what caused the matter converter's overload, do you? You don't know the energy's source. *Do you?*'

Adam's white brow furrowed darkly. 'I . . . we . . . my silicon brothers . . .'

'You messed up, Adam. You messed up big-time.' And there was a sneer in Cally's taunts, a contempt. 'You're a failure, a loser. You don't deserve to lead the hybrid race. You're not worthy.'

'I am. I am worthy. I am the first.'

'And the last.' Derisively. Not letting up for a second. 'You're nothing, Adam. You're an experiment gone wrong. You're a kid with a chip in his head as well as on his shoulder, that's all. You're a boy playing at being a robot. You're not the next stage of evolution. You're a dead end.'

'Be silent. Be—'

'You think you're what the Hybrid really wanted? Adam, you think your parents would be proud?'

'*Shut up!*' Specks of colour on the pale boy's cheeks. 'You mustn't say . . . I am the hybrid. I am the mind of the machine. I am the computerised man. I *am*—'

'Second choice, Adam. Second best. You're second best. You know that. They didn't want you. They wanted me. I was supposed to be the one. Remember? You know that. You're nothing. The booby prize. No wonder you're not up to the job. Your parents *knew* you wouldn't—'

'I don't *have* parents!' Anguish. Rage. Turmoil. 'No

ties! No people! No carbon form human beings! I don't
need them. I only need my brothers, my silicon brothers,
and—'

'Failure, Adam! Failure!' Shouting it, screaming it.
'Failure!'

'I *hate* you Calista I *hate* you *hate* you *hate*—'

His fingers grasping for her throat. They'd been there
before. They could break her neck, Cally knew. Maybe
she was the one who'd failed.

His fingers freezing. His hands, in front of her face
like a little boy proving to his mother that he'd washed
them before supper. His hands, as cold and pale as ice.
Ice, cracking.

Adam wailed. Cally grimaced.

Fissures in his skin. His skin, splitting open. And the
shiny black hardness of the circuits and grafts beneath
like the bodies of insects.

'My God.' Ben or Jimmy, one of them forgetting
Adam's warning to stay silent. It didn't matter. He was in
no position now to have tongues plucked out by the
roots.

'Calista, what have you done?' His entire form was
vibrating, juddering with increasing violence. The flesh
of his face, unseaming, a robot's face revealed. And
under his clothing, his torso, his limbs, bulging and
swelling as if infested with crawling things. 'No. *No!*'

This was what Cally had gambled on. She'd hoped
something like this would happen. *Like* this, but *not* this.
Part of her felt ashamed, even as the cables holding them
lost their incentive to do so and dropped like dead
snakes to the floor and the Deveraux agents fell too,
quickly scrambling to their feet again.

'Cally, what's *happening* to him?' Definitely Ben this time.

And Adam was crumpling, shaking, like a man in a fever, and he was making small, pathetic moans as he subsided to the walkway, and his skin was like wallpaper half stripped from a wall. His last conscious movement, assuming the foetal position.

'Emotion,' said Cally. 'I forced him to feel it. I goaded him. He lost his temper. He put the barrier back between man and machine.' She approached Adam Thornchild softly, almost tenderly. 'His cyber-self rejected the parts of him that were still human, like a host body can reject a transplanted organ. His silicon brothers have disowned him. He's shut down.' She knelt beside the body of the hybrid. 'I wish there could have been another way.'

His voice, faint, distant, as if receding into the past. 'Mommy, where are you? Mommy, I'll be a good boy. Don't leave me here . . .'

Cally stroked the child's white hair. 'Oh, Adam . . .'

Then silence in Cyberia.

The clean-up team had arrived. They'd taken possession not only of the wretched remains of Adam Thornchild but of Cyberia too and everything in it. The hybrid's tech was to be analysed, classified and evaluated down to the last circuit, standard practice after the seizure of an enemy's base. Deveraux wasn't proud. If those who would endanger the world commanded new technology that could just as easily be put to its defence, then the tech was appropriated for that very purpose. No compensation paid. There were no patents in espionage.

Cally had seen it happen before, many times. One time in particular kept her thinking all the way back to Hong Kong with Jimmy and Ben.

The acquisition of the starstone.

It seemed quite crowded in the briefing room below the Shop, though to be fair only three of those attending were present physically. Head Tech Thurby and the head of Jonathan Deveraux took part holographically.

'Your assumption was essentially correct, Agent Cross,' Thurby was saying, nodding approvingly. 'We'll make a scientist of you yet.'

'Don't you believe it,' Ben whispered in Cally's ear. 'You'd never cope with those spectacles.'

Cally grinned. Jimmy watched her. He watched her and Ben, their fingers seeking each other out as if magnetised. He'd been watching them for a while.

'At the same time as your and Field Handler Kwan's mission reports estimated the activation of Thornchild's matter converter, we registered a massive increase in the starstone's energy output, though the power was directed *internally* rather than *externally*, something of a first. When we examined the device after the phenomenon, we discovered something rather interesting.'

Thurby paused for dramatic effect, a technique wasted on Jonathan Deveraux since the day he lost the capacity to feel shivers down his spine, along with his spine itself. 'Is something wrong, Thurby?' he said.

'No, sir. Not at all,' the Head Tech flustered. 'No, ah, what we discovered, what we found was, ah, the *absence* of one of the energy signatures that up to that point had been located within the starstone.'

'Meaning?' prompted Cally.

'Meaning hi, honey, I'm home,' said Ben.

'We'll find things out sooner if we' – Jimmy wished he hadn't spoken; he felt painfully like a teacher – 'keep the interruptions . . . well, to a minimum . . .'

'*Meaning*,' continued Thurby, 'that it seems certain the energy was transferred, transported, like a radio signal between two terminals, between a transmitter and a receiver, the starstone and the matter converter. Meaning that Agent Stanton is the energy. The energy *was* Agent Stanton, but transmuted by the starstone into a different form.'

'I've still got some whys here, Thurby,' said Ben. But one of them wasn't why did Field Handler Kwan seem to have such a down on him: that was obvious.

'Why did the starstone reconfigure your molecules in the first place?'

'I told you it hurt,' Ben quipped.

'We now believe it to be a teleportation device,' Thurby explained. 'Once a subject is absorbed by the starstone, it can expect to be teleported to another such machine within operational range. That range must be thousands of miles at least, obviously, but even so, until Thornchild's matter converter, the starstone could locate no suitable receiver for its cargo.'

'So it kept me inside it?' Ben clarified. 'A mass of energy, like a package on a shelf?'

'Exactly,' said Thurby. 'Without an address, post cannot be delivered. The matter converter supplied that address. Its function, its technology, while not identical to the starstone's, the product of a different planet, were similar enough to effect the teleportation. The starstone simply did its job. Dispatched Agent Stanton. Reconstituted his original form.'

'And saved me into the bargain,' mused Cally.

'See?' Ben said, glancing pointedly at Jimmy Kwan.
'Even when I'm just a bunch of molecules you can still
rely on *me* to get you out of trouble, Cal.' He turned back
to Thurby. 'So you're saying everyone else, every*thing*
else that I saw zapped into the starstone in Wallachia is
still in there?'

'We think so, Agent Stanton. There remain energy signatures.'

'So why was I the lucky one to get sprung?'

'Good question,' said Jimmy.

Thurby had to admit they weren't sure. 'We think it
might be because you were the last *living* organic subject
absorbed by the starstone, Agent Stanton. We're
working on it now. Mr Deveraux has kindly consented
to let us examine Adam Thornchild's matter converter
technology as well.'

'Indeed,' acknowledged Jonathan Deveraux, 'and
now, if there are no further questions' – which meant
there were to be none – 'perhaps you'd like to be about it,
Thurby.' A flurry of farewells and Head Tech Thurby
blinked out. 'As for you, Agent Stanton, it is agreeable to
have you back safely and in one piece.'

'Thank you, sir.'

'The Deveraux organisation can ill afford to lose an
agent of your calibre.'

'*Thank* you, sir.' Again the eyes straying towards
Jimmy Kwan. If the field handler fancied himself as
Ben's rival, he ought to have some idea of what he was
up against.

'There are more tests we must run to establish
whether your health is as excellent as it seems, Agent

Stanton. Then we must plan and execute your reintroduction to your parents and the world at large. *Then*, as Agent Cross has requested, a brief leave of absence for the two of you will be permissible before you return to active duty. That is all.'

A trio of yes, sirs.

Jonathan Deveraux didn't waste words. He didn't waste power either. He was gone.

'You've requested a leave of absence, Cally?' Jimmy tried not to sound hurt. Betrayed was a strong word, but he tried not to sound that, either.

'Ben and I' – not daring to look at Jimmy directly, almost back to square one, it seemed – 'we need some time together. After all that's happened, I mean.'

'Yeah. Come on, Cal, meet's over.' Ben took her hand. He didn't need to pull. 'Way I see it, we've got six weeks of lip action to catch up on.'

'Ben!' Cally protested, but playfully, and by the time they'd reached the corridor she was laughing.

And now the briefing room didn't seem crowded at all. To Jimmy Kwan it seemed very empty. Should have kept his distance. Teacher and student. Personal and professional. Should have kept them separate. Now what could he do?

A wry, resigned smile at his lips. There was one thing. Seemed he'd be paying the restaurant's cancellation fee after all.

She found him in his office. The paperwork under which he was practically submerged seemed more of a threat to Jimmy Kwan than any number of Triad members or Thornchild goons.

'Jimmy?' Tentatively, like if he didn't reply she'd be almost glad.

He did reply. 'Cally. Thought you'd be somewhere with Ben.'

'He's catching up on the newsfeed. IGC pumping six weeks of sports results into his brain.'

'It's refreshing to know he's got his priorities right.' Jimmy's eyeline drew his charge's attention to the mounds of paperwork. 'Is there something you wanted, Cally? I'm quite . . .'

'You could do all this on-screen now, if you wanted to.'

Jimmy knew. 'I believe in the old-fashioned virtues.'

Cally interpreted his words as a criticism of her. She'd expected it. Whether she deserved it or not was a different matter. 'I *was* going to tell you, Jimmy, about the leave of absence request . . .'

'Of course you were. An agent is obliged to inform his or her field handler of all proposed permanent or temporary alterations to their status.' He tried a sympathetic smile. It needed practice. 'You'll have a great time. You and Ben . . .'

'It's our second chance. I never thought I'd see him again. Jimmy' – she wanted him to understand; that was why she'd come here, to make him understand – 'you know that Ben was always the one for me. Him and me, we make sense. That's why, when he was gone, I lost it for a while. Nothing *made* sense any more. And if this stuff with the starstone had never happened, we'd have been together the whole time. I wouldn't have . . . if I gave you the impression . . . I didn't mean to kind of lead you on or anything, Jimmy. I mean . . . God, this is difficult.'

Jimmy Kwan sighed. He couldn't stay aloof from her or bitter or resentful. He liked her too much. 'This is the conversation we promised we'd have after the mission was over, isn't it? Only without the crispy duck.' This time, the sympathetic smile came more naturally. 'So it's business only from now on, is that what you're saying? All professional and no personal.'

'I'm sorry, Jimmy.'

'You don't have to be. If Agent Stanton is the one, then Agent Stanton is the one. I hope he appreciates his privileged position.'

'Oh, I think he does.' Cally paused. 'There's something else, Jimmy.' She wanted positives for him, too. 'What I said, about losing it when I thought Ben was dead. If it wasn't for you I'd have found no way back. I was on the brink, Jimmy, I was like dangling from a cliff and I was holding on by my fingertips and if it hadn't been for you taking my hand and pulling me up . . . I'll always be grateful for that.'

'Deveraux field handlers aim to please,' said Jimmy.

'You aimed higher than that,' said Cally. 'You gave me a chance to find out about my parents, and I did, and I've been able to help right the wrong that they were party to, it doesn't matter how briefly or misguidedly. I'm grateful for that, too. And I found *myself*, in the middle of all this Thornchild business. I know who I am, Jimmy, better than I've ever done before. By rights I should be Cally Lane. That's the name my parents gave me. Calista Lane. But I'm not her. Calista Lane perished with her mom and dad fifteen years ago. I'm someone new now, someone else, someone who's come to terms with her past finally and who's happy with who she is and proud of it too and ready to face her future. I've got a feeling it's gonna be good.'

'I've got a feeling you're gonna be right,' said Jimmy, 'and you'll deserve it.'

'And that's partly thanks to you as well, Jimmy,' Cally said. 'I'm just a whole heap of gratitude.'

Jimmy smiled. 'I appreciate it.'

'So, you know, I just wanted to be clear on one point.' The hard stuff was done now. Cally could afford to grin. 'When I get back from my leave, you'll still be here, won't you? Mei Ataki won't have made a sneaky comeback or something? You'll still be my field handler?'

'Cally,' said Jimmy Kwan, 'you'd better believe it.'

They were on a beach silvered by the stars. They were holding hands and Ben's was warm and strong in hers. Cally snuggled closer to him.

'Happy, Cal?'

'Better than happy. You?'

'The same. Maybe I ought to get sucked into alien teleportation devices more often if this is what we get out of it.'

Cally slapped him lightly. 'Don't even *think* that, Ben Stanton.'

He laughed. 'What? You, me, villa stocked with goodies, our own desert island?'

'You and me is all that matters,' said Cally. 'I don't care where we are so long as it's a *we*.'

'Yeah.' Ben grew suddenly serious. 'I'm sorry, Cal. For what I must have put you through the past couple of months. It must have been, well . . .'

'It was,' said Cally simply. She shivered. The night air was cooling. 'Let's go back to the villa.'

'Sure.' It wasn't far, a single-storey wooden-frame building that gazed out to sea like a castaway delighted not to be rescued. 'There's something I've been meaning to ask you, Cal.'

'Mean away.' He sounded cautious so she knew what it was. She was surprised Ben had been able to resist it this long.

'I could understand it if it's a yes. I mean, you thought I was dead and everything. Who didn't? And I mean, when you work *closely* with somebody—'

'It's a no, Ben.'

'What? Spy High agents have undergone mind-reading classes since I've been away?'

'Is there anything, *was* there anything between me and Jimmy? It's a no.'

'That's two tenses sorted. What about *would* there have been at some point in the future?'

Cally tapped her boyfriend on the chest. 'Well now that you're back, you'll have to work hard so I'm not *tempted* to stray.'

They reached the villa, entered rooms flooded with soft amber light.

'Yeah?' considered Ben. 'And how am I gonna do that, Cal?'

'Oh, I have one or two suggestions. Or three. Or four.' She led him onwards.

'Let's hope I didn't leave any important little bits of me behind in the starstone.'

'You know, it's weird being out here really,' Cally said. 'Back to nature. Miles from civilisation. Not a computer or a body sensor or a nanochip in sight.'

'You'd have to look pretty hard to see a nanochip in the first place, Cal.'

'Why are boys always so literal?' tutted Cally. 'No, I

mean, no sign of twenty-first-century technology any-where, and after the Thornchild mission, the absence is doing me good.' She twined her arms around Ben's neck. 'You, me, and not a lot else.'

'Time,' suggested Ben. 'Plenty of time.'

Cally tilted her head. 'I don't know, though. Maybe I'm getting paranoid. I know we're off-limits to the sur-veillance satellites but I still get the feeling we're being watched. Like there are people out there following our every move.'

'That *is* paranoid, Cal, but we sure wouldn't want an audience for what's coming *next*, would we?'

'So what can we do?' said Cally.

'This?' said Ben.

And turned out the light.